SNOWBALL'S CHRISTMAS

SNOWBALL'S CHRISTMAS

KRISTEN MCKANAGH

THORNDIKE PRESS
A part of Gale, a Cengage Company

GALE
A Cengage Company

**LIBRARY OF CONGRESS CIP DATA ON FILE.
CATALOGUING IN PUBLICATION FOR THIS BOOK
IS AVAILABLE FROM THE LIBRARY OF CONGRESS.**

ISBN-13: 978-1-4328-8423-9 (hardcover alk. paper)

Published in 2020 by arrangement with Kensington Books, an imprint
pf Kensington Publishing Corp.

Printed in Mexico
Print Number: 01   Print Year: 2020

To Evan, for all your support
and faith in me!

CHAPTER 1

"Lukas comes home today, Snowball."

At the sound of Miss Tilly's voice, I blink my eyes open. I've been sleeping curled up on my favorite chair in the kitchen, where it's warmer. The one that's extra soft because one of my two favorite humans sits there often. Waking up requires stretching. Half listening to her talk about this Lukas person she's been gushing about for days, I push my paws out in front of me with a big yawn that makes me squeak and then sneeze.

Miss Tilly chuckles as she stares out the window. "Do you think he'll stay longer this time?"

I don't know this Lukas person, other than listening to Miss Tilly talk to him on the phone, so I proceed to give myself a tongue bath, paying particular attention to my paws. My white fur is beautiful. At least I think so. My mama cat taught me how to

7

keep it clean before I lost her.

Or she lost me. I don't remember.

Tilly glances around the kitchen. "Do you think he'll notice?" This she almost whispers to herself.

I pause in my bath to see what she's looking at. Notice what? I get to my feet and knead the seat cushion with satisfying little pops of sound as my claws catch.

"No, no, no," Miss Tilly says in a singsong voice before she scoops me up under my belly.

Except she doesn't swat me on the nose like the cat who lives in the stable says she should when I do bad things. Instead, she tucks me in close and tickles me under my chin. I lean into her touch, a purr vibrating my body. The rumble means I'm happy.

My second favorite human breezes into the room, shaking her head at Miss Tilly. "I heard those little pops. You shouldn't let her get away with that, or she'll ruin the cushions."

Like I would. I purr louder, and Miss Tilly cuddles me. "Oh, Emily. Snowball's so tiny, what could she do?"

Emily reaches out to run a hand over my fur. "She'll get bigger and more destructive."

I don't know what she's talking about. I'm

8

an angel. Everyone says so.

"I need to get to my deliveries, or I'll be late." One more pat and Emily turns away, placing her gigantic purse on the kitchen table before moving to put on her thick winter coat along with gloves, hat, and scarf. As soon as that white stuff that makes my paws feel funny covered the ground, all the humans started wearing those weird clothes.

Why don't they just grow fur coats, like me?

Miss Tilly places me back on my cushion and moves to the sink. "I wish you didn't feel obligated to bake into the small hours of the night to help me make ends meet."

Emily pauses, then crosses the room to kiss Miss Tilly on the cheek. "I'm doing this to grow the business I'll have one day. People will be more likely to come to my shop if they've already sampled my food. Besides, Weber Haus is doing fine. We're bursting from the seams through Christmas and even into New Year's."

"With one guest room out of use," Tilly reminds her.

That's another thing they talk about a lot. Christmas.

While their backs are turned, I pop my head up over the kitchen table and eye Emily's purse. I love that purse. It's big enough

9

for me to crawl into with tons of funny things to bat around, but she *never* lets me play in it.

I sneak a glance at the two women, who are still talking about Emily's new bakery and the inn Miss Tilly runs. "Maybe when Lukas gets here, he'll help fix things up," Emily suggests.

"I wouldn't ask him to do that." Tilly shakes her head. "He has his own career and needs to travel."

Miss Tilly doesn't see it, but Emily rolls her eyes. Does she not like this Lukas human? I'm pretty sure Miss Tilly loves him. Her voice goes all soft and warm when she talks about him.

"How hard could it be for him to take a little time off to help the woman who raised him?" Emily asks.

With the two of them distracted, I focus on the purse. I'm going to make it this time. With a butt wiggle for added spring, I pounce. Up and over the edge of the table, across the dark wood, then, with a jump my littermates would've been jealous of, I plop into her purse with hardly a sound.

Ha! I made it.

Now I'll stay quiet and still for a minute to make sure Emily didn't notice.

Lukas navigated the streets of Braunfels with care. It had been a while since he'd driven in snow, and this was fresh. Not icy or slushy, though, which made it easier. The town had hardly changed since the last time he'd visited. The same Christmas decorations adorned lampposts, doors, and the tops of the buildings. Main street bustled with shoppers heading into all the small local businesses, which included everything from toys and ice cream to luxury home decor. The same businesses that had been there when he'd been a boy.

Which reminded him. He had yet to shop for Aunt Tilly beyond a few trinkets picked up on his travels.

"Did you hear me?" a feminine voice echoed over his car's speakers. His agent had the bit so firmly between her teeth it would take a crowbar to remove.

Lukas gripped the wheel. "I heard, Bethany. However, I can't say I'm all that interested in a job that requires me to travel over the holidays."

"But this is for *Geographic International*," she reminded him. "They loved the work you did at the Berlin Beer Festival this summer. They want the same type of feel for images in Lithuania, focused on how they celebrate the season. Particularly the International Christmas Charity Bazaar at Rotuse and the Cathedral Square Christmas tree in Vilnius."

"But they want me there in a week and through the new year," Lukas pointed out his biggest issue.

A year ago, he would've snapped up this opportunity. *Geographic International* had been his ultimate goal as a photographer, and that opportunity last summer had been a godsend. Working with them had opened doors he'd only ever dreamed about, skyrocketing his career.

But the constant travel was starting to wear. He had no home base. No close friends. His fault there, friends had never been high on his priority list. An on-again, off-again girlfriend who'd wanted more had once complained that, for a man who took such beautiful pictures of humanity, he sure didn't like people. Then she'd gone all amateur psychologist on him and informed him that his parents' sudden deaths had traumatized him and made him avoid deep connections.

Except she'd been wrong.

He had Aunt Tilly. His father's aunt,

Lukas's great-aunt, who'd never married, had taken in a shocked and lonely ten-year-old boy and given him a home and all the love he could ever need.

And you haven't seen her in a few years, a small accusing voice reminded him.

That realization had hit him with the force of a stampeding bull when he'd been in Pamplona to capture the event on film. Sure, he tried to call her almost every day, when he had cell service. He'd even gotten her to video-chat. But so long between visits? What kind of nephew did that make him? A horrible one, and he intended to make up for it. Tilly was all he had in this world, and he was all she had.

He'd start by spending this Christmas with her. Regardless of the opportunities thrown his way.

"At least think about it," Bethany urged, still on the phone.

Lukas grimaced, not that his agent could see. "Fine. I'll get back to you at the end of the week."

They ended the call about where cell service started getting spotty anyway. The road bent in a familiar way that had memories of driving it, past rolling, snow-covered hills, to the Victorian inn his aunt owned on the outskirts of town. The place where he'd

13

done most of his growing up after his parents died.

Lukas blinked at a new sight, his foot moving to the brakes even as he stared. "That wasn't there before," he murmured.

Someone must've bought the Turnstill property, because the big hill that ended in a nice flat field at the side of the road had been converted into a sledding hill. Not just a "haul it up yourself" kind of hill, either. A motorized rope pull had been installed at the far side, a small parking lot paved over near the road, and a permanent structure put in place at the top of the hill. The wood siding painted red, the building sported a sign that read, "Tickets & Food." Smoke curled lazily out of a small chimney on the roof, and several people stood inside a closed-in room with floor-to-ceiling windows. Allowing parents to watch their children in the comfort of warmth? Smart thinking by whoever put this here.

That wasn't what caught Lukas's eye, though. What had him slowing and pulling into the lot, even before he consciously decided to do so, was the idyllic picture the scene made. A Norman Rockwell painting come to life in the modern era. Not wanting to miss a second, Lukas didn't even bother putting on his coat as he hopped out

14

and pulled a camera from one of several bags on his front seat, fiddling with the lens and settings almost unconsciously as he walked closer.

The lighting was perfect. Slightly overcast, allowing the colors to pop.

Within minutes he'd situated himself at the bottom of the hill on one knee, uncaring of how the snow soaked through his jeans, snapping away, pausing to check the images on the digital screen. Children and families shot down the hill in a multitude of contraptions. The traditional wood sled on metal runners had been replaced by one- and two-seater plastic disks, black inflated tubes, long flat boards that looked more like bodyboards for the ocean, and other things.

Despite the modern rides and modern clothes, the scene carried an aura of nostalgia his camera couldn't resist.

A new layer of pristine snow covered everything, weighing down the limbs of the trees. Every time a sledder fell, a ploof of white went flying into the air, covering the tangle of limbs. Couples wrapped up in thick jackets, hats, and scarves stood at the top of the hill, calling down to their children. Moms or dads would ride behind small toddlers, trying to slow their speed with their feet. Those who'd reached the bottom would hook their sled onto the pully, if they could, and then tromp back up the hill beside it, their breathing crystalizing in the cold air in rhythmic puffs.

No one on this hill was worried — right in this perfect moment — about bills, or jobs, or where the next meal was coming from, or how to protect their children in a world descending into madness. In his travels, Lukas had seen plenty of the madness. Too much maybe.

This, though . . . this was like a time-out from life. A chance to revel in simple fun.

That contentment showed on each face on the small display screen of his camera. Even the toddler, crying because he'd been frightened when the sled tipped over. All it had taken was the promise of building a snowman, and tears departed.

A strong breeze flew across the landscape, swirling the snow, and a shiver skated up Lukas's back. He blinked and glanced down, realizing that in the rush of capturing these brief flashes of life, he'd forgotten his jacket and his knee was soaked. But he wanted to get a few shots from the top.

With an impatient huff, Lukas ran back to his car and grabbed his jacket, yanking a beanie over his black hair as well. Camera back in hand, he happened to glance up,

16

and paused.

Parked a few spots over, a woman was bent at the waist, the top half of her buried inside the back of her shabby SUV. A nicely rounded backside encased in tight jeans. Not a bad view. Lukas idly wondered what the top half of her looked like.

A second later she awkwardly backed up and paused, and a swear word reached him over the laughter and screams coming from the sledding run, followed by a grunt. Then she backed out the rest of the way, balancing a bunch of pink boxes precariously in her arms.

"Can I help with that?" Lukas called across the top of his car.

She jerked her gaze from the boxes to him and blinked even as her tower wobbled precariously. Lukas smiled, interest stirring as he encountered wide chocolate-brown eyes in a pixie face and lips that made him think kissing her might be as fun as whooshing down a snowy slope.

"That's okay," the woman called back, her voice warm, making him think of hot chocolate or hot tea with honey. "I have it stacked just right, and I'm afraid if anyone tries to take it, I'll drop the whole thing."

Unless he was mistaken, Lukas was pretty dang sure his interest was being reflected right back at him. Blessed with dark hair and green eyes and a decent physique, he was used to the opposite sex taking notice. He didn't take advantage often, not with his hectic travel schedule. Maybe this holiday would be enjoyable for more reasons than he thought. She had to be local, with all that stuff.

"You going up there?" He nodded toward the building at the top of the hill.

That spark turned more wary as she eyed him, then glanced around her surroundings before she seemed to come to the conclusion that she was safe enough here. "Yes."

"Me, too." He waved a hand for her to go ahead. "I'll follow you, in case you drop something or need help."

He couldn't tell from her expression if she thought that was nice of him or annoying. Did she not care for chivalry in a man? Tilly had insisted on good, old-fashioned manners, now a habit.

Right behind her, they headed for a series of steps farther off to the side, crudely fashioned by logs planted in the ground, leading to the building up top.

Ahead of him, the woman with the boxes huffed and puffed her way up the hill, her massive purse smacking against her hip, threatening to unbalance her with each step.

18

Lukas didn't mind the view — those long, long legs gave him ideas. Ridiculous to be this attracted this fast. He'd been out of pocket too long. That had to be it.

A flash of movement caught his attention, and Lukas focused on her bag. Another flash of white and he had to swallow a laugh.

"Ummm, did you know —" Lukas cut himself off mid-sentence as inspiration struck, lifted his camera to his eye, and waited, his lips twitching.

A small, furry white head popped up out of her purse, then back down in a flash. A tiny kitten that could give the snow a run for its money in the pure-white-things market. Following the mystery lady, Lukas couldn't help himself as he captured mischief personified on digital film.

With each step and each sway of her hips, her long, dark hair would bounce or swing. Every time it did, the kitten would pop up and bat at it with tiny paws. Fierce and adorable at the same time.

"Emily?" a male voice called from above them. "Let me help you with that."

The woman, apparently named Emily, shook her head, seemingly unaware of her passenger even as the kitten snagged a chunk of hair and hung on like Scrooge held on to his money. She tugged her head and the silky-looking tresses slipped from the kitten's claws. The animal ducked back down in the purse.

I should tell her. No sooner had the thought occurred and he stepped forward than she reached the top and went right inside as the man who'd talked to her held the door.

Lukas paused, then decided to wait. *I'll tell her when she's done.*

He set himself up where he wouldn't miss her when she came out, then lost himself in capturing more of the joy happening in front of him.

CHAPTER 2

Emily tried not to glance back and see if the man from the parking lot had followed her inside or not. One wrong move and all her beautifully packaged baked goods would tumble from her precarious hold.

It might be worth it, though.

She didn't tend toward instant attraction, always being more logical than emotional, but it would be hard *not* to react to a man like that. Tall, broad shoulders, and obviously in decent physical shape. Even all bundled up she could see that. But mostly what had gotten to her was the twinkle in his green eyes. Like he was in possession of a secret treasure map where *X* marked fun, and he wanted to take her along for the adventure.

Adventures are a distraction, and you can't afford distractions, anyway. Not now, she sternly reminded herself.

Navigating the people stuffed around the

square tables like peanut packaging in a box, she hardly absorbed the constant hum of chatter, the warm air laced with scents of mulled apple cider, or the Christmas music softly piped through overhead speakers. With a breath of relief, she made it behind the serving counter and into the small kitchen with all her boxes intact.

The Ables had originally planned to offer only coffee and hot chocolate here, but noticing how many of their guests left around lunchtime, they had added a lunch counter. Basic, with sandwiches and soups. They'd been more than happy to sell Emily's pastries and desserts for a small percentage of the profit, which meant they didn't have to bake them. Win-win.

Plus, she liked the Ables. They'd started this place after their youngest finished college. A sort-of-retired, but-not-retired venture.

Marlisa came out from behind the station where she made sandwiches and gave Emily a hug. "We sold out of everything yesterday. And people are requesting those little almond and orange breads."

"The stollen?" Emily smiled. "My grandmother's recipe from Germany. It's one of our family Christmas traditions."

"I'm not surprised," Erwin said with a

grin. "I've put on five pounds since we started selling your stuff."

Marlisa wrinkled her nose at her husband. "Would it be possible to double our order starting next week?"

What? Double?!

It wouldn't be professional to do a happy dance, but Emily sure wanted to. More sales meant more people eating her food. She managed to contain herself. Barely. "Of course."

More hours in the kitchen, but that was okay. She could sleep when she was dead.

Her mother would shake her head when she heard and probably threaten to send Emily's brothers over to help. Or worse, she'd send her brothers with friends with the hope that her only daughter would give up this dream of running her own bakery and settle down.

Her father, though, would wink over the top of her mother's head, giving his silent approval of her choices. Taught to bake by her paternal German grandmother, this had been Emily's dream since she'd first donned an apron. Dad got that.

Emily dismissed the conversation from her mind. Maybe she wouldn't tell them about the increased business. With Miss Tilly giving her permission to convert one of the

23

many buildings on the Weber Haus property to her shop, she was so close she could taste it.

All she needed was the loan for renovations.

After settling up quickly, Emily snapped up her purse and keys, which she'd set down on the counter, and practically skipped out the door into the crisp morning air. Pristine snow blanketed everything, sparkling in the bright sunlight. Perfect. That meant plenty of potential customers out and about to buy her wares from folks like the Ables. That was, if she could get her deliveries done.

She'd been up hours already, having cooked breakfast for the handful of folks staying at Tilly's inn, cleaned up, then packed her car to the brim with her wares. A backed-up toilet in the King's Ransom room, however, had slowed her down significantly.

Still, she'd get it done before she needed to be back to cook lunch for the few guests who chose to eat in the house rather than at a restaurant in town. After that was dinner, then baking for tomorrow. Somewhere in there she needed to get more of the gorgeous antique Christmas decorations up around the house. December was going way too fast.

At her car, her good mood took a back seat to frustration. The fob on her key chain was dying, which meant it didn't always let her in right away. After four or five clicks, she finally gave a *grr* of annoyance and opened the door with the key.

"Wait."

No mistaking the deep voice of the man from the parking lot. No way could he be talking to her, though, so she went to get in.

"Emily."

He is *talking to me.*

Surprise tinged with more delight than she'd let herself acknowledge had her pausing to look over her shoulder. "How did you know my name?" she called as he jogged down the last few steps.

He waved back up at the slope. "That man called your name earlier."

And he'd paid attention? Wow. A blush warmed the skin of her cheeks, making the sting of the cold air against her bite more. "Listen, I'm flattered and everything, but I'm running late."

He paused on a word, mouth open, then his eyes crinkled as he grinned. "I'm not asking you out."

Oh. Disappointment dropped over her like snow falling off branches on her head. *Ker-*

floop. Followed swiftly by embarrassment. The heat crept back up her cheeks, but for a much less fun reason. "Okay . . . What can I help you with?"

"Actually, I'm here to help you."

Help her? With what? She raised her eyebrows in question.

"I believe you've picked up a small passenger in your purse."

"My —" Realization rushed in with all the subtlety of a blizzard, and she closed her eyes in resigned horror. "There's a kitten in my purse. Isn't there?"

She opened her eyes in time to catch the full impact of her stranger's full-bodied laugh, his eyes alight with humor. "Does this happen to you often?" he asked.

"Only since this one arrived on our doorstep." More gently than she'd been handling it until now, she swung her purse around and opened it wide. Sure enough, two blue eyes stared back at her with all the innocence of angels.

"Snowball. You've got to stop this," she admonished as she lifted the small kitten out. Cuddling the ball of fluff against her chest, she lifted her gaze to her helpful stranger. Right in time to see him with a camera up to his eye. A soft click sounded as he snapped a picture.

26

"Uh — No, thanks." She lifted a hand to block any more.

"I'm only getting the cat in the shot. I promise."

Zero for two. First, he wasn't chasing her down because he was interested, and now he only wanted pictures of the cat. *My ego is going to need some chocolate therapy if this keeps up.*

Gathering the remnants of her tattered self-confidence around her like a cloak, Emily managed to smile as she tickled Snowball under the chin. The tiny stowaway leaned into the touch, the loud rumble of her purr immediate. "She is pretty irresistible."

This time when she raised her gaze, she was determined not to mistake anything he did or said as a sign of interest. In fact, it'd probably be good if she made a quick escape. "Thank you for letting me know. I'd feel awful if she got hurt or fell out and we lost her."

Miss Tilly would be beside herself with worry. In fact, she probably was already.

"Oh no." Before her stranger could answer, Emily dove inside her car. Then she swore for real when she realized she'd forgotten her cell phone.

Right. Drive to the next delivery and call from there.

27

"I was kind of hoping you might want to —"

"I have to go," she cut her handsome stranger off, lobbing the words over her shoulder.

Hurry dictated her actions as she deposited Snowball on the passenger seat, started the car, and reversed out. She gave another wave of thanks at her stranger, who watched her antics with a bemused expression, then headed to her next stop with a bit more speed than care.

"You are causing all sorts of chaos, you little dickens," she told Snowball.

By way of answer, Snowball delicately lifted one leg and proceeded to give her backside a wash.

Despite wanting to make sure Tilly didn't worry needlessly, not to mention the bazillion other things on her mind today, Emily still managed to think about the stranger all the way to town.

"I wonder if he's staying here for Christmas." She directed the thought at the cat, who stared back as though she understood. Which was silly.

Not that Emily would get the chance to bump into him again anyway. Her days were spent at the inn, the deliveries her only time away.

28

As soon as she reached McKitchens, one of the restaurants along the main street of shops downtown, Emily tucked Snowball back in her purse. "You stay in there," she told the kitten.

After all, she couldn't leave her inside the cold car. Even with a fur coat.

Then she gathered her boxes and rushed inside. Adam Larson, who managed the restaurant every weekday morning, led her to a phone in an office tucked into the back of the kitchen.

"Weber Haus," Tilly answered, her soft voice unmistakable.

"Hi, Miss Tilly, it's Emily. I wanted to let you know that I have Snowball. She stowed away in my purse."

Tilly managed to chuckle and tsk at the same time. "She does love to do that. I'm glad you called, because I've been searching everywhere."

"I thought you might be. I'll bring her home when I'm done with my deliveries."

"That'll be fine, dear —" A small scuffling noise sounded, then from a distance as though Tilly had put down the phone, garbled words came over the line. After another pause of silence, Tilly came back on. "Someone's here. I'd better go answer the door."

Before Emily could reply, the line went dead, and she replaced the phone in its charger. At least that was handled. *Now, deliveries.*

Her to-do list took her full attention as she stopped at three more locations that had agreed to sell her baked goods. Unfortunately, only the Ables were selling out. The others were selling well, though. That was something.

Driving back to Weber Haus, Emily had to keep from scanning the sledding hill for a black wool coat paired with jeans and a bright red beanie. Not that she had time to do more than glance on the way by.

He was more interested in Snowball, she reminded herself ruthlessly.

Back home, she pulled around to the garage — originally a carriage house — where she and Tilly parked. All guests parked in a graveled lot on the other side of the main house. She scooped Snowball from the front seat, not in her purse this time, and trudged through the snow, her rubber boots crunching with each step, to the kitchen side entrance.

"Miss Tilly," she called as soon as she walked in the kitchen. "I'm home."

Meow, Snowball protested, as though reminding Emily she wasn't the only one.

30

"*We're* home," Emily corrected as she set her purse on the kitchen table and Snowball on the floor.

"Oh, good," came a faint voice. "We're in the living room."

We? Emily glanced at Snowball and imagined the kitten shrugged in return. Tilly's favorite thing in the world was to chat with her guests. While Emily preferred to be behind the scenes, Tilly was front of the house. A perfect recipe.

She'd find out what Tilly was up to in a second. First, she had a carful of groceries to unload. Careful to keep Snowball from following, she hurried outside, grabbed two overflowing paper sacks, and returned. With both hands occupied, she backed through the kitchen screen door, then turned, only to smack into a wall of muscled male chest covered in a soft sweater. Inside the paper grocery bag, an ominous crack sounded, and Emily winced. There went the eggs.

Not too many, please.

She was planning an egg-and-sausage casserole as well as a bread pudding, and both needed eggs.

"Sorry," a low male voice sounded above her over the crinkling of the paper grocery bags. "I was trying to hold the door, but I'm afraid I just got in the way."

"No problem," she lied through her teeth. She didn't have time to go back out for more eggs.

He took her by the shoulders, carefully backing away. "Got it?"

"Yeah."

Emily set the groceries on the counter, then turned to address her unfortunate helper. She stumbled to a halt at the sight that greeted her. "You."

Green eyes crinkled at the corners. "Me."

Right. She sounded idiotic.

To cover, Emily bent and scooped Snowball into her arms. A kitty-shaped shield for the impact this total stranger had on her. At the same time, her brain kicked back on. She didn't remember any new guests checking in today. What was he doing here?

A sneaking suspicion crept up on her. *Please don't be who I think you are. You're too appealing for me to be mad at.*

I pause in my purring to peer closer at Emily's face. I know something is wrong because she's squeezing me tighter. A little too tight.

I give a mewl of protest, and she blinks, her frown morphing to vague confusion as she glances down at me. Emily blinks again, then loosens her grip.

32

Did she forget she was holding me?

That's strange. I look over to see what she was frowning at. Only it's not a what. It's a who.

That man from the place with all the white stuff and the kids laughing loudly. The one who found me in her purse. I cock my head, studying him. Why is Emily mad at him? Other than ratting me out — such an appropriate phrase I learned recently — he seems like a nice person.

The man reaches out and runs a gentle hand over my fur. I snuggle into his touch and start my motor back up. You can tell a lot from how a person pets. I like him already.

About then, Miss Tilly bustles into the room. "Excellent. You've met," she says.

"Not formally," the man says. I like his voice, too. There's kindness and something comforting in the deep tones. I'd like to snuggle under his chin and take a nap.

"Oh," Miss Tilly says in that floaty way she has sometimes. "Emily, I'd like you to meet my nephew, Lukas." Tilly is glowing with pride.

I tip my head and stare at the man. *This* is the Lukas person she's been talking about?

"Lukas," Tilly continues. "This is Emily Diemer. Emily helps me run Weber Haus and is a fine baker."

The Lukas man smiles. He has a nice smile, I decide. It reaches all the way to his eyes.

"A pleasure to formally meet you. Tilly's told me a lot . . ." He trails off.

I glance up at Emily because she's squeezing me again.

"*You're* Tilly's nephew?"

Her voice does *not* sound very pleased. What did this guy do to her? I'm the one he outed by telling her I was in her purse.

Lukas must be thinking the same thing, because his eyebrows scrunch up all funny. "Is that a bad thing?"

Emily opens her mouth, then her gaze strays to Miss Tilly. She seems to rethink her words. "I'm sure Tilly is thrilled to have you home. She's talked of nothing and no one else for weeks," she says. Only *her* smile doesn't reach her eyes. "How long are you staying? She wasn't sure."

Now she sounds too sweet. Not at all Emily-like. Emily is a lovely human, always quick to pet, but she's also straightforward. At least, that's what Miss Tilly calls her. Sweet sounds all wrong from her mouth — like too much cream, smothering her words.

I wiggle in her grasp, and she lowers me to the floor. I have instincts for humans.

Maybe if I show her Lukas is a nice one, she'll stop acting so . . . strange. I scoot over to him and wind myself around his ankles. Lukas chuckles. A deep sound that makes me happy. I like it even better when he bends over and runs a hand over my back. I arch up into his touch.

See, Emily. He's nice.

I glance over to make sure she's getting the message, only Emily is watching me with her lips pushing forward, kind of pinched.

"Traitor," she mouths at me.

A snort from Lukas tells both Emily and me that he caught that. Her cheeks go red.

"If you'll excuse me, I need to get the rest of the groceries before I get started on lunch."

Emily hurries out of the room, the screen door closing behind her with a bang that makes me jump. Lukas straightens and watches her go, the corners of his mouth lifting.

Is it just me? Or is there something going on between these two? Like a low hum in the air. *Two humans I like should like each other,* I decide. Maybe they need a little help to figure it out.

CHAPTER 3

The creaking of a door hinge pulled Lukas out of a light sleep. Given how much he traveled, some destinations not all that safe, he'd gotten used to more of a light snooze, rather than any kind of deep REM cycle.

Aunt Tilly needs to oil those hinges, was his first groggy thought.

He came a little more awake as he realized the sound was coming from *his* bedroom door. He cracked one bleary eye. No light penetrated the thick curtains drawn over his windows, but that didn't mean much. He should've remembered his childhood habit of not closing them all the way, or he'd never know what time it was.

Levering up on his elbows, he glanced at his bedroom door. Sure enough, it had opened a hair. Maybe he hadn't closed it fully, which was doubtful. Or perhaps Weber Haus had picked up a few new ghosts. He had a sneaking suspicion he was about to find out.

A few seconds later he caught a whisper of sound, a heartbeat, before Snowball landed right on his stomach. Even as tiny as she was, the impact made him grunt.

He dropped back to the pillow. "Hey there, fur face. You come for a visit?"

Meow.

Snowball headbutted Lukas's chin, and he chuckled. "Demanding little thing, aren't you?"

Meow.

Lukas reached to pet the kitten, but she hopped back, then meowed again and hopped a bit more. He gave her a cockeyed stare. The cat acted almost as though she wanted him to get out of bed and follow. With a groan, he sat, the sheets falling to his lap, and Snowball leaped off the bed and ran eagerly to the door. There she turned and he'd swear gave him an annoyed scowl.

With a meow that also sounded decidedly aggravated, she hopped back up on the bed and pawed at him before running back to the door.

"You must think you're a dog," Lukas mumbled.

Still, she obviously wanted something, and he was awake now anyway. With a grumble, he tossed back the covers, shivering as his bare feet hit cold wood flooring. He made a mental note to wear socks to bed, even if he did hate it.

A glance at his phone, he immediately reached for it and shot the kitten a glare. "It's not quite five. This better be good."

I must need a break. I'm talking to a puffball masquerading as a kitten.

Quickly, he pulled a T-shirt over his head. Already wearing flannel pajama bottoms, he was at least decent, on the off chance he bumped into anyone else at this hour.

As soon as he started following, Snowball took off down the hallway, pausing at the corner to make sure he was close behind. He reached the turn, and she scooted farther away. Half-amused and half thinking he should just go back to bed, he followed her down the back stairs that led to the kitchen. Nothing like the fancy grand staircase in the foyer; though it had a hand-carved balustrade, the balusters were narrower, darker, and had always freaked him out as a kid. Something about the way wind whistled up them.

You're a grown man now. World-traveled and having survived much more dangerous places than his cozy hometown. He still had to force down a shiver.

A warm light illuminated the last few

steps. Someone was actually up? It'd better not be his aunt. She shouldn't be working this hard at her age.

How . . . old . . . she'd seemed to him yesterday had been a shock. Still spunky, but frailer somehow. A fact that had him start wondering about Tilly's retirement. He'd never thought of her as needing to, but Weber Haus was a big job.

Lukas stopped paying attention to Snow-ball, curiosity growing. For some inexplicable reason, he took those last steps with more stealth, pausing to poke his head around the old-fashioned Hoosier cabinet that Tilly had had refurbished ten years back or so.

Over the years his family had updated the kitchen, bringing it more into the modern era with its copper farmhouse sink and built-in cabinetry. They'd kept the large butcher-block table in the center and the cabinet against the side, along with the original wood flooring. Though, come to think of it, the fridge, stove, and dishwasher all probably needed replacing. Once white, they'd turned more yellow with age.

He made a mental note to suggest that to Tilly.

Usually the warmest room in the house, it had also been Lukas's favorite. Guests ate in the dining room, leaving this room as his and Tilly's domain. He'd done his homework here, eaten most of his meals here, and generally kept out of the way here. Meeting people who wouldn't stay in his life longer than a few weeks at most had held no appeal.

The sight that greeted his curious gaze upped the kitchen a few more notches in his estimation.

Christmas music piped softly from a cell phone on the counter, an oldie, painting images of cold winter nights and cozy fires . . . and family.

He ignored the familiar, old pinch in the region of his heart that seemed to get worse this time of year and focused on the woman humming to herself.

Emily stood at the large butcher-block table in the center of the room. She had her back to him, but her long dark hair, pulled back in a ponytail, was unmistakable. Not to mention those legs. Encased in jeans and topped with a formfitting, pale blue sweater, the woman was a knockout in that freckled, sweet, girl-next-door way that managed to hit the right chord with him.

Except she didn't like him. At all. For a reason he had yet to unearth.

Meow.

He'd forgotten the darn cat, who now sat at his feet.

"Morning, Snowball —" Emily turned with a smile on her lips that froze the second she spotted him.

Jack Frost had nothing on Emily Diemer for chill factor.

"What are you doing here?" she asked. Granted, she attempted to rearrange her features to a more neutral expression, but the pinching around her lips didn't ease any.

Amusement and the strangest urge to win her over had Lukas affecting his most charming smile. "Good morning, Emily."

She lifted her eyebrows, visibly unmoved. "Not for any decent person," she commented wryly with a pointed glance at the microwave clock. "I came down to bake and get ready for the day. Plus, Christmas Eve isn't that far off, and we're hosting a large group, which takes early preparation. I'm freezing a few things ahead of time. What about you?"

Lukas didn't want to explain that Snowball had woken him up and insisted he come down here. He'd sound crazy. "This *is* my house."

The second the words left his lips he wanted to snatch them back out of the air. Definitely not the right way to go.

41

Emily turned her back on him, returning to the dough she was kneading, but not before he caught her scowl. "Technically, it's Miss Tilly's house. You moved away years ago," she pointed out.

She mumbled something else that sounded a bit like "And haven't bothered to come back all that often."

Was that what she was holding against him? Because he would've sworn she'd been interested in the parking lot when they first met. But the second she walked in the door and figured out who he was, she'd been frostier than the North Pole. Might as well get it out in the open. "I get the impression you don't like me much."

She paused, hands sunk deep into the dough. "I don't know you."

Right. An evasive answer if he'd ever heard one. "After you flirted in the nicest way at the sledding hill —"

She jerked her head up. "That was *not* flirting."

"That's too bad," he murmured, earning a scowl before she went back to her dough. "But then you found out my name, and, poof, no more flirting."

"I wasn't flirting," she grumbled.

He hid a smile and crossed his arms. "But you don't like me."

Emily blew out a frustrated breath. "From my point of view, you're the beloved prodigal son. An exciting career, jetting all over the world, and ambitious with it, good at it. With that charming smile, probably a girlfriend in every port. I guess Weber Haus isn't as exciting as what you've got going, but it needs help . . ." She trailed off and bit her lip as though she realized the words spewing from her were probably a bit too much.

Meanwhile, Lukas struggled to absorb everything lobbed at his head or, more accurately, lobbed at the blob of dough while he listened. But one thing was clear: in Emily Diemer's eyes, he was a charming, lazy, jerk of a nephew. Worse, before the gut instinct to defend himself kicked in, his initial reaction was a desire to wrap her up in a hug and try to make it all better. An oddly protective need. Maybe because he could see how much Emily cared.

Lukas moved to the other side of the table. "Has it been hard for Tilly lately?" he asked softly.

She didn't bother raising her head, punching and molding the bread with vigor. "She's had me . . . *this* year."

He didn't need a map to follow her thought process down the road. He glanced around the room, but the kitchen was in pristine condition if he discounted the flour currently covering the table and dropping on the floor in small white poofs as she worked. Maybe a bit dated — more than he remembered. And one cabinet hung slightly askew now that he looked closer. "So she *has* needed help."

Emily didn't bother to answer, and Lukas held in a sigh. He *had* tried to find out the state of things, but Aunt Tilly was never one to complain to anyone. Especially him. He'd assumed she had help, though. When he'd been growing up here, Tilly had run the inn, but she'd had a full-time cook, a handyman, and a groundskeeper to help. So far, Lukas had seen only Emily around.

"Where are the others?"

She paused and glanced up finally. "Others?"

He waved at the kitchen. "You've obviously replaced Mrs. McCready as the cook. If she retired, I imagine Mr. McCready, who used to maintain the grounds, did, too. And Big John, who converted the space over the carriage house into an apartment in exchange for being her on-call fixer."

Emily blinked at him a long second, then put her hand on one hip with an air of total disdain, heedless of the flour handprint she

44

was sure to be leaving. "You've got to be kidding me."

The nerve of Lukas Weber. If she had a skillet in hand, instead of a ball of dough, she'd smack him in the head with it. Was he really this oblivious? This was beyond neglect.

"Big John moved to another town, and the McCreadys retired to go be with their daughter, who got divorced. Years ago."

That oh-so-charming smile, which seemed to linger in his eyes even when his lips weren't tilted in a devil-may-care way, faded, replaced by confused concern that brought his brows down over his eyes.

Emily hardened her heart against the show of emotion. Too little, too late, as far as she was concerned. Tilly was the sweetest, kindest, hardest-working woman she knew. How could he, her only flesh and blood still alive, abandon her like he had?

"Tilly never said," he murmured.

"You mean the few times you bothered to call?" Emily bit her lip.

This was none of her business, and she was turning into a full-blown shrew. Except that Lukas's faults as Tilly's only family impacted her, too. *She* was the one who worried with Tilly about money and fixed the leaky faucets and mowed the overly large grounds in the spring and summers. *She* was the one taking care of things. *She* was the one who had to be ready to host twenty-five people for Christmas Eve dinner, getting ready for that on top of everything else.

Where was he? Running around living the high life. That's where.

Lukas placed both his hands on the wood-topped table and leaned closer, gaze searching hers. "Is that what you think?"

Rats. Antagonizing Tilly's nephew was not the way to get him to step up and help out. Still, she wouldn't lie, either. She tipped her chin up and held her tongue. There was no easy answer to his question.

"Wow." He shook his head. Like he was disappointed in *her*. "For your information, I call every night, unless I'm somewhere without cell service."

"I guess that happens a lot." Emily went back to her dough. She needed this to rise today so she could bake it tonight or she'd be way behind.

He reached across the table and put a large hand over both of hers, stopping her kneading, sending an unexpected and unwanted fizz of awareness through her. "I tell her when that's happening. You know, she didn't mention you, either. Tilly doesn't like

46

to share things if she thinks they'll worry someone." Frustration laced his tone now.

Some idiotic part of her wanted to believe him. Give him the benefit of the doubt.

Emily pulled her hands back. Too darn bad. She was frustrated with him more than he should be with her. "You have a job that takes you to out-of-the-way places. I get it. I'll even concede that Tilly doesn't like to burden others with her problems and may not have been open with you."

More than once she'd had to pry information like unpaid bills from the sweet lady.

"I hear a *but* in there."

"But . . . you haven't been home in several years. If you had, you would've found this all out for yourself."

And that, in Emily's unvarnished opinion, was unforgivable. Who didn't visit family? Especially at the holidays?

Lukas was quiet after that, though she was keenly aware of how he continued to stand at the table, watching her work. Emily finished with the dough, setting it aside to rise, then glanced at the clock.

She'd completed all her baking for today's deliveries and a few more things for Christmas Eve late last night. Again. Before she loaded up her car, the Bavarian cream puffs had to be filled and everything had to be

47

packaged. She had an hour before she needed to get the casserole in the oven and start frying bacon for their guests' breakfasts.

She was in the middle of cleaning up from the bread, keeping her gaze deliberately averted from the man still watching and doing her best to make her fluttering heart quit doing that. Why didn't he just go away?

"What needs attention first?"

His low voice broke the morning hush and the soft sound of "Carol of the Bells" playing on her phone, and Emily paused, mid-wipe, to stare at him. "Excuse me?"

"You said all Tilly's helpers have been gone awhile, which has to mean a lot has gone neglected since then. Right?"

And he was offering to help? That did not fit with the self-centered, jet-setting image she had of this man. He had to have some other motivation. Still, his getting involved was exactly what she'd hoped for. "That's true," she said slowly.

"I bet you have a list tucked away." His serious expression lifted for a moment, and she'd swear he was amused. Except he didn't exactly smile.

"I do," she answered. In order of most dire importance, in fact.

"If you give it to me, I'll see about getting

48

it taken care of." He held out a hand as if she had the list right there.

"It's in my room," she said. "I'll get it for you after breakfast."

He dropped his hand. "Fair enough."

"There's one tiny problem." One big problem actually.

"What's that?"

"There's no money." If her loan came through, Emily intended to earmark a portion of it to helping out with Weber Haus. After all, Tilly was being more than generous to allow Emily to start her business here rent-free, in exchange for cooking for the guests. Her dream. She'd been close once before. She wouldn't mess it up this time.

But the loan wasn't hers, yet.

"That can't be right." Lukas stated so emphatically that she snorted in response. The arrogance of the man.

"How would you know?"

He crossed his arms. "Trust me."

No way, no how. Trusting Lukas Weber would take a Christmas miracle.

"I'll have a talk with Tilly as soon as she —"

"Don't you dare." Emily whipped around the table to put a hand on his arm, ready to keep him from going off half-cocked.

Lukas glanced at her hand, then back up

at her with his eyebrows raised. Emily swallowed at the warmth she found in deep green eyes that reminded her of the peaceful pines all around the town, then swallowed again as an answering warmth bloomed inside her chest.

So what? She'd been attracted to him when they first met. That was before she'd known who he was, though. No way should she allow any emotion toward this man except disdain.

"If you talk to Tilly, she'll know I told you. She's so private about these things, she'll never trust me again. Plus, it'll upset her and —"

Emily clamped down on the words about to leave her mouth. The money she felt comfortable telling Lukas about before he went and hired expensive repairmen. Tilly's health — which wasn't failing, but the woman was nearing her eighties for heaven's sake — was another thing. Tilly wouldn't appreciate Emily bringing that up. She said often enough that she didn't want Lukas feeling tied here.

A statement that had Emily silently snorting in her head. He clearly had no problem with ties.

She took her hand back. "She shouldn't be upset," was all she said. "She has enough worries. All right?"

Lukas studied her for a long moment, and Emily found she was holding her breath.

"You really love my aunt, don't you?" he said quietly.

Not what she'd been expecting at all. "Of course." Emily glanced away. "She's been . . . kind to me."

One of the few people who openly and cheerfully supported Emily's dream. Not that her family didn't love her, but her dream made them worry. Especially after last time.

"I see," he murmured. Not that he possibly could.

His gaze traced her face, lingering on her lips. For the briefest, tension-filled moment, she wondered if he might kiss her. Which had her wondering what that would feel like. Soft but potent, and . . .

Quit it.

Almost like he'd heard her mental shenanigans, Lukas took a deep breath and a step back. "Right. I won't bother Tilly. I'm a cosigner on all her bank accounts, so I can check that way. Give me the list, and I'll see what I can do. Deal?"

He actually held out a hand to shake.

Emily still didn't trust the man. He was only here for two weeks, and she'd bet

51

money she didn't have that he wouldn't even last that long. Someone who traveled the way he did, someone who never came home, obviously didn't want to be here.

But if he wanted to try to fix a few things in the meantime, fine by her.

She gripped his proffered hand firmly, ignoring how warm his skin was against hers, or the annoying flutter in her stomach at the contact. "Deal."

I shake my head as Lukas leaves the room.

That had not gone the way I wanted. In the romance movies that Miss Tilly likes to watch on TV, getting the people to spend time together makes them fall in love.

Or at least like each other.

Apparently not. Because all Emily did was snap at poor Lukas. Though I don't understand why. Something about Miss Tilly, but Lukas loves Miss Tilly. Even I can see that.

I was sure when Lukas had first come into the room that he was going to sweep Emily into his arms. His face had done something funny, just like in those movies, and the way he looked at her . . . Only Emily had ruined it before he could. Darn it.

Curling up on my favorite chair, I rest my chin on my paws. This is going to take a little more work than I thought.

But that's okay.

Instincts that humans manage to ignore tell me I'm right. Maybe, just maybe, these people — Lukas, Emily, and Tilly — are supposed to be my forever family. Together.

CHAPTER 4

Instead of a creaking sound breaking into his first solid sleep in weeks — last night he'd oiled those hinges and all the hinges on the second-story rooms — Lukas woke to a rather brusque knock on his bedroom door.

Unfortunately, it coincided with someone hammering in his dream, so it took him a second to reorient and realize that no one was hammering, but someone was definitely knocking.

"Just a sec," he managed to slur. He stumbled out of the bed to the door.

Pulling it wide open, he found Emily — dressed in jeans and a cream-colored sweater, hair piled high on her head, beautiful, obviously ready for the day, regarding him with an irritated pull to her mouth and not a hint of warmth in her dark eyes. At the sight of him, though, her eyes widened, and Lukas suddenly remembered he'd worn only pajama bottoms to bed without a shirt again last night. Too late now.

She stared for a moment. Despite shock being the prevalent emotion in her gaze, he still managed to feel that look right down to his little toes. Right until she snapped her gaze back up to his eyes, as if suddenly remembering herself, and rearranged her expression to neutral, excepting a gleam in her eyes. Only he didn't entirely trust the gleam.

"Ready to get started?" she asked.

He was right not to trust. "Started?" What was she on about? What time was it anyway?

Her eyebrows winged up. Was that a hint of a smirk? "The list? I assumed you'd want to get going early."

Right. The darn list. She'd handed him multiple typed pages last night, and nothing on her list was insignificant. Painting. Repairs. Supplies. Paperwork.

If everything Emily had put on here was that needed, then the state of the house was beyond shocking. The Tilly he'd grown up with would never have let her beloved family inheritance degrade to such a level. The question was, how? Had she not noticed? Had old age slowed her down that much? Tilly was nearing her eighties after all. Was money that tight? If so, Lukas would be hav-

ing a strong discussion with her about helping. Or was there another reason?

"What time is it?" He glanced over his
shoulder at his bedside table, but his phone
was laying at an angle he couldn't see.

"It's five thirty," Emily informed him
cheerfully.

"In the morning?" The second the words
were out of his mouth he wanted to stuff
them right back inside. He held up a hand
and forced what he hoped came across as
an easy grin. "Scratch that. Dumb thing to
ask. My brain doesn't fully function until I
get caffeine."

Emily stood there with an expectant
expression. He was semi surprised she
didn't have her hands planted on her hips
as well. Which only made him want to
cuddle her. A terrible idea he studiously
ignored.

She did cross her arms. "I was planning
to fix the doorknob for the front door this
morning, before any of our guests were up,
but since it's on *your* list now, that'll let me
get started on my scones sooner."

Her expression screamed that she expected him to shirk his duties and leave her
hanging as he returned to the warm comfort
of his bed at this ungodly hour, thus prov-
ing her opinion of him correct. What she

didn't know was that Lukas had zero intention of letting Aunt Tilly down again. Plus, a part of him wanted to prove Emily wrong.

Guilt pinched inside him, clamping on his gut, because she wasn't completely wrong. He *had* been a bad nephew, worse even than he'd realized. But he could fix this. Be better.

"Let me get dressed and I'll be right down."

Emily blinked, suddenly reminding him of a bewildered owl, and he had to stuff the sudden urge to smile down deep. She would not appreciate it. At least he'd managed to surprise her. Much better than the disappointment that she'd radiated at him all yesterday.

With a curt nod, she swung away, hair bouncing on the top of her head. Lukas might have taken an extra second to admire the view as she walked away, wondering idly how long her hair would be if she let it down from the ponytail or bun she seemed to habitually keep it in.

Lukas closed the door, then regretted it as his room was pitched into inky darkness. Blindly, he made his way to the lamp beside his bed and, fumbling to feel for the switch, turned it on. Only to jump back at the sight of a white fluffball perched on the top of the headboard.

Lukas let out a sharp breath. "You scared me to death, Snowball. How'd you sneak in?"

The kitten cocked her head as if to say, *That's pretty silly. I'm adorable, and you're clearly not dead.*

After giving her a scratch under the neck, Lukas got dressed double time, gave his comfy bed one last regretful look, then opened the door. "Let's go fix things, furball."

This time, he wasn't surprised when the cat gave a small meow, then hopped off the bed to follow him down the hall.

Like the day before, they found Emily in the kitchen, the wonderful smells wafting up the back stairs. Also like the day before, Lukas paused to observe. She worked quietly and efficiently, slim hands making short work of whatever she was whipping up in the bowl she held, a small smile playing around the corners of her mouth. Baking obviously made her happy.

I wonder what else makes her happy.

His cell phone suddenly went off, and she jumped. He held up both hands as he came farther into the room. "I'm not trying to scare you every morning. I swear."

"You might want to get that."

He pulled it from his pocket and checked the screen. Bethany. This early? It could wait. He sent her to voicemail. "My agent. I'll call her back later."

She gave him a side-eyed stare, then tipped her chin at a pile of items on the counter. "The tools you'll need are right there."

"Great." He ignored the pile and opened the pantry door.

"Can I help you?" Her voice held a hint of weariness, sort of like a mother talking to a preteen kid. Not the relationship he wanted with her.

"I thought I'd have a quick breakfast before I get started," he said over his shoulder without turning around. "Most important meal of the day, you know." He grabbed an orange box. Cereal wasn't his favorite, especially with the delectable scents filling the kitchen, but it'd do in a pinch.

A soft football behind him came a few seconds before the box was snatched from his hands. "Sorry. That's for granola parfaits."

"Oh."

She put away the box. "Do you like cherries?" Her voice came out muffled from deeper inside the pantry.

"Yes."

She backed up and moved to the oven, which she opened and drew out perfect, mouthwatering pastries — triangles, golden brown, and appearing to be light as newly fallen snow. Lukas's stomach gave a loud gurgle.

"Cherry turnovers?" he asked hopefully, sniffing the air appreciatively.

She nodded and lifted each to a cooling rack with a spatula, then placed the last one on a plate that she shoved across the island table at him. "Careful it's —"

"Hot?" Lukas did grin now. "Just the way I like it." Then waggled his eyebrows.

That earned him a disdainful sniff before she went back to the dough. He couldn't help himself. Emily was too easy to tease.

He dug into his treat — trying not to groan his pleasure with each bite. He was right, light and buttery and the cherry filling the perfect combination of tart and sweet. "These are fantastic," he mumbled around a bite.

Emily's hands paused in her task, and she flicked him a glance. "Thank you. They'd be even better with a little Ceylon cinnamon, but I haven't had time to get any. Maybe after Christmas Eve is over."

Not a smile, but no frown, either, and she'd shared. Progress.

60

"You mentioned Christmas Eve yesterday. What's that about?"

"All of my family will be joining the guests here for Christmas Eve dinner before we go to the candlelight service at the church," she said. "I'm cooking for everyone, and I want it to be . . . perfect."

"I see."

She sounded as serious as a photographer who worked only with film. "Let me know how I can help."

"Thanks." Tone of voice was a big indicator with her, he was finding, and this tone said, *You . . . help? Yeah, right.*

"What made you want to get into baking?" he asked around another bite of turnover.

She was silent long enough that he wondered if she would bother to answer. He glanced down at Snowball, who sat at his feet and gave a blue-eyed-kitten version of *Heck if I know what she's thinking* in return.

"My grandmother," Emily finally said.

"Oh?" While he wasn't a journalist, he'd worked with enough of them and seen enough in action in interviews that he knew to get someone talking, sometimes he just had to give them the space to do so.

"I would go to her house after school every day. My parents both work."

Lukas nodded.

61

"Anyway . . . Oma loved to bake. Her parents had owned a bakery before they moved here. So, every day, after I finished my homework, she'd teach me a new recipe, then we'd get to eat it."

A soft smile graced her lips, her eyes hazy with the memory, and Lukas paused at the sight, cherry turnover halfway to his lips. What was it about Emily that he found so appealing? Given her patent dislike of him, he should be, at the very least, indifferent. Maybe his photographer's eye wanted to snap a picture of her like that — an image that would draw the viewer in with a feel of home, winter, and happy memories.

She glanced his way, caught him staring, and there went the smile.

He cleared his throat. "She sounds like quite a lady."

"She was."

He caught the past tense. "I'm sorry."

Emily twitched a shoulder in a shrug. "She lived a long and happy life, though Opa misses her."

"I bet you miss her, too."

She opened her mouth to respond, but paused, her expression softening. "I do," she finally admitted. "I wish she could see me now. She would've loved it here, I think."

"I understand."

She lifted a single eyebrow and he chuckled rather than get offended at her visible doubt. "I do. Aunt Tilly was always my cheerleader. I still send her the best pictures from each new project." Probably bringing up his relationship with Tilly to Emily was a bad move. Better to bring it back to her. "I'm sure the rest of your family is just as proud of you."

Her mouth settled into a surprisingly grim slash that, for once, he didn't think had anything to do with him. "They are," she said abruptly. "Don't you have stuff to do?" She glanced pointedly at his empty plate.

Lukas cast a longing look at the cooling turnovers on the counter. He'd hoped for one more, but clearly had overstayed his welcome. He cleaned up after himself and gathered the tools she'd provided and left.

Thank goodness for "how to" videos he could search up on his phone. In a jiffy, Lukas was an expert on doorknobs in Victorian houses. The one for the front door needed to be replaced, a new task he mentally added to his list. In the meantime, at least, he could tighten it so the thing didn't fall off the door the next time someone tried to open it. Snowball appeared and decided that he must be crouching there for her entertainment and proceeded to wind

63

around his legs, rubbing against him and purring loudly.

"Good thing you're little and cute, varmint," he murmured. Then ran a hand over her silky soft fur so she'd know he didn't mean it.

Suddenly, Snowball abandoned him to run off toward the staircase. Turning, Lukas found Aunt Tilly making her way slowly down, Snowball beside her as though carefully monitoring each shaky step.

Lukas paused, watching closely, a new twinge of guilt catching inside him like Snowball's claws on his jeans. He hadn't been wrong about his aunt's frailty. What if she fell down those stairs? He hadn't been gone *that* long. When had her health declined like this?

The other question was: What did he do now?

No way could he leave here with the house and his wonderful aunt in the state they were. Was it a question of getting her more help? Sending more money that she ignored? Maybe finding her a new home and getting a manager to run Weber Haus?

She'd hate all those options, no doubt. Pride and independence might be his biggest hurdle in finding an answer.

As soon as she saw him, she smiled,

delight evident in the twinkle in her eyes. "I've been meaning to fix that doorknob," she said. "Thank you, honey."

He sprang up to meet her at the bottom of the steps, in case her distraction led to a stumble.

"Emily mentioned it," he said. No way was he going to share the long list Tilly's personal Christmas elf had given him. Getting Emily in trouble with his aunt wouldn't win any battles and would definitely lose him the war.

"Well, we appreciate it." Tilly made it to the bottom of the stairs and gave his shoulder a squeeze. "Is Emily in the kitchen? I need to talk to her about today's guest list."

Lukas nodded, and his aunt made her way back there leaving him to his task, which didn't take much longer.

Thank you, internet.

Door fixed, Lukas moved on to the next item on his list. Painting the sitting room. He found Emily still in the kitchen and Snowball lying on the woven rug in front of the oven, obviously absorbing the heat. Tilly was nowhere in sight, but that wasn't unusual. No doubt she was bustling around getting ready for guests. Hopefully without breaking a hip, but she wouldn't thank him for butting in.

"Painting supplies?" he asked Emily.

She didn't even look up. "Already in the sitting room."

Of course. "Thanks."

He set the tools for the doorknob on the counter where he'd found them and left.

"Snowball." He heard Emily call the cat as he made his way across the once elegant open foyer to the small sitting room near the back of the house.

Apparently, Emily had been prepping in here already. The antique furniture had been pushed to the center of the room, including any paintings or knickknacks that had been on the walls, and covered with sheets. In a pile near the door sat more cloths, obviously to protect the floors, along with all the other paraphernalia he would need. The need for the fresh coat became immediately obvious. What had once been white walls had become so dingy, they appeared a sickly yellow. Around the fireplace, the plaster had turned even more dingy, no doubt from the smoke. Where the paintings had hung showed closer to what had to have been the original color, giving a stark contrast.

"Wow." When was the last time this room had been painted anyway?

He frowned, trying to remember any time

when he'd been living here that painting had happened. Only he couldn't. Not that adolescent or teen boys were all that observant. Seemed men nearing thirty weren't much better.

Hands on his hips, Lukas looked at Snowball. "It's been a long time since I've painted anything. Can't be that hard, right?"

She looked back with big blue eyes for a second, then proceeded to lift her leg and give herself a dainty bath.

Zero for two with the ladies in the house this morning. At least Tilly was glad to have him around. He winced at the thought.

The twinge of guilt was bordering on becoming a permanent tic.

Lukas got to work. After laying out the tarps, he taped off the baseboards, then mixed the paint and poured it into the roller bin and went to work. After a while, the quiet got to him, so he got out his phone and set it to his playlist, soft so as not to wake any guests. He hummed along as he rolled fresh paint onto the walls in long, thick strips, stopping every so often to observe his handiwork.

Vaguely he was aware of the sounds of the house stirring. The scents of fresh coffee and bacon wafted through from the hidden door behind the stairs that connected the kitchen to the sitting room where he worked. A few minutes later a burst of laughter came from the direction of the dining room. Breakfast was apparently served for the guests now.

"What on earth?"

Emily's yelp from down the hallway had Lukas jerking around. He took one step, looked down, then swore. He knew exactly what had upset her.

Snowball had apparently walked through the tray of paint he'd left on the floor to refresh his roller with. Perfect, kitten-shaped pawprints in pristine white traipsed across the drop cloths and onto the old hardwood floors leading away to the kitchen.

"Lukas —"

Even expecting it, Emily's call made him cringe. The upset in her voice made him feel like he'd stepped on one of Santa's elves. In fact, it sounded as though she was yelling with her teeth clenched while still trying to sound not-upset for the sake of the guests. More evidence against him was not helping his case to win her over any. Lukas would've paused to wonder why he wanted to, but she called his name again, her voice louder and sharper than before.

He picked up the tray and set both it and the roller in his hand carefully atop the ladder he'd been using, hopefully where Snowball couldn't get to it. Then he hustled to the kitchen, vigilant not to step in the wet paint and make it worse.

"Luk —"

He tried to stop the swinging door to the kitchen, but he'd shoved it pretty hard in his haste. It came to an abrupt halt with a loud thump as it obviously hit Emily, then swung back toward him with an accusatory squeak to reveal her thunderous expression, half-hidden by her hand, which she now held up to her eye. Snowball was clutched in her other hand, ears pricked, watching in adorable kitten-like innocence.

"Are you *trying* to ruin my day?" Emily asked through visibly gritted teeth. "Or prove your incompetence, because you really needn't have bothered."

In other words, she was already unimpressed.

Lukas's lips twisted and his usually laughing green eyes darkened with what appeared to be hurt, and suddenly Emily wanted to pull back the words. They were too harsh, spoken in the heat of her irritation.

Wait. Doesn't he deserve it?

Not only had he been a neglectful nephew when Tilly needed him most, leaving a total

69

stranger to hold things together with duct tape and willpower, but now he was making more of a mess for her to clean up. The man should have the word "nuisance" printed on his forehead as a warning for all who came near him.

Be fair, Emily, a small voice whispered. *Anyone could have an accident like that. Especially with Snowball around.* The kitten had a nose for mischief.

Not only that, but she'd been in the back of the hall when Tilly had come down the stairs, and witnessed Lukas jump up to try to subtly help his aunt the rest of the way. Then there was the gentle way he handled Snowball. And the cheerful way he went about his tasks.

None of it added up. Like a Rubik's Cube she'd got for Christmas as a child. A total mystery she'd obsessed over and eventually given up trying to solve. His good behavior had to be for show and wouldn't last. She'd had experience with his kind before.

"Of course I'm not trying to ruin anything," he said, with way more calm than she felt right at that moment. "Come on, let's look at that eye."

Was he not thinking of the ruined floors? "The paint will dry, and we need to —"

"*I* need to fix my own mess. Which I will."

70

He moved into the kitchen, taking her by the arms and backing her up until she plopped down on a stool. Shock had her letting him. Then he quickly put ice in a baggie, wrapped it in a towel, and handed it to her, at the same time taking Snowball from her hands.

Emily's eyebrows rose steadily until they had to be in her hairline as, without a word, he grabbed lemon juice from the fridge and took the cat to the sink, where he proceeded to wash the paint from her paws.

After drying them, he set her down in Emily's lap, where he caught her expression. "What?"

"Nothing." Nothing except he was moving around like he'd lived here the last decade, rather than not having set foot in the place in some time, and knew exactly what to do in an emergency.

"Hold on to her while I clean up the paint on the floor," he instructed.

"It's ruined." She only just managed not to wail as she stared in horror at the prints that Snowball had traipsed into the kitchen and could picture the path back to the sitting room, each tiny paw shape darker than the next.

"Nope." Lukas didn't sound nearly as upset. "I've sadly had experience with this before. When I was fifteen, I decided to paint my room black in a misguided Goth phase and spilled a paint can in my room before I even got started. I had to clean it up before Aunt Tilly found out." He shook his head at the memory with a grin. "I never did end up painting the room after that."

All her righteous indignation had nowhere to go in the face of both that grin, which had her heart lifting inexplicably, and his calm demeanor as he went about getting done what had to be done.

"Do you have any rubbing alcohol?" he asked.

Her eyes went wide and her hand flew to her eye. "Is there a cut?"

"No. For the paint."

She slowly lowered her hand. "In the cabinet below the toaster oven."

"Got it." He retrieved the bottle. He also grabbed a rag from the drawer where it must've still been when he was growing up, then got started. Emily sat in total silence, clutching her ice and the kitten, and watched as he methodically worked on each paw print.

Sure enough, he managed to get them up without damage to the old wood. Or, at least, no noticeable damage to worn wood that needed to be refinished anyway. Hunkered over, gradually he made his way out of the kitchen and down the hall where Snowball no doubt had tracked it from. Emily stayed where she was, trying to reconcile her image of the man on his hands and knees, cleaning up paint without a qualm, with the spoiled, inconsiderate man she had set in her head.

Was she a teensy bit wrong about him?

Not that it mattered. He'd be gone in a few weeks, and she should be cleaning up from breakfast. She'd been in the middle of doing the dishes when Snowball had made her grand entrance, and, after that, needed to make her deliveries. But now that she was seated, she didn't mind the break so much. It wasn't often she got to just sit during daylight hours.

The door swung open, more carefully this time she noticed. "All cleaned up," Lukas said.

He bustled about putting away his cleaning supplies, washed his hands, then came to stand in front of her. Gently, he took Snowball from her grasp and placed the kitten on the floor. "Let's see that eye."

And have him in her space muddling up her thoughts? No, thanks. "It's fine. You didn't hit me that hard."

"That's not what the door told me."

Ignoring her protests, he took her by the wrist and lowered her hand, then leaned in closer. "You're going to have a lump."

"Oh." Holy cow, the man smelled incredible. Aftershave, lemon, paint, and something just Lukas. Who knew that could be such a heady combination? She needed to give her eyeballs something to do other than look him in the eyes, so while he studied the bump on her face, she tried to disassociate herself by cataloging his features.

Up close, she could see a slight crook to his nose, like he'd broken it a long time ago. *Sports or a fight?* she idly wondered. Thick brows that were straight slashes over his eyes. Crinkles at the corners of his eyes. No surprise there, the man was clearly a grinner, never taking things seriously. Strong jaw currently sporting a day's growth of beard because she hadn't given him time to shave when she'd got him up at the crack of dawn. Did the man have any flaws?

He cocked his head to get a closer look at her eye, and she smiled to herself. His ears stuck out. *Ha. See. He's not perfect.*

He ran a finger softly over the spot on her face where she'd got hit hardest and she sucked in sharply not because he'd hurt her but because that touch *affected* her. Like she wanted to lean into him, close her eyes,

74

breathe him in.

What is wrong with me?

He stilled, gaze zeroing in on hers. "Sorry." His low voice skated over her, leaving a trail of shivers.

Emily cleared her throat and straightened her spine, trying her hardest to stamp out her reaction to Lukas Weber like she would a small kitchen fire. A reaction she didn't want. Even if she was a smidge bit wrong about him. "It's fine. Like I said."

And this needed to stop. Now.

She hopped off her stool, forcing him to back up. "I need to finish the dishes and do my deliveries."

Lukas glanced at the sink. "You go do your deliveries. I'll take care of the dishes, then get back to painting."

Suddenly, she found his helpfulness annoying. "I need to make the beds in the rooms first."

"I can do that, too. Anything special I need to know?"

Emily regarded him with narrowed eyes and reached for her previous irritation, because she did *not* want to like this man. All this Good Samaritan stuff had to be a show. Clearly, he was a person who traded on his copious charms, easy grin, and offers of help. He knew exactly how to butter her up. That had to be what was going on here. After his holiday visit was over, she and Tilly would probably never see him again, given his track record.

She glanced at the clock on the microwave. She'd be a solid hour ahead of schedule if she went now, though.

"The couple in the honeymoon suite are leaving today. We'll need to change the sheets in that room as well as swap out the towels. Otherwise, just make the beds." She tipped her chin at the dishes. "Handwash the china."

Before he could answer, Tilly opened the swinging door. "We'd better get to the beds," she said.

Emily stiffened, hoping he realized that he shouldn't share their morning-chores plan with Tilly, or that wonderful lady wouldn't let them. Fixing the door was one thing. Running Weber Haus was another, and she looked on her nephew as a bit of a guest.

"Emily was about to head upstairs," he said before she could. Not really a lie, as she'd need to go up and get on her boots.

A laughing green gaze met her over his aunt's head, and he winked. The man actually winked, drawing her into a shared conspiracy to save Miss Tilly from her own pride.

A dangerous connection to cultivate. She didn't want to be connected to Lukas.

Except Tilly happily left the room to go get through paperwork.

"Thank you," Emily murmured when she was out of earshot.

Lukas's eyebrows shot up, and she thought he was going to comment on the thanks. Instead, he shrugged with that frustrating insouciance he carried off so well. "My pleasure."

Then he turned to the sink, and, after a moment staring at that broad back, she gave herself a shake and got busy loading up her car.

Christmas could not come soon enough. Once the holiday was past, Lukas would be gone, and things could get back to normal.

Maybe the trail of prints leading Emily to Lukas had not been a good idea.

I thought it would be so cute, showing her the way to him, but instead she got mad. Really mad. I mean, Emily would never hurt me, but she looked like she wanted to.

Next time I'll stick to the shiny things I like to bring Emily. She doesn't get mad about those. Maybe a trail of shiny things leading to Lukas would work better.

I lick at my paws and make a face. Why

are they sour?

Better clean them, even if it tastes awful.

Lukas shuts off the water and turns to face me. He gives me a scowl, which I can tell he doesn't mean, so I continue on with my bath.

My poor paws taste awful.

Lukas throws his head back and laughs, and I realize he's laughing at me, which raises the fur at the back of my neck. Hey . . . I got these nasty-tasting feet trying to help him out. He should be thanking me. I haughtily turn my back on him and continue my bath.

Except he scoops me up and pets me. "Serves you right, getting me in trouble with Emily that way."

I give him a tiny lick on the hand by way of apology for that part and he pats my head. "I know you didn't mean to. You were just having fun."

I was trying to get you two to spend time together. Only Lukas doesn't speak Meow, so he chuckles.

Then he takes me upstairs to where Miss Tilly sits in her room. She's got a quilt from one of the bedrooms and is doing that thing where she puts lots of string in it, something she calls sewing. "I'm surprised that one

78

hasn't fallen apart it's so old," Lukas comments.

"Anything worth keeping is worth keeping in good repair," Tilly replies.

Lukas watches her for a moment, petting me, though I can tell he's not paying much attention to what he's doing. I nip at his finger, and he gives a little jerk.

"This one wants to play in my paint, and I'm not finished," Lukas says. "Can you watch her?"

He sets me down on her lap. I love Miss Tilly. Besides, it's been a long morning, so I curl up and close my eyes.

I'll have to think of a better way to make Lukas and Emily spend time together.

CHAPTER 5

Lukas offered to do the dishes after dinner, which freed Emily up to start her baking prep for the next morning. They worked in companionable silence. At least, he hoped the silence was companionable. He'd yet to catch a scowl or frown from her, but maybe she was just tired.

The woman was nonstop.

After delivering all her baked goods, she'd come home to make lunch for anyone in the house who wanted it, cleaned up from that, then knocked off three things on the list she'd given him, despite his protestations that those were his tasks now. After that she'd cooked and served dinner for the entire household.

He'd disappeared for that part, citing an errand that took him to town, where he had a lonely dinner at a local pub. Bar food that in no way matched Emily's cooking. Hanging out with total strangers in the place that was supposed to be his escape from the world had never been his favorite thing.

Meanwhile, thanks to applying two coats of paint in the sitting room taking most of his day, Lukas was about as tired as he ever remembered being. After practically falling asleep on his burger, he'd come home, entering through the back door to the kitchen to find Emily still hard at work. Despite his own fatigue, he'd gently pushed her away from the sink and taken over.

"Breakfast tomorrow? Or —"

"Getting a head start on Christmas Eve," she said.

Why did he get the feeling she was nervous about that night? "Good thinking."

She ignored that.

"Um . . . What would you like me to tackle tomorrow?" he asked, his back to her as he dried the last piece of fine china.

Silence.

He carefully set the plate down and turned to discover Emily sitting on a stool pulled up to the center table, head resting on her folded arms, fast asleep. A small snore confirmed it.

He smiled. "Guess I'm not the only one worn-out tonight."

He crossed the room and crouched beside her. "At least now I know you're human and

81

not Superwoman in disguise." Trying not to scare her, he gave her arm a gentle shake. "Emily."

No response.

He shook again. "Em."

She blinked those big brown eyes open and hazily focused on his face. "Hi," she mumbled.

A spark of warmth lit inside his chest. She wasn't snapping or glaring or pulling away. "Hi," he answered quietly.

She blinked again and tilted closer. "Hey . . . your eyes have a little blue in them."

His smile widened to a grin. "I guess they do."

Another blink, filled with a vulnerability that knocked him sideways, before she slowly lifted her head. Tendrils of her hair had pulled loose from her bun and spilled around her face as she cast a confused gaze around the room. "I'm in the kitchen," she grumbled.

"Yes. You fell asleep baking."

With a sucked-in breath, Emily straightened, eyes wide, vulnerability gone behind a door slammed shut, keeping him out. "Oh my gosh. I've never done that before."

Lukas rose to his feet with an odd reluctance that tugged at him to go back to where he'd been closer to her. "You must've been more tired than you realized."

She took another deep breath and nodded. "Long hours lately, I guess."

And another log of guilt to add to his pile. "Why don't you go to bed now?"

Emily's nose wrinkled in a way that made him itch to have his camera out. Adorable. "I need to finish in here first, or I'll have to get up even earlier than usual."

"Heaven forbid," he teased in mock horror.

And won his first genuine smile since she'd learned who he was, a warmth in her eyes that drew him, like seeing a house lit from within on a cold winter night. What would it be like to have her friendship instead of her distrust?

You're leaving after Christmas. What does it matter?

Somehow it did.

The lure of bed calling her, she glanced around. "I'll clean up first. The rest can wait I guess."

She reached for a bowl at the same time he did and looked at him with eyebrows raised. "You don't have to help."

He shrugged and gently pried the bowl from her fingers. "Aunt Tilly always did say that two hands halve the work."

Maybe he shouldn't have brought up his aunt, but she nodded, and in quiet harmony they cleaned up the kitchen from her baking stint. Then he followed her up the back stairs, doing his darndest to keep his eyes from wandering. She had a flour handprint on the back of her sweater, but how on earth had she got that there?

She stopped at her door and turned to face him. "Tomorrow I could use your help with setting up Christmas trees."

"Trees? As in more than one?" He'd seen that on the list but assumed it had been misspelled.

That gleam, the same one from this morning, entered her eyes, which he did not trust at all. "Yes. We put one in several rooms so that, no matter where the guests go, they have a tree to admire and the scent of pine fills the house. It takes most of the day to do." The last she said with a challenging glint in her eyes.

Terrific. "I can see how it would."

"I'm going straight after my deliveries. So . . ."

"I guess we're decorating Christmas trees." Not his favorite activity. He still remembered the glob of lights Tilly would toss into a box until the next year, and the hours spent unraveling before searching for the one missing or burnt-out bulb to make them work.

"The good news is, Martin Johnson knows exactly what I need and promised to set the best trees aside for me. We can pick them up in my SUV and get started."

At least he didn't have to shop for the trees then. "Sounds fine."

"See you in the morning." With an almost gleeful smirk, Emily slipped inside her room, and Lukas went on to his, stopping by Tilly's room first.

"Hi," he said upon finding her awake. Snowball lay beside her in bed, curled up into a tiny fluff of white. "You shouldn't still be up. It's late."

"Oh, tush." Tilly waved a hand at him. "I'm old. Plenty of time to sleep in heaven."

Lukas shook his head, not wanting to think of that hopefully far-off day.

Tilly patted the bed. "I've hardly seen you today. Just this morning when you were fixing the door handle. What did you do?"

Lukas shoved yet a new layer of guilt down deep. He *was* supposed to be here to spend time with Aunt Tilly. "I helped Emily with a few things. Tomorrow we're going to put up the Christmas trees." Lukas settled beside her on the bed. Snowball's ears pricked, but she didn't deign to lift her head.

"That's nice," Tilly said nodding slowly. "I love that she started that tradition, but it takes her several days usually. I'm sure Emily will appreciate the help."

He gave a noncommittal hum. "Aunt Tilly . . . What happened to the checks I've been sending you?"

Faded blue eyes narrowed and her lips compressed. "What do you mean?"

He wagged a finger at her. "You're a terrible bluffer. I checked my bank account and not one check has been deposited."

Tilly's chin went up, a sure sign she was about to be stubborn. "I'm not taking money I didn't earn."

"Of course you earned it. You took me in —"

"That was a privilege." Her hand flapped, and he knew he'd offended her.

Even Snowball lifted her head and glared at him as if Tilly's sudden tension was all his fault. "I know. But you took care of me, now let me take care of you a bit."

Even as he said it, the guilty twang got more pronounced. Had he been using money to buy him out of what she really needed . . . him here with her?

"No, honey." She reached over and patted his hand, hers so much frailer than what he remembered. He could see the veins through the thin skin. "You keep your money. I'll be fine."

"Sons take care of mothers, and that's what you are to me, you know."

Her eyes glistened for a moment, but she shook her head. "I can't let you do that."

Except he could be as stubborn as his aunt. He'd use that money on Emily's list. After he left, he'd set up an account for Emily, or whoever he got to run this place for Tilly, to draw from discreetly, and no one had to be the wiser. Maybe that was the answer.

Except for Tilly's age and health.

"We'll talk about this again later," he said. Then he levered off the bed and leaned over to kiss her cheek good night.

Tomorrow, he'd make sure to spend some quality time with her, maybe involve her in the tree decorating.

I'm sitting with Miss Tilly after breakfast is over and the guests have all headed off to whatever they do during the day. She's in her room reading her newspaper. She still does this every morning, though she's the only human I've ever seen with this habit.

This is one of my favorite times of day, because as she finishes a sheet, she'll drop it on the ground so that I can pounce on it and tear it to shreds.

In fact, I'm ready to spring into action, lightly balancing on my paws, tail out, muscles all bunched.

A paper flutters to the ground with a rustle of sound and I'm on it in an instant. I manage to pin it in one leap and rip into it with claws and teeth. That paper stands no chance as I shred it in the most satisfying way.

I could do this all day.

The sound of the kitchen door creaking open before it clunks closed again catches my attention, my senses better than humans I've learned, and I pause.

Only Emily, Tilly, and Lukas go in and out that door. Did Emily leave without me?

I abandon my shredded foe to leap lightly up to the windowsill and peer out. From Tilly's room, I can see only the front of the house, though.

Are they walking around the back? Maybe I should use my secret passage to get out and go find them.

Awareness of the man following her out of the house was starting to become a thing in a way that made Emily want to grind her teeth until they were flat nubs. Instead, she clicked her key fob to unlock her car with a bit more oomph than usual.

Nothing.

Darn batteries. She needed to write that down on her list, because she kept forgetting about it. She tried again. And again.

"Brrr . . ." Lukas rubbed at his arms. "Hurry up, slowpoke. I'm freezing."

She paused in her clicking to shoot him a miffed look over the top of her car. "I'm not being slow. My key fob isn't working."

He raised his eyebrows, lips buttoned up in a way that appeared suspiciously like contained amusement. "Do you have a key?"

Emily stilled, muffled an inward sigh and the urge to smack herself in the forehead, then used the key to unlock the door and let him in with the button that unlocked the rest of the doors.

Lukas shot out a hand to stop her from starting the car. "Maybe I should drive."

"Why?" He sounded so serious.

"Well, your mind is obviously elsewhere, and you know what they say about distracted driving . . ." He blinked at her with total innocence.

Emily rolled her eyes and shook off his hand so she could start the car. "I'm fine."

"Good." He put a hand to his throat. "I was worried there for a second. I mean,

89

unlocking a door seems pretty simple but —"

Don't laugh. Don't laugh. Don't laugh. It would encourage him too much.

"I tell you what . . ." she interrupted, voice sweet enough to give a candy maker a toothache. "You let this one go, and I'll stop bringing up how long it's been since you bothered to visit your aunt."

The humor wiped out of his expression so fast, Emily instantly regretted the words. He'd just been teasing.

"Generous of you," Lukas said.

She cleared her throat. "I'm known for my sweet and kind nature." Usually, she was.

Then she hit the button to turn on the radio before she did something silly like apologize. Or kiss him.

No need to change the station, already set to the one that perpetually played Christmas music. Emily hummed along softly, concentrating on guiding her small SUV, which had all-wheel drive and handled like a dream under any conditions, to the outskirts of town where the tree lot waited.

Doing her best to ignore Lukas, she hopped out, grabbed the box she'd set in the back seat, and moving faster than Santa on Christmas Eve, headed for Martin, who ran the place.

90

Coming here was one of her favorite parts of the Christmas season, and not just because of the scent of fresh cut pine. Martin had set up fire pits in safe locations around the area and sold the best hot chocolate around so that people could take their time selecting trees. Each evening around dinnertime he brought in a different group of singers or carolers or musicians. Starting last year, he'd invited food trucks at the same time so that families could enjoy dinner and the music before heading home with their tree.

One of the best times to be had in town. If only she had an extra second to spare to stay and enjoy it.

"There's a face I've been looking forward to seeing." Martin's long, gray beard twitched as he smiled.

If he wasn't skinny as a rail with dark brown eyes, he could've had a permanent posting as the town Santa thanks to that beard.

Seeing him here always put her in the Christmas spirit.

Lukas stepped closer, and Emily introduced them. "Martin, this is Lukas Weber, Miss Tilly's nephew —"

"I remember you," Martin boomed.

Emily winced. Martin only had two volumes. Loud and louder.

"You were a scrawny boy last time I saw you." Martin patted his concave belly and grinned.

To her surprise, Lukas grinned back. "Yes, sir. I remember you."

Martin ran a hand down his beard. "I expect I'm hard to forget."

"Especially at Christmas," Lukas said.

Lukas's low chuckle sent goose bumps cascading over her skin. Despite her thick jacket and jeans and practical boots, not to mention the heat lamp radiating warmth nearby, she did her best to put that reaction down to the cold weather.

But the man had a nice laugh. Warm and inviting.

Martin turned to her. "I have your trees right here. As soon as you give the okay, I'll wrap 'em up and strap 'em to your car."

They followed him to a corner under a tent, roped off with a sign that read, "Reserved."

"Here you are," Martin said, indicating the trees with a flourish of his hand. "Three Douglas firs, with the usual height requirements, like you asked."

"Those look great. How much do I owe —"

"Hold on," Lukas cut her off. For once,

the man was not smiling.

She crossed her arms. "What?"

"Three of the same type of tree?" He shook his head and clucked his tongue like Tilly did sometimes when she was scolding Snowball. "I'm surprised at you."

"I said the same myself last year," Martin exclaimed.

I do not have time for this. "It's fine."

"Huh." Lukas crossed his arms, imitating her stance. "I'm shocked Aunt Tilly let you get away with this. Granted we only ever had the one tree, plus the smaller one up in her room for our family-only present opening, but still." He shook his head and Emily might as well have been on Santa's lap finding out she'd made the naughty list.

She bit her lip, looking over at the trees again, then back at Lukas.

Emily caught the twinkle in his eyes, though, and so she paused and, for once, managed not to rise to the challenge that was Lukas Weber in a teasing mood. "You can take that up with her next year. We need to get going."

When she went to lead Martin away to pay, Lukas snagged her by the arm and turned her to face the lot. "Can't you picture Tilly's happy face when she sees three distinct trees? You know how much

93

she *loves* each room of the house to have its own personality."

Emily actually *could* picture Tilly's pleasure, with way too much ease. Come to think of it, there might have been a hint of disappointment from that lovely woman last year. Not that Tilly would ever say anything. Still . . .

"And just think what the folks coming for Christmas Eve will say."

Unfair.

"What did you have in mind?" she asked with resignation.

CHAPTER 6

Yes.

The fact that Emily caved was a minor victory. Like winning her over was important and this was a small step down that line.

Plus, Aunt Tilly would love the different kinds of trees. "We'll pick the best of these three, then pick two other types. Preferably different kinds with different looks."

He looked askance at Martin, who ran his hand thoughtfully over his beard. "I might suggest a blue spruce. They're in the section over to the left."

"I was thinking that would be good."

Martin nodded. "And also a white pine. They need lighter ornaments because their branches aren't quite as sturdy, but the color and texture of the needles is lovely. They're with the specialty trees in the back."

Beside him, Emily made a small sound somewhere between a cough and a groan but said nothing.

"If you don't mind, I'll help a few other customers while you browse. If you want to pick the one of these three you want to keep, and put the other two outside the rope, that would help. I'll come check on you in a bit."

With a wave, Martin left them to it.

Lukas chuckled. "I forgot what a character Martin is."

That, at least, pulled a smile from Emily. "He's a total hippie, and I kind of love him for it."

"It's a bit ironic that he runs a business cutting down trees," Lukas commented, turning back to the selection before him.

"He'll acknowledge the situation himself if you ask him," she said. "The tree farm is only a small part of their family business."

"I remember." The Johnsons owned a ton of acres and operated a massive orchard, which was popular in the fall, and the tree farm around Christmas.

He cocked his head, no longer seeing the Douglas firs, his mind further away. An idea was in there. Something to do with Weber Haus, but he needed to think it through more thoroughly.

"So . . ." He rubbed his hands together with more eagerness than he'd expected.

He hadn't originally wanted to spend any time shopping for Christmas trees. Except now that he was in it, he couldn't regret it. "Let's pick out our trees . . ."

"Tilly's trees," Emily corrected. "And specialty trees are expensive," she muttered under her breath as she checked over her shoulder to make sure Martin couldn't hear.

Lukas leaned closer and in a loud whisper said, "This is my treat."

She lifted a single eyebrow.

He shrugged. "My idea. My aunt's happiness. My treat. No one has to know but you and me."

Emily just shook her head. "We could've used you and your deep pockets last year."

He ignored the comment and strode to the three trees Martin had picked out. He stuck his hand inside the branches of one to grab it by the trunk and tipped it upright. Then studied it for symmetry before he spun it slowly around to search for holes or gaps in the branches. Then leaned in and sniffed before nodding to himself.

He proceeded to do the same for each of the other two, then, third one in hand, turned to Emily to find her watching him with wide eyes and . . . Was that a twitch to her lips?

"That's . . . errr . . . quite a process you

have there," she said.

Lukas grinned, more happy than he should be that no hint of sarcasm lingered in her words. "Pretty basic, I'd say. Why? How do you pick a Christmas tree?"

"I don't. Martin does because I don't have time to hang around here." She pointedly glanced at her wrist like she was looking at a watch, not that she had one.

"Fine. I can be quick."

Except his cell phone went off. With a sheepish smile aimed in Emily's direction, he checked the screen. Bethany. He sent it to voicemail and stuck the device back in his pocket. Bethany wanted to talk more contracts, and that could wait until Emily wasn't listening.

"Let me guess," Emily said. "Your agent."

"I'll call her back when we're done." He gave the tree he was still holding a shake. "This is the one. I'll put the others over here."

One selection down, he ushered her toward the blue spruce section of the massive lot. As they passed by, he caught Emily sneaking a furtive glance filled with surprising longing at a quaint stand. One he happened to know had once been a storage shed but had been converted to look like a building at the North Pole and sported the sign "Hot Chocolate and Cider."

"Would you like some hot chocolate?"

Being thoughtful only earned him one of her dubious frowns. He was starting to catalog her frowns in his head. This one he classified as faked.

"We don't have time," she said.

That wasn't a no. "There's always time for hot chocolate."

With a hand at her back, he managed to scoot her in that direction. Luck was on his side, and the line cleared out in time for them to walk right up to the counter. Otherwise, he seriously doubted he could've got Emily to stick around.

Surreptitiously he watched as she blew on hers, then took a sip. Emily closed her eyes and gave a soft hum of appreciation. An answering hum of tension spun through him at the sight and sound, and Lukas paused to enjoy it. Only for a split second, though. Before she could catch him, he forced himself to get them moving.

He might be on a bid to win Emily's trust, or at least make her stop doubting him, but attraction was a bad idea. He was leaving, and she disliked him.

For good reason, unfortunately.

He started walking. Emily, after a beat of hesitation, hurried to catch up, cocoa in hand. "They've always had the best hot chocolate," she said. "I've tried for years to figure out the recipe, and Martin refuses to share." She eyed her cup like she could discern the secrets with her own version of Santa-vision.

"That's because it's a store-bought mix."

"What?!" She jerked her head up, then looked back at her cup like it had sprouted legs and turned into a spider.

"Yeah. I helped out one Christmas for extra money, and the hot chocolate stand was where he put me."

"Don't tell me that," she wailed. "It ruins the mystique."

Lukas laughed. "I've always thought the touch of salt in the mix is what brought out the flavor."

She shook her head, expression comically tragic, but also light in a way that he got the sense she was teasing. Progress.

"Let's go pick these trees fast before you ruin another one of my Christmas traditions," she said.

He couldn't let that stand. Lukas stopped and tugged her around so that he could wrap her in a hug. Granted, as stiff as she went, it was sort of like hugging one of the trees. "Sorry," he murmured in her hair. "I promise no more spoilers while I'm in town.

Not even a hint that reindeer can't fly, Rudolph's nose doesn't glow, and elves are crap at making toys."

Emily didn't say anything, but he caught a soft chuckle and, a little at a time, the tension drained from her body . . . and Lukas found he didn't want to let her go. Because this was nice. Really nice.

"Come on, slowpoke. We should get moving," she grumbled into the front of his jacket.

Dang. He'd have to let her go.

"Lift higher." Lukas's strained voice reached Emily from over the top of the SUV.

However, she couldn't see his face through the thick branches of the white pine they were attempting to carry into the house. Buying the trees had been an adventure in and of itself. Not because of her, but because of Lukas.

The man had issues when it came to Christmas trees, picky to the point of it being a disorder, but he'd ended up with the exact three he wanted.

Which meant they'd taken a lot longer to be done with their selection before Martin had helped them strap them to her SUV in a massive pile.

"I *can't* lift higher," she retorted now. "I'm

on my tip toes."

"I'm surrounded by shrimps," she thought she heard him mutter. Hard to tell when she couldn't see him.

A shadow passed behind her a split second before the weight of the tree was lifted from her hands. Freed of her burden, Emily stepped back, then laughed and threw her arms around her brother's waist.

"Peter —" she practically squealed.

Peter's answering laugh vibrated against her cheek. "Give a guy a break and let me help your boyfriend get this tree off your car."

"Oh." She let go and hopped back. "Sorry."

Once they got the tree down, Peter looked at Lukas over the top. "Which way?"

"Follow me," Emily said.

As soon as the two men had laid it down in the formal living room, they faced off with similar expressions of wary curiosity.

"Pete, this is Lukas. Tilly's nephew. *Not* my boyfriend." Better to get that straight right away or her horde of a family would descend Christmas Eve with expectations and a heck of a lot of teasing.

"Lukas, meet my brother Peter. He's in the navy and is on leave. I haven't seen him in months and months, and apparently he's forgotten what email is for."

"I'm not much of a writer," Peter said. "And it's not like I had a ton of time, Em."

"Whatever." But she hugged him again to show no hard feelings.

For his part, Lukas's wariness dropped away, and he held out a hand to shake with a grin. "Nice to meet you."

Peter, however, sent her a significant glance before shaking. "Likewise."

Emily winced. She'd forgotten about complaining to Pete in her last few emails. She'd just been so tired, taking care of Weber Haus almost entirely on her own and worrying about Tilly. Not that she'd been any warmer to Lukas when she'd discovered who he was. Still, he'd tackled his tasks with gusto the last few days. Maybe he was obliviously negligent more than useless or a terrible person.

Does he deserve a break? Maybe a little Christmas charity?

"Do you mind helping us get the other trees?" she hastily asked before her brother could say anything.

In short order, Christmas trees were set in their stands in the dining room, living room, and newly painted sitting room, as well as in the foyer tucked into the curve of the main staircase. Lukas had talked her into that extra one. He also had bought a smaller one for Tilly's sitting room. The fresh scent of pine filled the house, making everything smell like Christmas, and Emily stood there inhaling happily.

Then she turned to find her brother rolling his eyes. Granted she had a tendency to do this every Christmas. What could she say? She was a baker. Smells were a big thing to her. Almost as important as taste. "Did you come from Mom and Dad's?" she asked.

He shook his head. "On my way there now, but I thought I'd stop and see you first."

"What do you do in the navy, Peter?" Lukas asked.

"Computer systems, mainly," Pete said, then turned his back on the man and faced Emily. "I'm surprised you're still working here."

Emily plonked her hands on her hips. "I get it enough from the rest of the family. If anyone understood, I thought you would."

Her brother crossed his arms and set his feet. "You've lost weight since I saw you, and you were already skinny."

"I'm fine," she assured him firmly. A flicker of a glance told her Lukas was now inspecting her from head to toe with a discerning eye, not that he'd be able to tell much under her thick sweater and jeans.

Peter grunted, then reached out and ruffled her hair. "I can't stay."

She wrapped him up in another hug, not wanting to let him leave. Though, if he'd just got back, Mom and Dad would want to see him as soon as possible. "I expect more time later, sailor. Let me walk you out."

Lukas didn't follow.

As soon as the door closed behind them, Peter gave his head a shake. "You're making nice with the deadbeat?"

Emily gave a hiss of annoyance. She loved her brothers more than she could say, but her family's tendency to get all judgy and protective about everything drove her nuts. Granted, she'd been the one to complain first. "Please. I have a plan . . . I have him doing all the chores around the place while he's visiting Tilly for Christmas."

That finally got Pete to grin. "I've taught you well, little sister."

"Hey! I get *some* credit here," she insisted. "I always managed to wheedle you into cleaning the bathrooms for me."

"Only because you'd gag and threaten to throw up if you had to do it, and then Mom would make me clean them anyway."

"And yet I manage to clean bathrooms

here from time to time with nary a heave."

Pete stopped walking abruptly. "You did that on purpose?"

Emily inspected her nails with feigned interest. "I'm just saying you're not the only one with tricks in this family."

He grunted, which was Pete for "whatever" and continued down the drive. He paused at his truck, which he'd parked behind her SUV and pulled her in for a long hug. "How about lunch tomorrow?"

Emily's first reaction was to say she couldn't, but then she cocked her head and tossed a glance toward the house and grinned. "Lukas can deal with the lunch tomorrow. I'm due a day off anyway."

Technically, *this* was her day off and she was using it to decorate.

"Great." Peter kissed her cheek, then hopped in his car and drove away.

Back indoors, Emily dragged the boxes of decorations she'd used last year from the spots where she'd stashed them after hauling them down from the attic. As soon as he caught sight of them, Lukas grimaced. Was he about to grinch-out on her? He'd promised to help.

"Ready?"

"Sure." He almost visibly had to gather himself.

Emily hid a grin behind the fall of her hair and opened the first carton, pulling out neatly bundled strings of white lights.

"Hey." Lukas snatched one from her hands. He stared at the thing as if it had grown elf ears.

"What?"

"This is not a tangled mess." He held it out to her, accusation in his tone.

Emily laughed and realized exactly why he'd been reluctant. "I organized things after the first year I helped Tilly."

It had been a twisted, time-consuming muddle.

"Wow." He shook his head, then lifted his eyes to stare at her with a strangely intent gaze. One that set her blood flowing faster. "I'm impressed."

Bands of tension wrapped around Emily's rib cage, making it hard to breathe. Sheesh. This was Lukas Weber, Tilly's inconsiderate nephew, for heaven's sake, even if he'd been nothing but helpful since arriving. She shouldn't care about impressing him. And yet, a tiny glow of happiness ignited in her heart.

"I wrapped the lights up to unravel more easily." She did her best to give a nonchalant shrug. "No big deal."

There went that charming grin of his.

With the dimples. Her heart joined the inappropriate fizzing going on inside her, setting it off double time.

"It's a big deal to me," he said. "I was dreading this part all day. Now it'll be easy."

So saying, he unwrapped the strand he held, tested it by plugging it into the wall, then unplugged it and proceeded to start wrapping the tree as if he did this all the time.

Which was the opposite of the spoiled, bohemian traveler she'd been picturing for months and months.

Working side by side, they got into a rhythm, going to each room. As they finished up the foyer, with her on a step stool wrapping lights around the top of the tree and Lukas feeding them to her, the sound of the front doorbell jingled.

A young couple stepped inside, both glowing, though from the chill in the air or from love was anyone's guess.

"Welcome," Emily greeted with a smile and a wave. Below her, Lukas just nodded, suddenly quiet in a very un-Lukas-like way.

Before Emily could climb off her stool to help them, Tilly came slowly down the stairs. "I've got it, dear," she said to Emily, and led them to the small desk tucked off to the side where they checked in guests.

Emily paused to listen. "Must be our honeymooners," she whispered to Lukas as Tilly then led them upstairs.

"Ah."

She shot him a closer look, his tone and the stiff way he held himself catching her attention. She pursed her lips as she studied him, then suddenly found herself the recipient of an equally curious stare.

"What?" Lukas asked.

"You're not a fan of the guests being here, are you?" A total guess, mostly based on how he'd disappeared during dinner last night only to show up for kitchen duty. Most people would have done the opposite.

Lukas held up another strand of lights to her. Seeing he didn't intend to answer, she took them and kept going, wrapping the top of the tree.

"I moved here right after my parents died," Lukas said slowly.

Emily paused, then kept going. Maybe he found it easier to tell her this way. Though, even with her back to him, she could hear the pain in his voice.

"All I wanted to do was be alone. Instead, all these people were constantly in and out. Total strangers. And I had to put on this brave face and be polite."

She couldn't help herself. Emily paused

and faced him, her chest constricting again, but this time in direct reaction to the lonely, heartbroken little boy she could see lurking in the depths of his eyes, turning the color of moss.

"That had to be hard," she said quietly. Was that why he tended to stay away?

Lukas opened his mouth to answer, then horror flashed over his face. "No —" He reached for her, but he wasn't fast enough.

A streak of white flashed from the corner of her eye the millisecond before Snowball jumped off a stair and landed on Emily's head, sinking her sharp claws into Emily's scalp.

Unable to help herself, Emily squealed and reached for the kitten before she could scratch an eyeball. Unfortunately, her violent thrashing set the ladder she was perched precariously upon swaying, and Emily tumbled backward with another screech. Instinct had her bracing to hit the ground hard. Instead, Lukas caught her with a grunt, strong arms wrapping around her.

"I've got you," he said, mouth close to her ear. In the same instant, Snowball leaped lightly to the floor.

"Jiminy Christmas. That could've been bad." Emily clutched Lukas's shoulders tighter as she pictured the worst catastrophe.

"Thank —" She lifted her gaze and paused at how close he was. Right there. If she wanted, she could lean in and —

Good grief, what am I thinking?

"Thank you," she got out in a rush.

She expected him to put her down, only his arms tightened fractionally around her. "Are you okay?" he asked. Had his voice lowered?

"Mm-hmm." She had to hide a wince at how squeaky that came out. Then she took a deep breath, determined to make the next sound out of her mouth normal. "Fit as a fiddle. Although I should probably check for scratches."

Which reminded her . . . She swiveled her head to find Snowball sitting at their feet watching them with avid interest and, of course, her appearance of angelic innocence.

"What was that all about?" Emily demanded of the kitten.

Snowball canted her head as if trying to interpret human, then meowed, looking between Emily and Lukas.

Lukas's low chuckle vibrated against Emily's side, and she squirmed in his grasp. Mostly thanks to her own reaction to that low laugh. "You can put me down now."

As soon as her feet touched the ground, Emily backed up a few steps despite how Lukas's eyebrows went up as she did. She didn't care. The distance was necessary, or she'd do something idiotic like kiss the man. Then she scooped Snowball up in one hand. "Why don't you finish wrapping the top of the tree," she said to him. "I'll go lock this mischief maker up in a room and get the ornaments."

She was out of the foyer in a shot, needing space to reorient. She was supposed to be mad at him.

Lukas's confused sounding "okay" followed her up the stairs.

"I can't believe you did that to me," she scolded Snowball.

And got a rumbling purr in response.

Ha! I knew it.

I might be a kitten. Everything is new to me, and human behavior is especially odd, but I *knew* Lukas and Emily had something. Even I could feel the tingle in the air when he held her, and they stared at each other — like a strange sort of quiet passed over them and they settled into each other.

Since I've been living here, I've got to see many human pairs. The ones who stay in what Emily and Miss Tilly called the honeymoon suite always seem to be the most in love, and every once in a while, that quiet will surround them, too. I've felt it before.

And I felt it again just now.

Emily might be mad — she's squeezing me a bit too tight again, but I don't squiggle or meow. I'm too pleased with myself. A few more attempts like that one to push them together, and Lukas is sure to change Emily's mind and make her fall in love with him. I already see how he looks at her when she's not looking back.

Maybe then she'll realize what that quiet really means.

CHAPTER 7

The first clue Lukas got that he was not alone was the sound of a loud, rumbling purr from the ball of fluff curled up and sleeping in the center of his back.

Again?

Mornings were turning into a routine. How he had managed to sleep through Snowball pushing his door open this time he wasn't sure — he needed to figure out how she did that. She'd also managed to jump up on the bed, climb on top of him, and get settled before she started purring. Given the last couple days of unaccustomed activity, no doubt he'd been sleeping pretty hard, though he walked and hiked a lot for his job and worked out in hotel gyms when they had them. He'd thought of himself as in decent shape until now.

It didn't help that, in the middle of the night a whistling sound coming from the unoccupied room across the hall had woken him. After an hour of trying to sleep through it, he'd gone into the Knight's Suite and fiddled with the window — which had been partially cracked open but otherwise didn't want to budge — for a good long while until he'd finally shut it.

Mental note to fix that window.

As the lethargy of slumber faded, Lukas lifted his head and checked his phone to see the time, then paused as the numbers on the screen sank in — 6:00 a.m.?

That can't be right.

Why hadn't Emily woken him as she'd been so patently eager to do, well before his alarm?

The homey aromas of fresh-brewed coffee and Emily's superb baking drifted through his wide open door. Which meant it was already time for breakfast. Lukas tipped to the side to dump Snowball off his back as gently as he could. She rolled with a thump, then lifted her head to glare at him in a totally offended feline way.

He pushed out of the bed and made a face at her. "Why didn't you wake me sooner?"

In answer she hopped to her feet and spun in a circle, kneading the mattress before curling back up, paws tucked under the fluff of her ruff, and watched him with idle curiosity.

"I thought you were on my side." He turned away to grab fresh clothes from his armoire. After showering last night, he'd fallen into bed like a useless lump of coal. Now he was talking to a kitten like she was his ally and responsible for waking him. Clearly this place, and a certain spunky brunette who was maybe warming toward him a tiny bit, were getting to him.

Lukas dressed in a rush before he hurried down the back stairs, Snowball on his heels, reaching the kitchen in time to see Emily disappear out the door leading to the dining room.

"Dang." Looking around he could see that not only had she cooked breakfast, but she had cleaned up from most of it as well.

Before he could decide what to do, Emily came back through the swinging door. She paused at the sight of him, then took note of Snowball at his feet. The kitten proceeded to prance over to Emily and lay something at her feet. When had the scamp picked that up anyway?

"Another present?" Emily said as she bent to retrieve it. Something silver and metallic glittered in her grasp. "A piece of tinsel. Oh my, how lovely."

In answer, Snowball rubbed against Emily's ankles, chin tipped up as though supremely proud of herself.

"Does she bring you gifts often?" Lukas wondered.

"Sometimes." Instead of a cool expression or ignoring him, he actually got a half smile. "I figure it's better than presents of dead mice or bugs." Emily shuddered. Snowball nipping at her feet, she moved to a cabinet and pulled out a bin of kitty food.

"Sorry," Lukas said. "I guess I slept through my alarm." No way was he going to admit that between Emily and Snowball the last couple of days, he hadn't needed the alarm. In fact it was entirely possible he'd forgotten to set one in the first place.

"It's fine. But I think we now know who the slowpoke is here."

Teasing? She was actually loosening up enough to tease him?

She turned her back to him as she loaded up her tray with the carafe of coffee and glass pitchers of milk, water, and orange juice.

Lukas rubbed a hand over his face, not entirely sure how to deal with an Emily who wasn't sparking at him. "I'll get that." He moved closer and reached around her to pick up the tray.

Emily said nothing but let him. He backed out of the kitchen into the dining room only to turn around and discover five sets of eyes trained on him. His aunt, an older couple who looked to be perhaps in their seventies, and a younger couple in their early twenties, the new honeymooners who'd arrived yesterday.

Aw, heck.

He'd forgotten that bringing breakfast out meant dealing with the guests. Not his favorite thing to do. No matter, he would simply put down the tray and be on his way, politely of course.

Lukas fixed a stiff smile to his face. "Who needs coffee?"

Emily came in behind him and took a seat, draping a pristine white napkin across her lap. "Why don't you join us this morning?"

"Oh, yes!" Aunt Tilly practically bounced in her seat at the thought. When he'd been growing up here, she had to resort to bribery to get him to spend any time around the guests.

Lukas shot Emily a narrow-eyed glance. She knew about his thing with the guests. And here he'd thought she was warming to him. Was this payback for not waking up earlier this morning to help her? While she might not like him all that much, he hadn't pegged Emily as a vindictive person.

Emily must've caught his frown, because she stilled, then glanced from him to the guests and winced. "Sorry," she mouthed.

So . . . not on purpose?

He gave her a small shrug in response as he pulled out a chair and sat beside her. The food smelled amazing, but he had to admit, the woman at his side smelled even better — like her baking had infused into her skin, making her permanently smell like sugar cookies.

I wouldn't mind a nibble.

"Everyone, this is my nephew, Lukas," Tilly announced, interrupting his thoughts.

"More like a son," he corrected. "After all, you pretty much raised me." He shot his aunt a wink.

She gave a happy hum in response. "Lukas, I'd like you to meet Katie and Miles Bauer." She indicated the younger couple with a wave. "They've just been married."

"Congrats," he offered.

The couple smiled at each other, happiness shining from their eyes that, like staring directly into the sun, was almost painful to witness. No doubt under the table they were clasping hands. Suddenly, Lukas itched to get out his cameras and capture their happiness on film, because he knew it wouldn't last long. Not that the happiness

119

wouldn't last, necessarily, but that sheen of newness would eventually give way to something else — comfort, friendship, partnership — as they grew through the phases of their lives together.

Unaware of his thoughts, Tilly continued the introductions. "And this is Louise and Bill Hoffman. They have been coming every year for Christmas for about the last five years."

While he'd been to visit once or twice in the earlier part of those five years, his trips home hadn't been at Christmas.

"Nice to meet you," Lukas said.

Then he cut himself a slice of still-warm banana bread and slathered butter all over it. He took a bite and groaned before he could stop himself. "Emily, I didn't think it possible, but this is even better than the cherry turnovers."

Emily's cheeks turned rosy in a way that had nothing to do with the fire crackling cheerily away in the fireplace at their backs. "Thank you."

"I beg to differ, young man," Bill Hoffman said around a healthy bite of the bread. "This is excellent, but those cherry turnovers are now on my list of favorite foods ever."

"He couldn't stop talking about them all

day yesterday," Louise affirmed. "When are you going to open the bakery, Emily?"

Lukas sat up straighter. "You're going to open a bakery?" And what? Leave his aunt without help? She clearly had taken over from Tilly as the driving force behind the inn. Particularly the food.

Although . . . maybe Tilly wouldn't need Emily's help for long.

An idea had been percolating. One he thought everyone involved could live with. What if they sold the property and used the money to find Tilly a smaller place, maybe one of those fancy retirement communities where she'd have plenty of people her own age? He'd make sure to visit much more often, already planning to tell Bethany to schedule quarterly breaks for him to return home.

With the repairs Lukas was helping with, hopefully it would help the value a bit. However, selling might be more difficult if Emily went off and started her own bakery and wasn't part of the package deal with the inn. In the vague idea that had been forming, he'd seen her as included in the sales agreement.

"Of course," Tilly said. Her tone indicated that he should have already known this somehow. "Opening a bakery is Emily's dream."

Is that why she's doing so much for Aunt Tilly? For the extra money?

The second the thought popped into Lukas's head, a squelch of shame followed. What a horrible thing to think. Emily was working herself to the bone, if her brother was to be believed about her having lost weight. As far as Lukas could tell, she wasn't getting paid extra for any of it. Besides, Lukas could see the affection Emily held for his aunt.

That's why she pushed herself.

The problem was now he had to sell Weber Haus without a cook. "When is that going to happen?" He directed the question to Emily.

She shifted in her chair slightly. "I'm working to secure a small-business loan that will cover the renovations, equipment, and goods I need to get started."

Mind still spinning like an old-fashioned top over all the implications and impacts, Lukas hid all that behind a bland smile. "No more early-morning deliveries. That will be nice."

Emily's brows beetled and her lips flattened. Apparently, that had been the wrong thing to say to her, though he couldn't for the life of him figure out why.

"The deliveries are to help build the business by word of mouth before the bakery opens," she said in a flat voice. "I happen to have both a culinary degree *and* a business degree."

"Having seen you in action, I have no doubts you have everything well planned and well in hand." He popped another piece of banana bread in his mouth and smiled at her as he chewed.

"Yes, I do." On that note, Emily stood from the table, grabbed her mostly empty plate, and marched back into the kitchen.

Lukas watched her leave, then turned a confused gaze on his aunt. "Was it something I said?"

"You'll have to ask Emily." Aunt Tilly gave him that disappointed shake of her head that he remembered from growing up. Apparently, he was the one in the wrong here. A situation that was becoming a sad state of normal.

"No time like the present, son," Bill Hoffman prompted. Louise flapped her napkin at him in a shooing motion.

Lukas looked longingly at the rest of the food on the table — fluffy eggs, crisp bacon, and grapefruit — which he had yet to sample. They were right, though. He should figure out what he had done wrong and apologize. Taking his own plate, he also got up from the table and headed into the kitchen, where he found Emily standing at the sink staring out through the window into the side yard. Snowball had jumped up on the counter to perch beside her, balanced on the small counter space between the edge and the sink, staring out the same window, her long fluffy tail dangling down behind her, twitching lazily.

Any residual irritation disappeared at the sight of Emily's shoulders hunched over like she carried the weight of the world. "I didn't mean to offend you," he said softly.

Emily stiffened before she turned on the water and started rinsing off dishes. "You didn't."

"Clearly I said something wrong. Though I'm not sure what."

Slowly, she shut the water off and dried her hands on a towel. Then she turned to face him. "I'm not mad at you."

He could tell she meant that. No irritation or animosity lingered in her gaze, but a weary sort of sadness peered back at him.

"Then why —"

"My family doesn't understand my dream of opening a bakery. I got the business degree for my parents, plus I figured it would help. I paid for the culinary degree myself without their knowledge. They found out thanks to an unfortunate incident with a . . . business partner . . . who backed out on me at the last minute."

The way she hesitated over the business partner bit had him wonder if a romance had also been involved.

"Now I'm going it alone, and they worry that I'm going to get myself into debt. Like restaurants, most bakeries fail pretty spectacularly." She shrugged like that was no big deal, but he could tell it was a very big deal.

If he knew anything about Emily it was that she was driven and she cared, a heck of a lot. Otherwise, she wouldn't have been so angry with him when he arrived.

"You know what Tilly said to me when I decided to be a photographer?" he asked.

Emily's lips twitched. "What?"

"She said that following a dream is one of the scariest things in life a person could do . . . and the most fulfilling. She warned me that talent wasn't enough, that I would have to work harder than every other photographer out there if I wanted to make it. But that if this was in my heart, no amount of hard work, or failure, or roadblocks, or empty stomachs should be able to stand in my way."

Emily did smile at that. "Sounds like Tilly. Was she right?"

"About everything. I had years of living with multiple roommates and still barely getting by, eating ramen noodles for every meal, not being able to afford things like health insurance, being told no more times than I care to count. I could wallpaper this house in rejections. I almost gave up several times, and probably would have if Aunt Tilly hadn't always been there cheering for me."

Emily cocked her head, listening with interest. "But you obviously made it."

He gave her a wry smile. "Success didn't come all at once. I built it little by little. One project leading to another. One contact leading to another. One step down the road, often followed by three or four steps backward. And lots of waiting. Now, yes, I'm successful. But I have to keep working or that all goes away. In my profession, you're only as good as your last project, your last award, your last publication . . ."

"Is that why you never stop?"

Lukas would've expected that question to come out as more of an accusation, given who was asking. Except Emily truly seemed to want to know, dark eyes curious and clear.

Which was probably why he found himself

126

sharing. "I love what I do and the fact that I can make a living at it is a blessing that I will never take for granted." If he told her the other part, though, the part where he hadn't felt like he had a home base to return to, even with Tilly here, he would definitely ruin this moment. So he kept that to himself.

"I know I had Aunt Tilly to encourage me, and now you do, too. Your food is excellent, and I have faith that the bakery will be a huge success. Of your family, I've only met Peter, but going by him they obviously care for you. So I say don't worry, and they'll come around. They're just concerned about the practical, and most dreams are not practical or easy. Otherwise, everybody would chase their own."

Emily glanced away, seeming to think about that, then stepped into him and wrapped her arms around his waist. "Thank you, Lukas," she murmured into his chest. "I think I needed to hear that."

An unexpected longing caught Lukas off guard, and he stiffened against her even as he wanted to wrap around her and keep her close.

She must've sensed his hesitation, though, because Emily let go and turned sharply back to the sink. "Do you mind clearing the table for me? I'd like to work on the loose railing on the porch before I go to lunch with Pete."

"I don't even get a day off?" Lukas teased.

Emily chuckled, a rich, sweet sound that he wanted to hear more of. A lot more of. "Nope. In fact I'm putting you in charge of lunch." She tossed a devious grin over her shoulder.

"Of course you are." But he laughed as he went into the dining room to gather more dishes, his steps lighter than they had been in a while.

A fact that must've showed, because Bill gave him a thumbs up and Aunt Tilly nodded as if he were a ten-year-old who needed to understand he'd done the right thing.

An hour later, Emily stood on the front porch with Lukas, both of them bundled up against the chill. At least the sun was shining today, the sky that perfect clear blue that only happened on pristine winter days.

As Emily watched from where she stood on the top stair, Lukas gave the white wooden banister a jiggle. Then proceeded to bounce gently on each wooden step all the way up to where she stood.

"Well . . ." He ran a hand around the back of his neck, still focused on stairs. "The good news is I don't think we need to

128

replace anything. The wood is in decent shape; I'm not seeing any signs of rotting. I think we only need to shore things up in a few spots."

Hopefully. What he knew about carpentry could be written on the wings of a gnat.

"And you can fix it? Before Christmas Eve, especially. I mean I have a handyman we can call." She didn't hide the doubt from her voice, but that only made him want to prove himself worthy.

He put a hand to his chest. "You wound me with your doubts."

Emily rolled her eyes and crossed her arms, giving him a look that clearly brooked no funny business, but different than before. Now, no animosity lingered.

Lukas relinquished his comical pose and shook his head. "Let me give it a shot first. I'm still figuring out Aunt Tilly's finances, so I'm not sure about the handyman."

"Okay," she agreed slowly.

"Don't worry," he assured her. "If I mess up, it has to be fixed either way, right?"

"Hmmm . . ." She pursed her lips. "You make a fair point."

Unable to help himself, Lukas put a hand to his ear dramatically. "Hark . . . What do mine ears hear? Emily Diemer thinks I had a good idea? I need this recorded for posterity." He pulled his cell phone from his back pocket, pretended to hit an app to record, and held it up toward her. "Say that again."

Emily snorted a laugh and shook her head at him. "Come on. Let's see if Big John left what you need to do the repairs."

"Tell you what . . . You go let Aunt Tilly know we'll be making noise out here and I'll go check the barn."

Luckily, he didn't have to convince her. As soon as Emily was out of eyesight inside, Lukas pulled up videos for repairing stairs. He watched as he walked around the back to the small workshop attached to the barn, where he knew Jim used to keep his things.

Unfortunately, he needed a few things that were more specific than the generic tools and extra pieces of wood he managed to scrounge up. Around the front of the house again, he found Emily waiting. "I need to make a trip to the hardware store. I'll probably be gone about an hour. Do you need anything while I'm out?"

Emily blinked at him, then made a face like she was debating with herself. "How about you drop me off at the grocery store and pick me up when you're done?"

"Fair enough."

Ten minutes later, they were in his car and headed into town.

"We are planning to do the tree toppers and light the trees tonight for the guests," Emily said. "Do you think you could join us and take pictures?"

When they decorated the trees the other day, beyond testing the lights worked, Emily hadn't let him turn them on. Nor had she allowed him to put the final touch atop the trees. Now he knew why. "A new tradition?"

She nodded. "One of my family's favorite traditions is to decorate the tree together. I tried that two years ago, but I couldn't manage to get all the guests together at the same time for long enough. Most of them have plans around the area. Then, last year I got the idea that doing the tree topper and lighting the trees was pretty quick. We do it right after dinner, which most of the guests come back for."

"For someone whose heart is set on baking, you certainly have a lot of good ideas when it comes to the inn." Maybe he could convince her to stay?

She was quiet long enough that he chanced taking his eyes off the road for a quick glance and found her playing with the tassel at the end of her scarf.

"I do enjoy coming up with things that I think the guests would like, but all the practicalities of running that house stress me out." She wrinkled her nose at him as if she was embarrassed to have shared that fact.

"You don't think the practicalities of running a bakery would stress you out?"

Emily huffed a laugh. "It's certainly possible. But they are different practicalities — equipment, supplies, taxes, and setting up the legal parts of a business. Not running a full household and entertaining guests on top of all that."

So, no offer to run the house permanently. Clearly, she only wanted to have her bakery. He'd have to find another cook for Weber Haus. Unless . . .

"When you start the bakery, would you want to continue cooking the meals for the inn?"

Again she was silent. This time, however, when he glanced over, she was staring at him with her brows tucked into a cute little frown. "Why do you want to know?"

"No reason. Just wondering."

When she continued to stare at him, Lukas raised his gaze to the ceiling. "God, rescue me from women who have trust issues."

He meant the words to be teasing, He even shot a good-natured grin her way only

132

to encounter a wall of frost that had nothing to do with the chill outside.

"I don't have trust issues," she said. "I'm just not sure what to think about you."

"Me?"

"Uh-huh. You with the charm, and the toothy grin, and the dimples. And the hair," she tacked on the last almost accusatory, flinging a hand at the offending follicles.

Lukas lifted a hand to his head. "The hair? What did my hair ever do to you?"

"It's floppy on top and falls into your eyes and gives you this lost little-boy look. Like you're all innocent and charming or something. It's very annoying, I'll have you know."

Lukas had to clamp down on his lips to keep from laughing. She thought he was charming? Tension banded his ribs, making it harder to breathe all of a sudden. A nice tension. Like he wanted to scoop her up into a hug or kiss her until she glowed.

He did nothing of the kind, keeping his eyes on the road. "I'll try to keep my hair under better control, ma'am."

Emily just shook her head and stared out the window. "I'm sure you're perfectly aware of your effect."

That wasn't as funny or as nice to hear. "Do you think I'm not genuine?"

Because if anything, he'd been more himself around her and being home with Aunt Tilly than he had been in years wandering the globe.

"I haven't made up my mind yet. In person, you come across as kind and thoughtful, but from a distance . . ."

She let the thought trail off, but he got the point, and it stung.

"I honestly didn't know." How many times could he tell her that or apologize for letting his aunt get into such a financial muddle and the house in such disrepair?

Emily tipped her chin up, not looking at him but out the window. "All you had to do was come home."

"To the place that only reminds me of losing my parents at a time when a kid needs them around? That's all I used to see when I came here. That's what I was getting away from when I left."

The second the words left his mouth, Lukas regretted them. He was well aware of how selfish he sounded. Because he also had happy memories here. Tilly had done her best to make his life wonderful and help him feel loved and wanted. Maybe he'd allowed tainted memories, and a bitter and ungrateful teenage heart, to color his life too much.

He pulled into the parking lot of the grocery store and parked, but Emily didn't get out. Lukas looked over, fully expecting to see accusation in her eyes. Instead, he encountered a sweet sort of understanding that he hadn't expected from the one woman who seemed to see right through him.

Emily placed a hand over his, where it rested on the gear shift and squeezed. "I can't pretend to understand what that must've been like or not having my parents around. I'm sorry you had to go through it."

He searched warm, dark eyes that he could get lost in way too easily, then flipped his hand over to link their fingers together. He'd meant it as a show of thanks, a quick squeeze. Then got distracted by the sight, her fingers, paler, softer, laced with his, which showed his travels, the skin darkened and rougher.

"I shouldn't complain," he said in a low voice. "Because I did have Tilly, and she was wonderful."

Her warmth seeped into his skin through that innocent contact.

"But I imagine a bit quirky as a mother figure," she murmured.

Lukas had to resist the urge to run his

thumb over her knuckles. That would be taking an innocent gesture of friendship too far. Wouldn't it?

"She used to dress up as Mrs. Claus for Halloween."

Emily snorted a laugh, the sound drawing a chuckle from him.

"I haven't thought of that in years," he confessed.

"Has it gotten easier for you? Coming back?" she asked.

Lukas thought about that for a second, but in the end, it didn't really matter. Because if they sold the house, things would change. Or, maybe without being tied to the inn, his aunt would want to travel and see him instead.

"You don't have to answer that," Emily said in a rush. "My brothers are always telling me that I stick my bossy nose in where it's not wanted."

She glanced down at their entwined fingers and tried to tug free of his grasp, but Lukas tightened his grip, suddenly reluctant to lose the contact. "I kind of like your bossy nose. It's cute. Especially with the freckles."

Emily's gaze flashed to his. At the same time, her mouth dropped open and she gave the most adorable little squeak as if she wanted to say something but couldn't quite find the words.

Lukas watched her reaction with interest. What would she do if he kissed her? Because he wanted to. Badly. Her lips were pink, and soft, a temptation he wanted to sample.

As he went to lean closer, drawn by those delectable lips still parted, Emily choked a gasp and sat up straighter. She managed to surprise him and tug out of his grasp. Before he knew it, she had her door open and one leg out.

"If we're going to get done with the stairs in time for me to go to lunch with Peter, we better get moving." She sort of tossed the words over her shoulder into the car at him, then closed the door with a forceful *thunk* that rocked the vehicle, and walked away, purpose in every stride. She didn't even glance back.

Lukas sat there gathering his wits. "Smooth, Weber," he muttered to himself. "Real smooth."

CHAPTER 8

Lukas was nothing like what Emily had built him up in her head to be. Only now she was having trouble reconciling the kind man who seemed to have no problem working around the house and who clearly adored his aunt, with the neglectful nephew who never came to visit his only living relative.

Plus there was the kissing thing.

He had almost kissed her when a gesture of friendship and understanding had somehow turned into . . . more. She was sure of it. What she wasn't sure of was how she felt about it. Because, caught up in him, she had wanted to lean in and meet him halfway and find out what kissing Lukas Weber would be like.

Regret chipped at a vulnerable place inside her that she hadn't.

No. It needed to be a hard no, regardless of her wondering. A very bad, no good idea.

In fact, in her history of bad ideas, kissing

Lukas Weber probably topped the charts. Worse even than the day when she was six and she decided to do a cake stand but had used salt instead of sugar in the recipe and had to give everyone their money back. Possibly even worse than the fiasco with Greg. Her business partner, and she'd hoped for more, had left her high and dry and broke, pulling out too late for her to recover deposits and payments already made. All so he could flake off and start a different venture with a different business partner.

Lukas could only end in anger, or worse, heartbreak. Because no matter how charming he was, or helpful around the house and kitchen, his being here at all was temporary. He'd go back to his life as a famous photographer and forget all about the small needs happening at Weber Haus.

Her included. For him she was probably just a bit of fun, or perhaps a challenge. Someone to win over.

"Okay, I think I'm ready," Lukas said.

His voice popped her thought bubble like a balloon hitting a sharp blade of grass. Emily almost jumped but managed to control herself. They were repairing stairs, that was it. They had both organized their purchases once they got home, then they'd bundled up and come out here, where he'd started some Christmas music playing on his phone which sat on the top rung of the railing.

"What do you need me to do?" she asked.

He didn't even glance up, bent over as he inspected things, a look of concentration scrunching his face. On her, that face would be awkward, on him . . . pretty dang cute.

"You see where this stair is splitting right where it hangs over to the next stair?"

Emily yanked her gaze to where he pointed. "Yes."

"Eventually we will have to replace it. But the internet gods have blessed me with the power of knowledge, and I think I can repair it well enough to hold us over for a while. First, I need to put some wood glue inside the crack. If you can pull it back enough to give me a wider gap to work with — but not so much that you risk breaking it more — that would be great."

"Got it." Emily knelt on the bottom step and did as he asked.

Starting at one end, Lukas squished glue into the crack. Unfortunately for her, when he got to where she was kneeling at the other end, instead of making her scoot over, he stood on either side of her legs and bent over her. Emily held her breath because after all the stupid thoughts in her head, this was way too close, too much in her personal space.

Surrounded by Lukas.

Just like the other day, she suddenly found the scents of aftershave and wood glue and Lukas Weber appealing. Last time had been aftershave and paint and lemon. Which meant she was losing her ever-loving mind.

He glanced up, and they both stilled. He searched her expression, his green eyes turned that darker, mossy color, and Emily was suddenly back in the car, warm despite the chilly weather, and longing for something she shouldn't let herself even consider.

Lukas stepped back, seemingly completely unaffected, but at least none the wiser as to his ridiculous effect on her. "Okay, you can let go."

Instead of standing, she moved to sit on the lower step. Lukas did, too, now pulling out bits and pieces for a drill that apparently he had bought at the hardware store. The song on his phone changed to a classic, and to her surprise Lukas started to sing along. Not even under his breath, either.

And he was terrible.

Tone-deaf, oblivious to his tone deafness, and loud. Which would've been sort of adorable if she wasn't determined to keep him in the "charming but useless" box in her head.

She winced at a particularly sour note. "Who sings the song again?" she asked innocently.

He made a face at the question because everybody should know the answer to that one. "Bing Crosby," he said.

"Then you should let him sing it." She grinned to soften the words a little. But not too much.

"Ha, ha, ha," he gave a fake laugh. "I take it you don't appreciate the acquired taste that is my singing?"

So he wasn't oblivious; he just didn't care. "Let's say I prefer the original version and leave it at that."

"Would you deny a man one of his great pleasures in life?"

Emily snorted. "When that great pleasure can take place in the shower and save the rest of us? Yup."

"Heartless woman." Lukas resumed singing — full-on crooning more like — and louder this time, along with emotive hand gestures and even a pretend microphone. About three lines into it, Snowball appeared out of nowhere and ran down the steps as if on a mission. She hopped in his lap and, standing on his knees with her back feet, balanced there lightly and placed both front paws over his mouth.

Emily buttoned her lips together to keep in her laughter.

Lukas gently removed the kitten's paws. "Hey. I'm singing here."

He tried again, singing along with Bing with gusto. Again, Snowball put her paws over his mouth to shut him up.

He pulled his head back. "Listen, you —"

The kitten didn't even let him speak, putting her paws back over his mouth.

Emily lost it. She threw her head back and laughed until the tears came to her eyes and her cheeks ached. Then she looked over at Lukas, who lifted the little cat up and put her on the stair above with a mock scowl. That only made it impossible to contain the gales of laughter that wanted to burst from her.

For his part, Lukas mock frowned at her. "I don't know what you find so funny."

In starts and fits, through her laughter Emily managed to shake her head. "That's what makes it funnier."

His disgruntled expression, in combination with twitching lips, set her off again.

This time he chuckled with her, the deep roll of it making her want to hear him laugh out right. Which was a silly wish to have.

Emily finally managed to get herself under control, wiping the tears from her eyes. "I

143

haven't laughed that hard in a long, long time. Thank you, Snowball."

While the kitten lifted one paw to give it a dainty lick, Lukas straightened. "Snowball? And all at my expense, too. I should be offended."

"I get the impression you don't get offended easily, Mr. Weber."

He shrugged and went back to setting up his drill. "I don't see the point of going around angry at everything in this life, or looking for the fault in others, deliberate or otherwise."

Emily could've taken that as a dig at her, but somehow, she didn't think it was. So she decided to take his advice and assume it wasn't. "Seems the world would be a better place if more people did that."

Lukas had moved positions so he could line his drill bit up with the edge of the stair but paused to glance up at her, eyebrows raised. "Did you just agree with me?"

"Don't let it go to your head," she said dryly.

The crunch of tires on gravel had them both raising their heads to find her brother pulling his truck up the long drive that led to Weber Haus. When Peter got out, he wasn't alone. Emily sat up straighter as Daniel, one of Pete's best friends growing up, got out, too. Both men walked up to where Emily and Lukas sat waiting.

"Hey, little Em," Daniel boomed, then swept her up and spun her around before setting her back on her feet, dizzy and breathless.

"It's been a while," she said with a tight smile.

Honestly, it had been years. Long enough that she figured she'd got over the almighty crush she had on him in high school. Tall, with broad shoulders, he wore his sandy-brown hair a bit on the shaggy side and had grown a beard that was neatly trimmed but managed to suggest rugged mountain man. The jeans and plaid button-down under a thick black coat only added to the impression. She waited for any trace of the old, awkward Emily she would become around Daniel to appear. Other than being vaguely pleased she'd done her hair and makeup today, she didn't feel much of anything.

Except the strangest urge to take a peek at Lukas's reaction.

"You remember my brother Peter," Emily said to Lukas who'd got to his feet and watched the byplay with a vaguely interested, slightly disappointing expression. "This is his friend, Daniel Aarons."

"Nice to meet you. I'd offer to shake, but

I've been handling wood glue," Lukas greeted with an apology.

"You, too," Daniel nodded back. He eyed the drill in Lukas's hand and the other paraphernalia scattered about the stairs and porch. Then he sent Emily a quick searching glance. "Fixing a stair looks like? I'm a carpenter, maybe I could help."

Emily wrinkled her nose and sent Pete a glare, getting a confused "What?" mouthed at her in return.

"It's no big deal," she rushed to say. "A few home repairs that don't need a professional."

Her parents and even Pete had mentioned asking Daniel for help several times this last year. Something she couldn't contemplate, because, knowing him, he'd offer to do it all at no cost to her, which she wouldn't accept. After all, he was building his own business and couldn't afford pro bono work, and she couldn't afford to pay him. Or rather Miss Tilly couldn't afford to pay him.

"A carpenter, huh?" Unfortunately, Lukas didn't know any of that. Or he knew about the not-affording-it but not the avoiding-dragging-Daniel-into-it thing. "Actually, before I do more, let me at least ask you if I'm on the right track."

The two men knelt down in front of the

146

stairs. "I'm planning to drill holes, then insert these wooden dowels that will hopefully keep the two parts together and give the splitting part a little more strength to hold up to people using the stair."

Daniel nodded. "That could work. It would probably be better to replace the board."

Lukas opened his mouth to answer, but Emily beat him to it.

"Didn't you make a reservation, Pete?"

"Why would I —"

Emily dug her elbow into Pete's side, and he grunted. Rubbing at the spot, he frowned at her, but at least he got the message. "Yeah . . . I wanted to make sure Emily's favorite restaurant had a table for us."

Daniel looked over his shoulder, eyebrows raised. For that matter, so did Lukas, but at least Daniel got up. "You're on the right track," he said to Lukas. "Make sure when you drill the holes you keep it as straight as possible. You don't want to come out the top of the step."

"Thanks. Will do."

Emily managed to drag her brother and Daniel to the truck, tossing hasty instructions over her shoulder at Lukas. "I put soup to warm on the stove for lunch. Serve it with the loaf of rye in the bread box, and

147

the fruit salad in the fridge."

"I thought I was in charge of lunch?" he called.

"I have my reputation to think of," she shot back without turning this time.

Then she hid a grin as the sound of his laughter chased after her.

After fixing the broken tread on the stairs as well as shoring up the loose banister — both of which looked pretty darn good for someone who was not a carpenter, even if he did say so himself — Lukas not only served lunch but also cleaned up afterward, then hit one more task on Emily's list while he was at it. Now festive garlands he'd found in the attic hung over each doorway throughout the house.

The place was eerily quiet. Even the ghosts didn't dare to make a peep. After lunch, all their guests had gone into town, and Emily wasn't back yet.

"Aunt Tilly," Lukas called as he wandered through the rooms.

He rounded the corner in the foyer to head upstairs only to catch a glimpse of her in the formal living room. Tilly was standing at the bay window staring out, seemingly lost in thought. Natural light, dimmed by the cloud cover that had moved in, washed her in a brilliant glow.

Lukas sprinted upstairs for his camera, then quietly snuck back down, not wanting to disturb the moment or the peaceful, yet slightly wistful expression on his aunt's face. In rapid succession, he managed to shoot several frames of her before she turned her head and caught sight of him.

"Lukas Weber," she said in that school-teacher tone she sometimes used. "You know how I dislike having my picture taken."

Lukas chuckled because she always said that, then proceeded to ask if her lipstick was on or how her hair looked before posing. "You'll like these," he assured her.

He walked over and showed her the digital display. Raw, these were already some of his personal favorites of the year. The white light coming in through the windows highlighted a beauty that shone from within her — Tilly's heart and spirit which age could never touch. In her expression, he'd managed to capture both the memory and experience of her past along with a hope for the future, despite her years. Just wait until he got them on his computer.

"Oh, these are lovely," Tilly murmured. "I don't think I have looked so young in years."

"This is what you always look like to me.

Young at heart."

Tilly chuckled but shook her head at him. "You always were a charmer."

"I'm wounded that you wouldn't think me sincere." He clutched his chest.

That earned him another dry chuckle. He'd always loved Tilly's laugh. Something he couldn't ever put into words or describe. Not a cackle exactly or a cough, but dry and lingering, full of mirth and warmth and a love for the ridiculous.

"What were you thinking about?" He looked at the display again, taking in her expression. "You appear almost happy and sad at the same time."

She flapped her hand as if waving off the question, but he waited, knowing she'd tell him eventually.

"Only the musings of an old woman. With the garlands up around the house, I was reminded of my childhood Christmases. When I'm alone, and it's quiet, sometimes I can hear them."

"Who?"

"Not ghosts exactly. More like memories. My father calling out as he brings in freshly chopped wood for the fireplaces, or my mother singing as she cooks in the kitchen. Sometimes I hear my brothers, usually arguing over some new silliness. If I close my eyes, I can see them, though the images in my mind grow fainter every year. But the sounds remain." She grinned. "Sometimes I hear other memories. Our guests chatting over a nice meal. The crackle of real wood in the fireplaces instead of the fake gas logs in them now. Or you as a child, though usually those memories involve loud music coming from your room."

Lukas glanced around, trying to picture a younger Tilly surrounded by her family, and later by strangers who were never strangers to her but friends. "You have a lot of history here."

"You do, too." She patted his hand. "More than you realize."

"My history is wherever you are."

Still, her words had him thinking. His aunt wasn't going to like the idea of selling her beloved Weber Haus. He'd have to make sure he found her the perfect place to go instead, somewhere she could continue to make memories like those, without working herself to death or having to worry about money. He would take care of her, make it wonderful for her.

"Oh my goodness."

Tilly's exclamation yanked Lukas out of his thoughts. Following the direction she was looking, he smiled. Snow was falling outside, coming down in big fluffy clumps.

"Oh dear," Tilly said.

Lukas nodded. "I hope all our guests can get back to the house okay. If it keeps on like that, they might have trouble driving."

Tilly shook her head and pointed. "No, Snowball."

Lukas peered closer. Sure enough the little white monster perched on the railing that wrapped around the front porch. Only she was clearly readying herself to jump, tiny butt wiggling and tail slashing as she stared with serious intent at something beyond. Another moment Lukas had to get on film. He rushed outside and brought his camera up right in time to get her last butt wiggle before she leaped. Snowball cleared the manicured bushes that sat in front of the porch only to ploof into about two feet of snow, disappearing entirely.

"Oh, help her, Lukas," Tilly wailed from behind him.

He was already on his way down the steps, which he was happy to notice didn't creak under his weight. Before he could wade into the yard, Snowball came flying out of the kitten-size hole she made. She landed beside him on the walk, which was already covered by more of the falling flakes.

Again Lukas brought his camera to his

eye, snapping happily away as the tiny cat kept picking up her paws and trying to find a non-cold place to set them down, giving each one a shake in the process. At the same time the fat snowflakes kept landing on her fur, and she'd pause periodically to shake them off. Gradually, she made her way back over the steps. As soon as she hit one protected by the awning that didn't have snow, she sprinted up the rest of the way, right to Tilly, who scooped her up and snuggled her against her breast.

"What are we going to do with you?" Tilly scolded.

"How are you even getting outside?" Lukas asked as he bounded up the steps, then tickled under her chin, which she leaned into. This was the second time today she had managed to sneak out, and he was sure he had been careful when he brought her in after fixing the stairs.

Snowball answered them both with a loud purr.

I snuggle against Miss Tilly, who brings me inside from the cold. That white stuff felt funny on my paws, and I did not like it as much as I thought I would. Besides, I couldn't find the one flake I was chasing from the sky.

Worn out from my morning, I'm pleased when she sits down in the living room on the sofa nearest the fire and cuddles me on her lap. She picks up a book to read, which I know means we'll be there for a while. Long enough to have a lovely nap. All curled up and warm, I close my eyes.

"You spoil that cat," Lukas warns Tilly. His voice vaguely breaks into my sleep.

I don't bother to lift my head and argue.

Shows how little he knows anyway. After all, Lukas has proven he's not too bright. He didn't even kiss Emily when he had the chance. Again. This human needs a lot more of my help.

Besides, sometimes a kitten just has to have a little fun.

CHAPTER 9

"Are you ready to order?"

Vaguely Emily heard speech happening all around but didn't quite register that words were directed at her.

"Ma'am?"

The second question still didn't penetrate. Emily stared at the menu in front of her face without seeing, her mind a million miles away. Or, technically, closer to five miles away with the unwanted guest currently fixing the stairs of Weber Haus.

It was completely unfair of Lukas to be the kind of funny she found irresistible — both playful and sarcastic. And, despite his being well aware of her opinion of him, he certainly hadn't let that affect his attitude. He didn't act awkward around her or even uneasy. If anything, she was the one who kept having uncomfortable moments. Mostly because she kept having random thoughts like wondering what his stubble would feel like against her palm, or what it would be like to snuggle with him on a couch, or what she could do to make him laugh, too.

And the almost kissing seemed to be turning into their thing . . .

Inappropriate. Inadvisable. Heck . . . incomprehensible.

Because, when it came down to it, he was still the same guy at the heart of the problem. Lukas was unreliable, absent, and had one foot out the door already. If his agent called one more time, that might be a record.

He'll be gone after Christmas, and then my life can get back to normal and I can get back to focusing on my bakery.

"Em?" Peter reached over and shook her elbow. *That* got her attention.

She jerked the menu down to find both Daniel and Peter staring at her, as well as an irritated waitress.

"Drink?" the waitress asked, in a tone that indicated she'd asked several times now.

Emily had been planning to have water, but after making the girl wait, she decided to act as though she'd been perusing the drink menu.

"I'll have an Irish coffee, thanks," she said the first warm drink that came to mind. The

156

day might be sunny, but after sitting on the front porch, her bones were as cold as the outside of her.

Peter's eyebrows shot up. Not surprising, given that she rarely drank alcohol.

She smiled at him sweetly. "This is my afternoon off, might as well enjoy it."

"Whatever you say."

She caught his secret grin as he raised his own menu.

She glanced at Daniel, who sat on her left across the table from Pete, only to find him watching her, a speculative light in his hazel eyes that she hadn't encountered from him before. If he had looked at her like that even a year ago, her heart probably would've done a tap dance across the inside of her ribs. She'd had a crush — a small one, mind — on her brother's best friend since middle school.

But right this second, Emily couldn't conjure more than a mild reciprocal interest. She had to be more tired than she realized. "How's business going, Daniel?"

He smiled as though she'd asked him something way more important than what she had. "Business is going well, though it tends to slow down this time of year. People are saving their money for Christmas gifts and decorations and parties. Plus the weather can get in the way."

"Makes sense." Emily arranged and re-arranged her silverware on the tablecloth, needing to channel nervous energy some-where. "I'm not sure, of course, but I imagine the bakery business will also be cyclical. Heavier over holidays, I would think."

Her items were selling better in all the shops, which lined up with the idea. She made a mental note that, assuming she was up and running in her own space this time next year, she'd need to hire extra help.

Daniel nodded his agreement. "But I've been doing this long enough that I plan for the swings up and down, making sure to spread out my expenses and setting aside money for the slower months. The hard part in my business is managing my contract workers, who will go to my competitors if I don't have regular jobs for them." He gave her a stare that she tried to interpret as direct, rather than patronizing. "You'll have to think about that for your servers in the bakery."

Ugh. She'd forgotten Daniel's tendency to lump himself with her brothers in the "Emily needs our protection" view of the world. Even from herself, often. At least that was something Lukas didn't do. "I have already incorporated seasons into my business plan," she assured him.

"I don't doubt it." He grinned. "You always were the smartest of the Diemer family."

"Hey —" Peter protested.

Daniel ignored him, giving her a wink. "And the prettiest."

Emily tipped her head back and laughed, though mostly at Peter's disgruntled expression. "That wouldn't be hard, given I'm the only girl out of five. Although . . ." She tapped her finger on the table as if she were thinking. "Of the boys, I'd say Oscar has to be the prettiest."

"I'm sitting right here, you know," Peter grumbled loudly.

"Oh, Pete. Didn't see you there, buddy." Daniel pretended to lower his menu and suddenly notice his friend.

"Yeah, yeah."

She and Daniel exchanged mischievous grins. Emily didn't know about him, but she had every intention of messing with Pete the rest of lunch.

"So, Em. What's good at this place?" Peter held up his menu and gave it a shake.

Right. In theory this was supposed to be her favorite restaurant, except Peter was the one who had picked it out, being the only new place in town since he'd been gone. One Emily had yet to visit.

"Mmmm . . ." Emily picked up her menu as if trying to decide what to advise him to get, when really, she was frantically reading through the items on the page, which she hadn't actually glanced at when her head had been focused on a certain photographer.

What did this place make again? Oh, right. Nepalese.

"Anything. Although I hear the tikka masala is excellent." In actual fact, she had no clue, but it seemed like a safe guess.

"Will I like it?" Peter asked.

"Given your picky taste buds, who knows." Emily shrugged, then reached over and poked him in the bicep. "Maybe it will help with your scrawny muscles. Put some hair on your chest. Then you can be as pretty as Oscar, too."

Daniel snorted, then choked on the water he was drinking. Emily reached over and thumped him on the back until he stopped coughing.

"You've gotta give a guy a warning before you say funny stuff like that," he said.

"Yeah. Real funny." Pete leaned back in his chair and crossed his arms, pushing up his military muscles in an obvious display.

He bent what Emily had secretly dubbed his *military man* stare on her, but she still caught the twitch to his lips.

The waitress chose that moment to return and take their orders, then whisked away with their menus.

"Speaking of funny," Pete said when she was gone. "What happened to not liking this Lukas guy?"

Daniel glanced back and forth between them. "What's this about? The guy fixing the stairs at Weber Haus?"

She gave Pete a pointed glare. "Nothing that's anybody's business but Lukas and Tilly's."

Pete ignored her. "I've been getting emails from this one," he jerked a thumb in Emily's direction. "Talking about how rundown the inn is getting, and how old Miss Tilly is, and how there's this nephew running around taking pictures of this and that all over the world when what he should be doing is helping fix the situation, since Miss Tilly raised him."

"Wow. I did not get that vibe from him," Daniel said. "He was doing a pretty decent job on fixing the stairs. I thought he was another carpenter and you'd hired him instead of me."

The hangdog expression with that statement was not adorable at all. "If I needed a carpenter, you'd top my list," she said dutifully, not wanting to hurt his feelings, and he brightened.

Emily shot Pete another pointed look. "At least while Lukas is home, he's doing his part to pull his weight. Like I said, it's none of our business."

"Well, you certainly seemed chummy with him," Peter said, ignoring her hints that this was not a conversation she wanted to be having.

Good thing he hadn't witnessed the almost kiss.

"We were deciding on what to do for the stairs," she said in a dry voice. "I'm not sure how chummy that is."

Her brother snorted. "You could cut the tension with a buzz saw."

Emily seriously needed to get them off this topic. "Speaking of chummy, have you seen Lauren yet?"

Daniel set forward. "Lauren Bieler?"

Pete's turn to shoot her an accusatory look. "I haven't talked to Lauren since before I was deployed."

Emily tsked and shook her head in total mother-hen fashion. "That's too bad. Because you couldn't stop talking about her before you left."

"Really?" Daniel looked at Pete with interest.

Peter sat back, glancing between them, expression stoic as always. "How are preparations for Christmas Eve going?" he asked her.

Emily laughed. "Changing topics, huh?"

He did his silent, military stare again.

She laughed again but answered anyway. "I've gotten a lot done ahead of time but feeding that many people is tricky."

"Especially when one is Mom," he muttered.

He wasn't wrong.

"How's the loan going for the bakery?" he asked next.

She should've expected the question but made a face anyway. "I need to find a cosigner because I don't have collateral to put up." Not after the Greg incident.

"What about Mom and Dad?"

Emily pursed her lips. "You mean Mom, who is trying to convince me not to open a bakery in the first place?" She shook her head. "Besides, I know that this is a risk. I'd rather not drag them into it. I'll find another way. I'm looking into venture capital or possibly angel assistance, or maybe even crowdfunding, to get the collateral I need for the loan. I don't want to put anyone else's head on the chopping block except mine."

"Crowdfunding?" Daniel's voice said it all, even if his face hadn't scrunched up with disdain. "You'd let other people give their hard-earned money?"

Even Peter shot his friend a questioning frown. "Crowdfunding is voluntary," he pointed out.

Would it be rude if she whacked her old crush on the head with her napkin? Emily managed to grit out a calm smile. "The way I'm thinking of doing it, investors would get a small something in return for their investment, cookies for a month any time they come into the shop or along those lines. Pete's right, though, I'm not *taking* people's money. Crowdfunding is people giving because they believe in what I'm doing and want to be a small part of it."

Fatigue seeped into her, the weight of her dream dragging, piling on top of her. All the decisions, all the worry, the money, the time and energy. It would all be worth it someday. The picture she had in her mind was one she held on to tightly, but right now, she was exhausted. Why was it she seemed to be constantly defending herself to the people who should be supporting her most?

Suddenly, Lukas's words came back to her. That no amount of hard work, or failure, or roadblocks, or empty stomachs, should be able to stand in her way. She straightened her spine.

"Have you finished all your Christmas shopping yet?" she tossed out. That had to be a safe topic of conversation, right?

Both men groaned.

"Don't remind me," Pete grumbled. Then he suddenly brightened, eyeing Emily in a way she didn't trust. "Maybe after lunch you could help me pick something out for the parentals."

Emily's first thought was that she was already leaving Lukas and Tilly with lunch responsibilities, and they had the tree topping and lighting thing tonight. Then she reminded herself that she hadn't had a day off in months. Not really.

"Sounds like fun."

Lukas dried his hands on a dish towel after finishing cleaning up from lunch, then folded it and hung it back over the rung attached to the sink cabinet. Good thing Emily had made as much food as she did.

As soon as he'd seen that both the Bauers and the Hoffmans were there, along with the Andrews, a family of four who had

165

checked in that morning, he'd had a hard time not letting the disgruntled surprise show on his face. Hadn't Emily said usually only she and Tilly were around for lunch and that most of the guests ate out? Still, the huge pot of soup he'd been warming had suddenly made more sense. Emily Diemer definitely knew what she was doing when it came to the inn.

He had to find a way to keep her so that she came as a package deal if they sold it. She was too valuable to lose. Which meant figuring out the bakery situation.

Lukas glanced between his feet where Snowball sat, curled into a ball on the mat. "Wait. Why can't she have her bakery here?"

Snowball raised her head and tilted it to the side, ears perked. Clearly agreeing with him.

"Right." Purpose in his stride, Lukas ran upstairs to his room and grabbed his coat, gloves and hat, then headed outside, careful to make sure to close the door behind him before Snowball could sneak out.

A ton of unused buildings littered the Weber Haus property. Built in the early 1900s, the property included the main house, as well as stables, a carriage house, the manager's cottage, and a gatehouse, all of which had been used for various purposes

166

through the years. One of those structures had to be perfect for converting to a bakery.

Trudging through the snow, he visited the manager's cottage first. Big John used to live here, and it had been remodeled to have central heating and air, electricity, and running water long ago. Except as soon as he got to the house, Lukas found it locked. Which meant he had to trudge back through the snow, deflect a curious Tilly when he asked for the keys, and return to let himself in.

Only as soon as he walked in the door, he knew it wouldn't work for the bakery. The setup was too much like a cottage, and the kitchen was way too small. The space would take a lot of money to convert.

Next, he visited the stables, which he also ruled out due to the size as well as the fact that it was not fitted for any amenities. But the second he walked into the carriage house, Lukas stopped and grinned.

"The third bed Goldilocks tried was just right," he murmured to himself with satisfaction.

He'd forgotten that around the 1950s, the carriage house had been used as a small shop for selling trinkets and clothing and such to the folks who stayed in the house. They had found that most tourists in town didn't come out so far for one shop, and there weren't enough guests to keep it going and had quickly shut it down.

Lukas frowned over that.

He wouldn't want Emily's bakery to fail because of location. Except the town had expanded out this way since, and hopefully foot traffic might be better now that the sledding hill brought people in this direction. Although, they might have to do something else, like open the house as a restaurant as well as an inn. Which would be a ton of work for her.

"That'll take more thinking on it," he muttered to himself.

In the meantime, though, at least he'd found a perfect space. The area of the carriage house converted to a shop was nice and open, already had built-in countertops, and was fitted for electricity and water, as well as heating and air. Retrofitting this for a bakery would not be nearly as difficult as any of the other buildings on the property.

Maybe Emily would finally put her guard down after he told her about his idea.

The ring of his phone disturbed the quiet, and Lukas pulled it out of his pocket to find his agent's name on the display.

"Hi, Bethany," he answered.

She didn't even bother with niceties,

jumping right into it. "Have you given any further thought to Lithuania for *Geographic International*? They're looking for an answer now."

"Tell them I can't do that one. Between us, my aunt needs help, possibly transitioning to retirement. I need to be here longer than I thought, and definitely can't travel to Lithuania before Christmas."

A pregnant pause greeted his words. "You're passing up an incredible opportunity," she warned.

"I know." He should've been getting a pang of regret or a twinge of impatience or even that tickle that used to scoot him out the door to whatever next assignment he could find. Only nothing came beyond perhaps a small sigh of relief that he didn't have to immediately pick up and leave. "Please tell them that the next assignment I will be happy to take no matter where, as long as it's after the new year."

"That might smooth ruffled feathers," she agreed.

"Good. In the meantime, I need your help . . ."

"Why do I get the feeling you're about to wrangle me into something I don't do?" Bethany's voice was as dry as the Sahara in the summer. And Lukas would know, be-

169

cause he'd been there during that season trying to capture a haboob on film.

"I need to find a realtor who specializes in selling Victorian inns as a business rather than as a home sale. Just for a valuation at this point. Is there any way you could track down somebody like that for me?"

Bethany's sigh carried a strong whiff of reluctant patience. "You know that's not my specialty, right?"

"Of course. But you're brilliant, smart, and know a ton of people."

"Brilliant and smart are the same thing."

"See. You're smarter than me already."

"Huh," was all she said in return.

"Listen, B. The faster I sell this, the faster I can get back on assignment," he wheedled.

Bethany growled into the phone. "Fine. Only because you're my favorite client."

"I bet you say that to all your clients," he teased. "But I am extra appreciative."

"Yeah, yeah. I'll get you the information as soon as I find a few options, then it's up to you. I'm not actually talking to these people or helping you sell this inn thing."

"Of course. You're an angel."

"I'm glad you noticed."

He could easily picture his agent, with her smart clothing and the Coke-bottle-thick glasses perched on her nose, and an expres-

170

sion of haughty disdain.

"I'm well aware I couldn't do anything I do without you," he said.

Bethany chuckled. "Charmer."

Lukas paused at the word. Maybe Emily's attitude toward him was coloring his reactions, but did all people regard him as inauthentic? "I meant it."

Bethany had been crucial to all the most important steps of his career. The woman had been in this business almost thirty years and had contacts he could never have gotten to on his own. Signing with her had been one of the best things he'd ever done.

"Well . . ." Bethany sounded almost taken aback. "Thank you."

Lukas made a mental note to tell his agent more often how much he valued her. "Thanks again for the help. I'll keep an eye out for an email."

"Sounds good." Bethany was all back to business.

After saying their goodbyes, they hung up.

Meow.

Lukas jumped, then laughed at himself. Snowball had managed to follow him into the carriage house, even though he'd been so careful to make sure she didn't get out the door. He scooped her up. "You're going to get lost, young lady," he scolded, even as he cuddled her close. "How are you getting out of the house, anyway?"

That darn Lukas is going to ruin everything.
I squirm in his grip, too angry with him to sit still. Besides, he's holding me all wrong. Only I'm small, which means he has a pretty tight grip on me. Still, I squiggle around until I manage to get my back paws under me, then grab on tight with my front claws and bat at his hand with my back feet.

"Hey —" He transfers me to his other hand while he's walking through the snow toward the main house, his breath making a heavy mist in the air with each puff.

I do my boxing-with-the-back-feet maneuver again.

"What's the big deal?" he yelps. Again he switches hands, only this time, he scoops under my bottom, holding me more securely.

Usually, this is how I prefer to be held so I can cuddle properly. Not this time.

Meow. Translation: *Thanks for the boost.*
Using the leverage I gained having a solid surface of his hand under my back paws, I twist around in his grasp and sink my front claws into his jacket, then proceed to climb up to his shoulder with every intention of jumping down from there.

172

"Snowball, quit it," Lukas said.

It takes him several tries to get me off, since I have all four sets of claws hooked into his clothing, but he finally does it just as we arrive back in the house. As soon as the door bangs shut behind us, Lukas sets me on the ground with a glare.

I give him the stink eye right back, back arched.

Miss Tilly walks in at the same moment, and I shoot over to her, meowing to be picked up. Which, of course, Miss Tilly does. Immediately, I snuggle into her hand as she cuddles me against her chest, that loud rumbling coming from my belly.

I look directly at Lukas who gazes back, then shakes his head at me. "What was that all about?"

"What?" Miss Tilly asks.

"Snowball went wild when I was bringing her back inside."

Tilly glances down, and I blink up at her in total innocence. She's not the one making dumb decisions. Lukas is. Now he knows I'm not happy about it.

"Well, she seems fine now." Tilly smiles and pets my fur.

My purr rumbles louder.

"Huh. I thought she liked me."

I turn away so he knows I'm still mad. I'll

173

like Lukas better when he figures out that he shouldn't be thinking of moving Miss Tilly somewhere else. I may be young, but I'm not dumb, and that's exactly what he was talking about.

Not if I have anything to say about it.

CHAPTER 10

I will not feel guilty for spending the day away from the house.

Emily had to repeat that to herself several times and did so again as Peter drove them up the long snow-covered drive to Weber Haus, the wheels of his truck crunching in the now thicker drifts as they went. Tomorrow, weather willing, she'd send Lukas out to clear the drive and walkways. No point while snow was still coming down.

Can't feel guilty about weather. You don't get to control that. More's the pity.

Christmas shopping with Peter and Daniel had been mostly them following after her as she made suggestions, but she'd had fun all the same.

And I'm glad I went.

Tilly had Lukas. No one had called screaming about lunch or a burned-down house. After the work she'd been putting in, she deserved a day to herself. Or sort of to

175

herself, shopping and eating with her brother and his best friend. They'd worried a bit about the snow when it started falling in heavy chunks, but Pete's truck was four-wheel drive, and the snow had let up after an hour or so, coming down in smaller flakes and at a trickle.

Now the sun had already set, blanketing the land in darkness and dropping the temperatures rapidly. The house glowed white thanks to the combination of the pristine surroundings and the flood lights that lit up the front. You could even see it from the road, despite how far back it sat.

I need to get the Christmas lights up on the outside.

They should have been up by Thanksgiving, but that hadn't happened. Food wasn't the only thing she needed ready for Christmas Eve.

No. *Lukas* needed to do that. The task was already on the list she'd given him. She made a mental note to point that out as a priority item.

"Do you want to stick around for dinner? Afterward we're going to light the trees." Emily looked at Peter, then at the back seat where Daniel rode, to gauge their reactions. After all, hanging out in an inn with mostly strangers wasn't exactly a rollicking time.

"Wait. Who's cooking?" Peter asked.

Emily waggled her eyebrows. Her family might worry about her pursuing it as a profession, constantly quoting failure statistics for restaurants and bakeries at her, but they did agree that Emily was a whiz in the kitchen. "I am. Or rather, I have. It's that spaetzle casserole Oma used to make, only with a bit of my own *oomph* added in. Plus salad and homemade bread."

"Twist my arm," Daniel said from the back seat.

Peter parked behind where she usually left her car around back by the carriage house, the headlights landing on what appeared to be footprints into the building. Who had been wandering around in there?

"I guess we're in." Pete distracted her curiosity.

They bundled into the house through the side door that led to the kitchen, pausing to stamp their feet on the mat outside, not that it did much. Once inside, though, the two men had to stop hard to keep from barreling into her when Emily almost left skid marks in her abrupt halt.

If she was honest with herself, she'd been expecting to find dishes in the sink. Though heavens knew why since Lukas had already done dishes for her several times. Maybe

177

because her brothers did dishes when they had to but not when they didn't have to, happy to leave them for anyone else. The kitchen, however, was spotless, and — she sniffed — he'd taken the time to use the special granite cleaner she'd bought for the counters.

However, what stopped her was the garland hung over the doorway.

"Give a guy a warning when you're going to slam on the brakes like that," Peter protested loudly, poking her to shove her forward.

Emily ignored her brother to wander out into the dining room — again pristine and with a garland up — through the foyer and into the living room where the sounds of voices and laughter could be heard.

There, she paused under the doorway. Yet another garland graced the frame above her head. The man must have put up every garland in the house. Had he worked all day?

Her surprise didn't stop there. Because Mr. Avoid the Guests knelt in the middle of the room, camera to his eye, laughing and snapping pictures of Snowball. Jakob Andrews, one of the two boys with the family staying in the house, dangled a curling piece of decorative gold ribbon over the kitten's head for her to bat with her little paws. Meanwhile, every other guest in the house as well as Miss Tilly looked on and laughed.

Emily didn't think she gasped or made any other sound, but Lukas suddenly glanced over his shoulder and pinned her with green eyes brimming with fun and those darn dimples that were close to irresistible. "Oh, good, you're home."

Home. Emily refused to acknowledge the spark of warmth that lit inside her, like a potbellied stove on a cold winter's night.

She managed a smile, though, for politeness' sake. "Looks like you're all having a nice time." She nodded at the ribbon. "You've found Snowball's obsession. Shiny things."

Lukas got to his feet and reached a hand behind her to shake Pete's and Daniel's. "You must've had fun, too. You've been gone awhile."

Not an ounce of sarcasm or ill intent lingered in those words, only good-natured well-wishing. Which only made the guilt at abandoning her post dig a little deeper.

"Or were you dawdling?" he asked. Then grinned slowly and mouthed the word "slowpoke."

The guilt eased up a smidge, the urge to laugh with him taking over.

"We got some Christmas shopping done," Emily said by way of explanation and winced internally at how prissy she sounded. When had she become the boring one? She half turned away from him. "I'll go preheat the oven for dinner."

"That's why I'm glad you're home. I already started the oven preheating. I just didn't know how long to put the casserole in for. I assume that's what you intend to do for dinner?"

Disappointment that he wasn't glad to see *her* was a ridiculous reaction, and Emily refused to give into it. "Great. I'll just go pop it in and set a timer."

While she was in there, nice and alone for a hot second, she decided to toss the salad and warm up the bread. For once not in the mood to join the others, she also set the table in the dining room. Usually on the weekend, she served buffet style from the kitchen, allowing folks to come and go as they pleased and making it easier on her for setup and cleanup. Since all their guests were here tonight, along with a few extras, going to the bother seemed worth it.

Plus, she could use the time to herself to stamp out this stupid attraction thing. Clearly her mind and body had taken separate paths the day he arrived, and she needed to find her way back together.

The swinging door popped open with a squeak, and Lukas appeared through it. He grimaced and glanced back at the door. "I'll add it to my list," he said before turning to face her. "Everything okay in here?"

Dang it. Couldn't a girl get a second alone to gather her scattering wits?

"All under control." She glanced at the timer she had set on her phone. "Five to ten more minutes and we will be ready to serve."

Rather than leaving Emily to her own devices, Lukas crossed his arms and leaned a casual hip against the counter before giving an appreciative sniff. "Smells wonderful, as always."

Go away. You're the reason my wits are on the run. "Thank you for putting up the garlands, they look wonderful."

The dimples came out to play as he shot her a ready grin. "Just tackling that list, ma'am," he drawled in a decent impersonation of an old-timey American cowboy.

She could picture him tipping the brim of his hat. Why couldn't he have been the spoiled, overindulged man she expected? A person she could legitimately not like for Tilly's sake. Given the extra work, even for her own sake.

Unfortunately, Emily wasn't quite sure what to do with the two seemingly incongruent sides to Lukas Weber.

Luckily, her alarm chose that moment to go off. Carefully, Emily got the casserole out of the oven, happy with the nice golden top to it and the way she could see it bubbling underneath through the glass of the dish. Not paying any attention to Lukas — or trying not to at least despite an awareness that niggled in the back of her mind — she sat one of the two casserole dishes on top of the stove to cool. Still avoiding eye contact, she carried the other dish through to the dining room and set it on two trivets. Lukas meanwhile followed behind her but kept going to call everyone into the dining room.

Thankfully, the rest of the evening went along without incident. She was finally able to relax as the group chatted amicably over a lovely dinner. Pete and Daniel helped clean up. Afterward, they turned off all the lights in the house, only the glows from fireplaces lighting their way, and went from room to room with the Christmas trees, taking turns putting toppers on them and plugging in the lights on each one until the downstairs shone as brightly as the northern star.

Tilly put a record on the old-fashioned player that sat in the formal living room as Christmas songs beautifully sung by a choir filled the otherwise quiet house and each person stood in the radiance and stared at the lights and basked in the joy of the season.

Emily let out a happy little hum, the last of her earlier tension draining from her body.

"This might be my favorite new holiday tradition," Lukas whispered in her ear.

He had spent much of dinner and the entire lighting ceremony behind his camera, the telltale *click, click, click* going off in rapid succession.

Emily couldn't find it in her heart to push away the answering glow inside her heart at his words. She'd come up with this last year, so two years didn't exactly make it a tradition, and last year hadn't felt quite this . . . magical.

"Me, too," she whispered back.

After they'd admired the lights, everyone had retired to their rooms and Peter and Daniel had left. Lukas lay in bed, trying his darndest to let the sandman do his job and drag him off to sleep, except his mind wouldn't shut down.

He'd had fun today.

More than he'd could remember having in a long, long time. Sure, seeing all the amazing sights and experiencing cultures he was exposed to regularly was a thrill, each and every time. But something about being home and surrounded by people he enjoyed — even the guests weren't so bad — and the Christmas lights and the wonderful meal had got to him.

And maybe a certain tart brunette.

Granted, he'd broken out his camera more as a shield to hide behind. When he'd started to get interested in photography as a teen, he'd done the same thing. Except he'd focused on shots of nature and buildings as an excuse to get out of the house. Like with the sledding hill, the setting and the cheerful crowd gathered at a table to share a meal had pulled that Rockwellian feel from him and he wanted it on film. He'd have to get breakfast on film one morning and take advantage of the lighting.

Closing his eyes, Lukas pictured Emily in that lighting, maybe in the snow, her hair down, dark eyes focused on him. On the camera.

With a huff, Lukas flipped his quilt back and jumped to his feet. He snagged his computer from his satchel on the floor and headed downstairs. If he wasn't going to sleep, maybe he could get some work done. Well, not work exactly, but photography.

A gift for Tilly.

Not wanting to wake anyone else, he winced with each creek of the floorboards as he made his way downstairs. The floors throughout the house really needed to be refinished and possibly replaced in a few rooms. Mental note to add that to the list. As he made his way down, a brightness like daylight had invaded the house when night clearly continued to hold sway outside, and told him the Christmas trees were all still plugged in.

Grumbling about fire hazards, Lukas went through the house and turned off each tree. At the same time, he made yet another mental note to get automatic timers so that no one had to be responsible for turning the lights on and off. One less thing for Emily or Tilly to worry about.

The second he walked into the formal living room, Lukas paused and grinned. Emily lay on the Victorian sofa, which couldn't be comfortable given how hard the thing was, along with the way the seat sort of curved like a bubble, not to mention how the dark-crimson-colored velvet was still stiff and kind of spiky rather than soft. She had to be cold, because she'd fallen asleep without a blanket and her knees were pulled up close to her chest as she lay on her side.

Where was his camera when he needed it?

He would've gone upstairs to get it and snap a few shots of the sweet scene, but Emily sighed and wiggled in her sleep.

Lukas tread closer at the sight of a tiny white fluff ball curled up in the small gap between Emily's knees and her chest. Snowball was keeping her company. He knew he should wake up Emily so that she could go upstairs and get better rest than what she was getting on that ancient sofa, but for whatever reason Lukas was reluctant to disturb her. Or maybe he wanted to appreciate the view.

The lights on the tree in this room were white and cast an angelic aura over both Emily and the kitten. Emily's dark hair, though still in a braid, spilled over her arm, dark against the pale skin, which was tucked awkwardly under her head as a makeshift pillow. A smudge of flour on her cheek told him she'd been baking again after everyone else went to bed. Her lips bowed upward, as if she were having good dreams.

Probably about kicking him out.

Lukas reached out and shook her shoulder gently, not wanting to startle her. "Emily?"

Emily didn't stir at all, but Snowball lifted her head and dead-eyed him through sleepy kitten blinks. Then she simultaneously stretched out her front paws and yawned, giving a little squeak as she did.

Lukas chuckled but continued to try to wake the woman who was disturbing his sleep way more than thoughts of photography. "Em," he said louder, and gave her shoulder a harder shake.

Emily sucked in a quick breath and opened eyes, which remained hazy and unfocused. "Lukas?"

"Hey there, sleepyhead." Lukas tucked a strand of hair that had escaped her braid behind her ear. "You fell asleep on the couch. I thought you might want to go upstairs."

She stared at him quietly, big dark eyes unfathomable. Then she smiled. If she had been awake and more guarded, no way would she have smiled at him like that. As though she genuinely liked him. An answering warmth started in the region of his heart.

"What time is it?" she croaked.

"A little after two in the morning."

"Ugh." She groaned as she maneuvered to sitting. "That's a terrible time. I'll never

187

get back to sleep before I have to get up at five."

Lukas moved to sit beside her. "Sorry. I would've left you to sleep, except I've had to camp out on this sofa a time or two and know exactly how uncomfortable it can be. You would've ended up with a major crick in the neck."

Emily rubbed at the back of her neck, suddenly looking younger. "Too late." Then she made a face. "Maybe I should just get started on the cooking now."

"At two in the morning?" He shook his head. No way was he letting her do that to herself. "Forget it."

"I'll never get back to sleep if I go upstairs. Or if I do, it won't be good sleep, and five a.m. will feel even worse."

Stubborn woman.

"How about this? I couldn't sleep, so I came down to go through some of my pictures, pick out the best ones, and work on them. You want to help me choose?"

Emily stared at him and even opened her mouth a few times before closing it again.

"I'm not asking you to sign your life away in blood, or anything," he teased. "I figure it'll give your mind something to do, but we can sit here in the dark, so it'll still be restful at least."

A series of emotions chase themselves across Emily's face — doubt, curiosity, resignation. Curiosity won out, apparently, because she gave a little shrug and moved so that they were both sitting close together, though not too close, just barely not touching. Lukas put his feet up on the tufted thing that pretended to be a coffee table, and she did the same as he propped his computer on his lap and booted it up.

"Which of these stands out to you the most?" With a few clicks, he pulled up a folder he'd already put similar photos in earlier — ones of Snowball in the snow and also in Aunt Tilly's lap and also playing. He set it up so that thumbnails were large enough to be able to compare details.

As soon as the images appeared on screen, Emily gasped and inched closer to see better. She was probably not aware that she now pressed up against his side, but Lukas was horribly, wonderfully aware, as her sugar-cookie scent wrapped around him, making him want to take a nibble.

"These are wonderful!" She turned her face to him with a glowing smile.

For some reason, that small bit of praise from Emily Diemer felt more important than any major critic, touching his heart in a way reviews and even his most recent

189

awards had not. "Thanks. Which do you like best, though?"

"All of them," she said eagerly, turning back to the screen.

Lukas chuckled. "I tend to spend a lot of time touching up each image I choose. I can't do *all* of them."

"That's a shame." She tipped her head to the side leaned in even closer, practically putting her nose against the touch-screen. "Of the ones in the snow, I think I like these two best. They capture her mischievous expression."

Trying to ignore the urge to slip an arm around her and snuggle her closer, Lukas opened the two Emily had pointed out, both of the kitten deep in the snow, her blue eyes just visible and her tail straight up as she prepared to pounce her way out. He added one more of her walking on the path, paused with one paw up and batting at the falling snowflakes.

"What next?" Emily asked, then covered her mouth as she yawned.

"Now, sleepy girl, we make them even better."

"Not possible."

"You'll see." He moved to her first pick and immediately adjusted the cropping. "I'm changing this to center Snowball better in the frame and cut out the excess background, which we don't need," he explained. "It enhances the composition."

"Mm-hmm." She watched beside him, not making any move to sit farther away, though she was close enough to be able to feel each breath. She must be super tired to forget herself like this around him.

And I won't take advantage. The stern lecture didn't help much, because he didn't say something to make her realize it, either, content to sit this way with her.

"I'm going to correct the exposure a bit. I want her blue eyes to pop."

"They already —" She paused as he worked, watching quietly. "Wow," she murmured when he was done.

"Better?" he asked.

"You're right. Her eyes really pop now, but it only adds to the overall feel of the image."

"That's the idea."

Quietly he worked on the other two images, taking a few more steps on the one of her batting at the snowflakes. Emily also fell into silence beside him, watching the progress from her position almost cuddled against him.

I could get used to this.

The thought snuck up on him. A dangerous idea born of a homey feel he'd maybe been missing without knowing it and a loneliness he hadn't even realized was part of his life until he'd come home. The sensation had crept up on him like a kitten in full mischief mode. Except it didn't matter. He had a job, one he loved and was good at, and he was leaving after Christmas.

There wasn't anything to get used to.

Finally, he tipped the screen so she could get a better view. "What do you think of this?"

"Perfect," she breathed. "I'd put this up on a wall."

Lukas laughed, and she turned to him, her gaze stern. "I'm serious. You must know how good you are. You *do* work for *Geographic International.*"

He shrugged. "I was only playing around."

Emily blinked. "If this is you only playing around, I'd love to see your not-playing-around stuff."

She gazed at him expectantly.

"Right now?" Lukas asked.

Of all the people in the world, he would've expected Emily to be the last to show even a smidge of interest in his photography. After all, she'd made it plain that his lifestyle was one she disapproved of.

But she continued to watch him with

192

expectation and a growing impatience, if her tapping foot on the coffee table was any indication, so he pulled up a few of his best pieces.

First, he showed her a lioness as she lapped the muddy water of a small stream. Only her head showed through the bright green grasses, and she'd glanced up, golden eyes pinning him, looking straight through the camera to him, just as he'd clicked. This had been his first picture to win an international award.

Next, he brought up an image of a cathedral in Saint Petersburg, Russia. Dusk had fallen, and the purple and navy sky glowed with color, illuminated by the moon, which sat directly behind the building, the brilliance of the colors of the cathedral illuminated by the dying sun from behind his back in the point of view of the lens.

Finally, he showed her his personal favorite. A tiny owl tucked into the knot of an old tree, its feathers the same browns and whites of the tree bark. If the little guy hadn't opened its eyes, Lukas never would've seen him there. He had been hiking through that forest on his way to a hidden lake higher up and happened to spot the owl. Sheer dumb luck.

"These are the images that have had the

most accolades and led to important next steps in my career." Would she hate that?

Emily thoughtfully studied each one in turn, taking her time. Lukas found himself leaning closer, eager for her thoughts even more than with others who'd seen these images.

"You are an incredible photographer," she said. "No doubt about that. But I think the picture of Snowball is as fantastic as these. Maybe not as exotic or even as dangerous, but that's one woman's opinion."

Lukas stopped himself from denying what she said, since Emily would probably bop him on the nose if he tried it. In pausing, he took a moment and looked closer. Was she right? Were the funny photos of Snowball, or even the pictures he'd taken of holiday activities and preparations in Weber Haus, worth more than his own amusement and a nice gift for Tilly?

Lukas turned his head only to become ensnared by the conviction and the warmth in her dark-eyed gaze. Losing himself in those eyes wouldn't be so bad.

"For someone who doesn't like me very much, you are certainly . . . supportive," his voice came out hushed.

He allowed his gaze to wander the beauty of her face highlighted by the dying glow of the fire — wide eyes framed by thick lashes, pert nose, stubborn chin, and lips worthy of more than a second look.

"Who said I don't like you?" Emily asked just as softly.

The moment wrapped around them. Could she hear how his heart galloped like reindeer hooves on the roof? Did she know how much he wanted to find out for himself if her lips were as soft as they appeared?

"You don't like me," he whispered. "You think I'm a scoundrel and a bad nephew."

"That's true," she whispered back, lips quirking, eyes warm.

"You'll regret it." And he'd hate that she would.

"Probably." She didn't pull away, though. Just watched him with expectation and a smile.

The fire gave a crack, as the last log broke in half, and somehow that tipped the tension in him over the brink.

With a groan, Lukas closed the distance between them, claiming her lips for his own, and almost groaned again. They were as soft as he'd been dreaming of . . . and sweeter. Heaven. And sugar cookies. The woman tasted of sugar cookies.

He went to pull away, wanting to be the

195

bigger person he was trying to prove to her existed.

Only Emily chased his touch and kissed him back, lips clinging. Another groan he couldn't hold back tumbled from him. He was completely lost. Scooching around to face her better, move closer, he threaded his hands through her hair to frame her face and deepened the kiss, savoring the feel of her in his arms and the taste of her on his lips.

She's going to regret this, a voice warned him.

With the last vestige of his will, Lukas broke away. He leaned his forehead against hers and took a second to catch his breath.

"Wow," he murmured. *Wow,* he echoed in his own head.

Emily wrapped her hands around his wrists, almost as though she was trying to keep him there. Then she gave an odd sigh and sat back, releasing him, and, like the ghost of Christmas past had come and gone, the moment disappeared into thin air. "I think the hour and the setting lowered our inhibitions," she murmured.

Like he'd guessed . . . already she was questioning her sanity for having allowed the kiss.

He'd play along. After all, he was the died-in-the-wool scoundrel here. "Don't hold it against me. Those lips would test a saint."

Despite a small smile of acknowledgment, she stood, shoulders stiffer than a second ago, putting more distance between them, leaving him colder. Emptier. "Maybe I will try to get a bit more sleep."

"A highly practical idea." God, he didn't want her to go.

After a pause, she gave a nod, almost like she was telling herself to move. "Well . . . good night."

"Sleep tight," he said.

She blinked, then turned on her heel and left.

Lukas blew out a long breath and ran a hand through his hair, then glanced at Snowball. "That was probably a bad move."

He got a definitive meow in response.

Yeah. Definitely a bad move.

Finally!

I hop up and pounce around the floor in a kitty dance of happiness. These two humans sure are slow figuring things out, but now they've kissed, which must mean that they are in love. People only kiss if they love each other.

I wonder if they'll put me in their wedding. A couple of weeks ago people got married at the house. They did this odd thing where a bunch of people sat in chairs and other people walked between them. Those silly humans did it outside in the snow and cold, but I got to see it from the window in Miss Tilly's room.

They had a dog that brought them some kind of pillow. I'm a cat, and cats are way smarter than dogs. At least, that's what the cat next door says. I've never met a dog. Still, I could bring Emily and Lukas a pillow.

Lukas settles back on the couch and plays with his computer more. I'm happy to stay with him down here, so I jump down from my seat and pad over to where the fire used to be in the fireplace. Only a few bright orange spots in the blackness remain, but the warmth reaches out and wraps around me, better than a blanket.

This is the perfect place for a bath.

After all, if I'm going to carry a pillow to Lukas and Emily when they get married, they're going to want my fur to look as beautiful as possible. I pause mid-lick of my back leg as a thought occurs to me.

I sure hope they don't put a big pink bow on my neck.

Chapter 11

Kitten claws to the chest was not the best way in the world to wake up. Especially when waking up meant realizing that you fell asleep sitting straight up on an uncomfortable old sofa with your computer in your lap.

"Snowball." Lukas groggily detached the kitten from his shirt and underlying skin. "We really need to come up with a better system for you to get my attention when I'm sleeping."

Looking at him like she did him a favor, Snowball squeaked happily, then hopped down to run to the stairs, just visible through the living room doorway. Lukas's brain, not fully engaged at this hour, took a second to catch up with what the mischief maker was doing, then realization gave him a shot of much-needed adrenaline.

Emily.

Lukas glanced at his phone and registered

the time — 6:00 a.m.? His nose was a usually a good indicator that Emily hadn't gotten up to start cooking yet, but he went through to the kitchen to be sure. Snowball zipped through the swinging door, hot on his heels.

The kitchen remained dark and cold, making him shiver. Lukas ran a hand over his face, trying to force himself to wake up more. "Not good," he muttered.

Together, he and Snowball hurried their way up the back stairs to Emily's door. When knocking softly produced no results, Lukas tried the handle, which luckily was unlocked. Carefully, he poked his head in the room. Darkness illuminated only by a nightlight in the hallway showed a human-size lump on the bed.

"Emily?" he called, keeping his voice down so as not to disturb other guests.

Déjà vu took over, both from last night when he'd found her sleeping on the sofa, but also from Emily cheerfully dragging him from bed early in the mornings.

A streak of white snuck past his feet and flew across the room. Snowball jumped in nimble silence and landed on Emily, who grunted, then jackknifed in the bed, making the cat hop back, only to freeze and blink at Lukas standing in the doorway.

"Morning, sleepyhead." He grinned. "Slow start today?"

"What time is it?" she asked.

He only managed to make out her sleep-slurred words. "Six, and I thought you wanted to be up by five."

A pregnant silence greeted his words for all of five seconds before Emily threw the covers back, unaware she'd buried Snowball.

"Oh my God." She sort of flung the words as she darted from the bed to her dresser. "I'm so behind." She paused and pointed at Lukas, then realized she was holding a pair of polka-dot panties, which she stuffed behind her back. "Why didn't you warn me sooner?"

Lukas crossed his arms as he leaned against the doorjamb, enjoying the view despite an inner voice warning him she wouldn't appreciate it. "I only just woke up myself."

She shot him a glare, her gaze running over him from head to toe before she resumed her flight-of-the-bumblebee impersonation. "You don't look it," she accused.

He chuckled at that. "Are you saying I wake up looking fresh as a daisy?"

"Ugh." She rolled her eyes and left him standing there. "I'm never going to get

201

everything done in time," she called from the bathroom.

Aware others in the house were sleeping, he stepped inside and closed the door. "Calm down," he called back. "I'll help you."

She stuck her head out the door, toothbrush in her mouth. "You have other things to do today," she said around it. Then disappeared.

Lukas turned away to snoop around her room, which he had yet to see since coming home. No surprise the space was spotless, inviting, and cozy. Not because of the antiques or the red-and-green Christmas quilt, but because of Emily. Personal touches filled the space that he had no doubt she'd placed there — a woven throw over the back of a comfy chair and ottoman, books stacked on her bedside table, and pictures on the mantel above the cold fireplace.

And the scent of sugar cookies.

"Actually, I hired help to hit a few bigger items on the list you gave me," he said over his shoulder as he went to inspect the pictures. "I'm sure I can squeeze in helping you."

He leaned closer to one of the framed images of Emily and four men who towered over her — one of them Peter. They had to be her and her brothers. The way they surrounded their sister, no doubt she'd been overprotected as a kid, probably even still. Not that Emily would put up with interference. The woman was way too independent for that. Lukas grinned at the thought of that combination.

Another image was of Emily graduating something — high school maybe — smiling at the camera with two people who had to be her parents on either side. Wow, she was a carbon copy of her mom.

In the center of the mantel stood what had to be an elaborate advent calendar. Made of wood, the three-dimensional thing was shaped and painted like a decorated Christmas tree. The traditional toy had numbered doors all over it. He opened a few but found them all empty.

"What's this about hiring someone?" Her voice came from directly behind him. Irritated.

Was it strange that he was starting to listen for that tone, like the mating call of some annoying bird?

Lukas turned and waved a hand at the advent calendar. "Do you fill this for yourself?"

Her brows lowered, and she glanced

behind him. "My grandmother used to. Now it's only for decoration. Who did you hire?"

"That seems sad," Lukas said. When she crossed her arms and stared at him, expectation evident in the scrunching of her eyebrows, he dropped the subject. "Your friend Daniel."

Emily's expression blanked out. "My brother Pete's friend Daniel?" she asked.

"Yes. He's a carpenter."

"I know."

Lukas glanced from side to side as if the paintings on the wall might be able to tell him what he was missing here.

"How exactly are we going to pay him?" she asked through gritted teeth.

"*I'm* going to pay him." He waited for her reaction and wasn't disappointed.

Emily's lips went flat, and disapproval beamed at him from dark eyes suddenly gone hard and cold. "I see."

Lukas set his feet and squared up to her, refusing to back down. This time, at least, he was doing something right. "I don't think you do. Several of the jobs you have listed are ones that need a professional. Besides, as you've so bluntly pointed out, I owe Aunt Tilly a lot. I'm happy to do this."

Plus, if he was going to sell the house, he

needed it in better repair.

After a minute, Emily shrugged, her expression slipping back to that neutral blankness, which was almost worse. "It's your money."

"We agree on that, at least." Guilt had kept him quiet until now, but Lukas was starting to tire of being cast in the role of bad guy.

Or maybe the stark contrast between moments like last night and this morning was too much to accept as passively as he had been up till now.

"What are you going to do with all that extra time?" she asked.

Then she went and said something like that. He choked on a laugh. "Extra time. Right. First, it looks like I'll be helping you with breakfast and maybe with deliveries. Speaking of, shouldn't we get started?"

"Oh, shoot," she muttered. "You're right." Then she rushed out the door faster than Santa could shimmy up a chimney, leaving him and Snowball to follow in her wake.

"Your news distracted me," she accused on the way down the narrow stairs.

"Well, your lips distracted me last night, so I guess we're even." The words were out before he could vet them.

Emily didn't even pause, already in the

kitchen with the freezer already halfway to open. "I'm going to pretend you didn't say that."

He couldn't take it back now. Might as well go for broke. "Probably for the best, or I'd be tempted to get distracted again."

"Oh. My. God." She pulled two cartons of eggs out of the fridge. "I can't deal with you right now."

Except the sweet pink color coming to her cheeks could, possibly, mean she liked it. He studied her closer and pushed his luck.

"Said the most kissable lips ever." Lukas had to swallow back a chuckle at her glare. The woman was adorable when riled. She reminded him of Snowball in a snit. But the color in her cheeks deepened, and he didn't miss the quick glance she cast at his own lips.

Then she shoved the egg cartons at him. "Beat twenty eggs with two tablespoons of milk per egg."

"Yes ma'am." He snapped out a salute but did stop his teasing to get to work, satisfied, at least for now, that the kiss last night hadn't been a fluke. She was interested. She just didn't want to be.

Emily kept breakfast simple — scrambled eggs, bacon, and cranberry scones she had stashed in the freezer that thawed quickly.

In short order, working together in relative harmony, they had the food cooked and the table ready right in time for the guests, who trickled downstairs, lured by the homey scents filling the house.

Meal taken care of, they returned to the kitchen to get started on prepping for Emily's deliveries, which she'd baked the night before. Before they got too far along, a knock sounded at the kitchen door and Daniel poked his head inside. The second his gaze landed on Emily, he smiled.

"Hey, little chef," he said, coming in the rest of the way, closing the door behind him. "How's it going?"

Lukas paused in folding together a pink box. Did the man mean to sound condescending? Or was this his way of flirting? Either way, Lukas had to beat back his inner caveman, who wasn't a fan.

"Fine." Emily sent Daniel an answering smile, one which was somewhat stilted if Lukas wasn't mistaken. The caveman retreated a bit, turning smug. Even if she didn't like him most of the time, at least she wasn't reserved with him.

You're being an idiot.

"Luke," the other man said with a nod. Instead of stopping to talk to Lukas about what needed to be done, Daniel moved to lean against the counter beside where Emily was working to box up several pies. "Thanks for giving my name to Luke here. I'm happy I can help."

Emily didn't stop in her task. "Sorry. I wasn't the one who came up with the idea of having you help."

Daniel gave her a benevolent smile that patently said he didn't believe her. "I figured you'd get around to asking eventually. This place needs work."

Watching from where he was set up, Lukas ground his teeth at that look and the words.

Emily remained pleasant, though. "You can thank Lukas for the business. He definitely needs help."

Based on her tone, he was pretty sure she didn't mean with the house.

Neither of them looked at him, though. Instead, Daniel inched closer, crowding into Emily's space as she tried to get stuff done.

Lukas frowned. How had he missed this last night? The guy had chatted in a friendly way with Emily during the tree lighting, but Daniel hadn't been like this, had he? Cloying, patronizing, and . . . clearly interested.

Or had Lukas been too focused on needing a carpenter for several of the items on his chore list?

"Excuse me." Emily politely moved Daniel so she could wipe off the countertops.

Daniel switched to lean against the center table, which didn't exactly get him out of her way. The guy might be built like a wrestler with broad shoulders and muscles bulging, and the ladies probably found him good-looking, but he was not exactly observant. "Maybe after we're both done with work tonight, we can go get some —"

In a bolting streak of white, Snowball suddenly shot through the kitchen and launched herself at Daniel's leg, climbing him like a tree to about mid-thigh where she got purchase with her claws.

"Owwww . . ." Daniel howled, and went to knock his attacker away.

Only Emily jumped in and grabbed his hand before he could hurt the kitten. Good thing she did, because Lukas would've had to tackle the guy, otherwise. Muscles or not.

"Snowball," she chided as she gently detached the cat from her brother's friend.

Tucked safely in her arms, Snowball's ears lay flat back as she glared at Daniel, emitting a sound that was probably supposed to be a warning growl but sounded more like a toy airplane.

"What is wrong with you?" Emily asked, and bopped the kitten lightly on the nose.

Lukas was tempted to give the tiny cat a

thumbs-up. He'd definitely slip her a tasty treat under the table tonight. A ludicrous thought given that he was the one who'd hired Daniel to be working here, day in, day out, for the next few weeks.

Well played, Weber.

He'd just been so happy to find a carpenter.

"I'll take her to Miss Tilly," Emily said.

Which left Lukas in the kitchen with Daniel, who he suddenly wasn't so sure about hiring.

Lukas had gone and dragged Daniel into the mess that was Weber Haus without discussing it with her.

Not that he had to, if she was honest with herself. This house, technically, was more his than hers. That had to be why she was so irritated. It couldn't be him inviting Daniel into the middle of . . . whatever was going on between them. That kiss last night had taken her expectations and raised them, blown them away. Like piles-of-presents-under-the-tree-Christmas-morning blown away.

A phenomenal kiss. Magical even.

Emily had to keep from sticking her tongue out at herself in the gilded hallway mirror as she passed. Kissing — good, bad, or otherwise — didn't have any bearing on the situation with Weber Haus. If anything, it muddied the situation. Having Daniel here would put a stop to her foolish wishing. She should be grateful.

So why wasn't she?

With a twitch, she prowled into her room, shutting the door behind her perhaps a little too hard. There she put Snowball down gently on the bed.

What she needed was a shower before she went out to do her deliveries. She hadn't had a chance to do that when Lukas woke her so abruptly the second time. Maybe after a nice, long soak, she'd feel more herself.

As she gathered fresh clothes from her drawers, she happened to glance in the mirror and catch sight of her advent calendar on the mantel of the fireplace. Emily paused, then slowly turned to look closer. Sure enough, a yellow sticky note was attached to one of the doors with "Open Me" scrawled in black marker.

Lukas. It had to be.

When on earth had he had time to sneak in here and do that? Probably when he said he needed to run to the restroom.

With the oddest combination of eagerness and wariness twisting in knots in her stomach Emily pulled the beautifully carved and painted Christmas tree with its randomly numbered doors off the mantel.

Her grandmother had given it to her as a child, and Emily had always loved it, cherishing it even more after Oma had passed away. Once she'd moved away from home, and no one was around to fill it but her, which seemed silly, it had become just a decoration. As she lifted the tree, several things rattled inside the small compartments. He'd had time to do more than one? The note was stuck to the door for day one, but they were further into the month. Interesting.

She tugged on the wooden knob and smiled to find one of her favorite chocolate candies inside. One of the kind she thought she kept well hidden in the kitchen. Maybe not, though. Unable to help herself, she popped it in her mouth, then opened the door labeled "two" to find a folded note that read, "Have a blessed and joyous Christmas." More chocolate and kind notes in several others. Even, a sprig of mistletoe with a tiny red ribbon.

Heat flooded Emily's cheeks, as her immediate thought involved kissing Lukas again.

Had he meant to remind her? Of how

beautiful she'd felt. How strong his arms had been around her. How her heart had pounded so hard, she'd worried he'd hear. Even now, her stomach tumbled over itself like a pineapple upside-down cake, all topsy-turvy.

He's leaving, and you have bigger plans to deal with.

With a few flips of her hand, Emily shut the doors on the calendar and hastily replaced it in its pride of place.

What was he doing anyway? Toying with her emotions like this?

Except she found it difficult to hold on to her righteous indignation over chocolates, a nice note, and mistletoe. A thoughtful act, on his part.

But also a tad thoughtless.

Maybe that was the trouble. Lukas was a good guy when the obvious was in front of his face, but thoughtless without a constant physical reminder of his responsibilities.

Only she couldn't make the giddy feeling go away. If she was honest, she didn't really want to. Which scared the heck out of her.

With a final look at the calendar, Emily shook her head and went to take her shower. She had too much to do to be standing around thinking about a man whose impact on her life, in the long run, would be —

should be — negligible.

In short order, showered and feeling at least clean and fresher, she made her way downstairs. As she went, somewhere in the house the distinct pounding of a hammer sounded. Daniel already hard at work? Good, a few less things for her to worry about.

With Snowball flying down the stairs, almost out of control, ahead of her, Emily stopped as soon as she hit the kitchen. Lukas was still in there. Along with a pile of pink boxes of varying sizes, her logo prominent on the top of each, already filled with the items she'd baked last night. He was leaning against the counter, scrolling through something on his phone, but looked up as she entered and smiled.

"I thought you were taking her to Aunt Tilly?" He nodded at the kitten, who'd leaped onto the table.

Oh. Right. Apparently, thoughts of Lukas were crowding everything else from her mind. "I heard Daniel working upstairs and decided it was safe to let her loose."

"Okay . . . Ready?" he asked.

Emily's eyebrows shot up. "Um . . ."

"I figured I'd save you a bit of time and go with you, as long as you don't mind stopping by the hardware store again. I'm going to try to fix the chipped paint on the cabinets in here and need to color-match. I couldn't find any leftover paint anywhere."

That hadn't been on the list she'd given him, though the task was on her personal list. Most of the guests didn't spend time in the kitchen, so it had remained low on her priorities as she was the only one who minded.

"Why don't you give me a list of what you need, and I'll pick it up while I'm out," she hedged.

Lukas, seemingly unaware of her discomfort, shook his head. "I also want to fix that cabinet that won't stay shut."

"That's been annoying me for a year." The words popped out.

"I thought it might. I've been annoyed with it, and I've only been in that cabinet once." That good-natured grin of his, so easily produced, might be her undoing. Either that or the kissing. She wasn't sure which was most likely to turn her into a fruitcake first.

Oblivious to the fact that she was stalling, he grabbed both their jackets from the hooks on the wall and handed hers over. "Come on, slowpoke. Daylight's wasting."

Don't look a gift horse in the mouth. Especially at Christmas.

That was Tilly's homespun wisdom sounding in her head, with the Christmas bit tacked on. Except Emily had been looking forward to a chance at getting Lukas out from underfoot so she could refocus her mind on normal, non-Lukas, nonidiotic thoughts. Distance was what she needed. Except on such short notice, Emily couldn't come up with a single excuse to leave him behind.

Hiding her reluctance, she shrugged into her coat and together they loaded the car. She grabbed her purse from inside.

"Whoops . . . Hold it." Lukas snagged her by the elbow and gently swung her around, suddenly close.

Too close. Even in the harsh chill of morning, the snow blinding in the sun, his body heat radiated to her. "What are you —"

"You have a passenger." He pulled one shoulder strap of her purse away and scooped a hand inside only to emerge with Snowball, who glared at him in full kitten miffedness. She pulled her small white back paws up, kicking at his hand.

"Oh my goodness," Emily scolded. "How does she do that?" She could've sworn she'd checked her purse before she picked it up. The imp was Houdini reincarnated as a cat with nine lives.

"Back in the house with you." Lukas opened the back door and set her inside, managing to close it quickly before she got out again.

Snowball sat on the other side of the glassed door and pawed at it, her mouth opening in helpless little meows that they couldn't quite hear from outside.

Lukas glanced at Emily, his green eyes alight with humor, a smile tugging at his lips, and she answered that look with a shared amusement of her own. Why it should feel as though only the two of them existed in that moment, Emily had no idea. But a growing part of her didn't want to break the spell. She wanted more. "She's nothing if not determined."

Lukas chuckled. "Like all the ladies in my life."

Emily lifted her eyebrows in question.

"Between her, you, Aunt Tilly, and my agent, my goose is well and truly cooked." He winked.

Emily didn't bother to hide her grin, suddenly feeling lighter, despite not wanting to. "My suggestion to you, Mr. Weber, is to just go with it. Don't resist the inevitable. You'll be happier in the end."

She headed to the car, steps lighter despite having to tromp through knee-high snow.

"You might be right." His low murmur reached her as she slid into the driver's seat, and a shiver skated over her at his tone.

Emily didn't look but suspected that if she did, Lukas would be watching her with a light in his eyes that would make her want to run up to her room and get that mistletoe out so it could do them some good.

"Let's go, slowpoke," she called before shutting her door.

They left without me.

I watch out the door as Emily's car slowly rolls by, tires crunching in the snow.

I can't believe they left without me.

CHAPTER 12

Lukas strolled through the hardware store,
the air filled with the scents of freshly cut
wood as he walked past shelves of different-
size beams and planks to the section he
needed. In addition to the tasks he'd set for
himself today, he'd also talked to Daniel
about a few other projects and had a list of
items. But his mind wasn't entirely on the
task at hand.

Too distracted by the woman walking
quietly beside him.

Rather than have her drop him off first,
he'd insisted on helping Emily with her
deliveries before doing his errand. Lukas
had given up on pretending he didn't want
to spend time with her. When she relaxed
around him, he enjoyed drawing out her
laugh, and the way she teased back, and the
way she asked a ton of questions like she
was truly interested. In the car, they'd chatted easily about Christmas gifts and what

they were looking forward to over the holiday. He'd wanted to ask if she'd liked what he'd left her in the advent calendar — after all, she'd gone up to shower — but decided that if she didn't bring it up, he wouldn't, either.

Maybe she hadn't seen it.

Or maybe she hated that he was the one leaving her stuff. His initial thought had been a wish to give her something to smile about. What if she took it the wrong way though? Emily wasn't exactly prone toward giving him, of all people, the benefit of the doubt when it came to intentions.

He stopped and perused the paint supplies.

"Do you need a caulking gun to fix the paint on the kitchen cabinets?" she asked.

Lukas paused and looked at what he'd been about to put into the basket. Nope, he didn't need that. "It's for the bathtub in my room," he made up on the spot, and grabbed a tube of clear silicon for good measure. Surely at least one of the bathrooms in the massive house needed a touch up in the caulk department. Or maybe a windowsill?

Focus, Weber.

Quickly, he made sure everything else that went into the basket was what he actually

220

did need, then he hustled them through check out.

"You hungry?" he asked as they loaded the SUV, the brisk air fogging with their exhaled breath.

Emily paused to look at him over the top. "I have to cook lunch for the guests."

Her tone said all she didn't with words. Basically a big question mark floated in the air between them along with their breath, asking if he remembered some people had responsibilities.

He grinned and enjoyed the way her eyes narrowed with annoyance at the sight. "Actually . . . no one will be home for lunch today. While you were showering, I happened to talk to each of the guests, all of whom have plans to eat out. Daniel brought his own, and Aunt Tilly said something about meeting with her bridge group today. So . . . no one to feed but you and me."

Emily wrinkled her nose, then yanked open her door and got in. "Don't you need to get started on the cabinets?"

He got in, too. "You don't have to cook, and we both need to eat," he pointed out gently.

He understood Emily's drive to achieve and accomplish and knock things off the To-Do list that never seemed to get smaller.

Someone needed to make this woman stop and relax every so often, or she'd put herself into a breakdown trying to do too much. He sort of liked the idea of being that someone for her. At least for now.

"What do you feel like eating?" she asked after a pause.

Lukas relaxed, shoulders dropping. It had been a fifty-fifty chance that she'd agree to lunch. Make that more like seventy-thirty, leaning toward the no side. "I haven't been in town much since coming home, and I'm sure there are a few new places since I was here last. Surprise me."

"Well . . ." She wrinkled her nose thoughtfully, and he had the strangest urge to kiss her just because she was adorable. Had she always had that small, white scar on the bridge?

"What do you like?" she asked.

He yanked his focus back to her full face. "Everything. I travel a lot and try local foods wherever I go."

Dang. Bringing up his travel and his job was a dumb move. The trouble was his job was entirely who he was. What else did he have to share of himself? Not much of interest he was starting to realize.

Instead of getting irritated, though, Emily turned to consider him. "What's the best

222

food you've had?" she asked, curiosity brightening her expression.

Progress, as far as Lukas was concerned.

Before he could answer, her cell phone beeped, and the screen lit up. The message was obviously from her mom and appeared to be an article titled "How Often Bakeries Fail."

Interesting. Even more interesting was the way Emily quickly turned off the screen, cheeks filling with color.

"Do you need to get that?" he asked.

Emily rolled her eyes. "Nope. So . . . best food?"

Obviously, she didn't want to talk about that message. He let her change the subject and gave her question serious consideration. "I'd say it's a toss-up between a beef and couscous dish in Morocco — heavy on the cinnamon — a sweet tapioca pancake sandwich with passionfruit and freshly shaved white coconut in Rio, or the sushi I had in Tokyo."

Emily eyed him with an undiluted interest that only had him wanting to keep her looking at him that way all the time. "That's quite a mix," she said.

Lukas shrugged. "I'm lucky that I get to try the best authentic foods around the world."

"Color me jealous." Emily smiled — she actually smiled when it came to his lifestyle — then started the SUV and put it in gear. "I don't have anything that exotic on offer, but I think I know a place you'll enjoy."

She managed to tuck her SUV in a tiny parking space right on the busy main street that ran through the center of town. They got out and joined the many folks on the sidewalks who'd ignored the cold, or perhaps were taking advantage of the sunny day, to come out and shop.

Seriously, Norman Rockwell would've loved this town, with decorations on every old-fashioned lamp and garlands strung over the street. At night it would turn into a winter wonderland with all the buildings decorated in white twinkling lights.

Emily took him into a place called Mc-Kitchens. Inside, the decor was all whites and blacks with one mint-green wall behind the bar. The ambiance leaned toward modern farmhouse, and the scents filling the air were scrumptious.

After they found their own seats, she handed him a menu. "Everything served here is seasonal and farm-to-table, locally sourced," she said. "You won't get the exact same menu from day to day, but everything is tasty."

The waitstaff was quick to take their orders, and the food was on the table before he knew it. Emily watched him closely as he took his first bite. Lukas pretended to seriously evaluate as he chewed, then winked. "You're right. Best food I've had in a while."

He had to hold back a laugh as she managed to simultaneously smile and frown. Teasing her was becoming as addictive as her cooking.

"Then again," he mused, drawing it out. "Nothing holds a candle to your cooking. Still, a solid recommendation."

Lukas nodded as if he'd pronounced an official review like he was a fancy food critic. Emily paused, bite midway to her mouth, then rolled her eyes. "You're a tease, Lukas Weber. Has anyone ever told you that?"

He shrugged. "Only you."

"Which makes me, what? The rudest?" Her brow pleated in a frown over that.

"Uh-uh." He shook his head. "It makes you honest. I find it refreshing. I always know exactly where I stand with you."

"I suppose that's something," she countered dryly.

"It also makes you the person I like to tease the most." Only he wasn't joking now. He gazed back with total sincerity as she inspected his expression.

Eventually, she shook her head as if she wasn't entirely sure what to do with him. "Definitely a charmer."

Only now she didn't sound quite as though that was a bad thing.

"Have you always been that way?" she asked around a bite, no judgment in her gaze. More . . . curiosity.

"What way?"

Emily's turn to shrug. "I find the combination of the charm and the aversion to spending time with strangers to be at odds with each other."

"Ah." Lukas thought about that, taking his time cutting his food. No one besides Aunt Tilly had ever witnessed his dislike of interacting with the guests, so no one had ever asked this question. "Actually, I enjoy spending time with people a lot. But that's now. Growing up, I disliked it because it felt as though my home was being invaded every single day. Living in an inn gave me very little alone time when that was all I wanted."

Hell, he'd been a mess after his parents passed away. Living that out under the concerned gazes of strangers had been . . . difficult.

"Makes sense," Emily said.

226

"However, these days, I have to interact with folks from all walks of life for my job. I'm rarely in my own space, constantly meeting new people." And this was the first time Lukas had connected the dots. He frowned.

"What?" Emily prompted.

"Nothing. I just did some mental calculations. My career is basically a traveling version of being a guest in an inn everywhere I go. I never realized that." The buzz of realization had him blinking.

Emily tipped her head and gave him a sympathetic moue. "Has your math always been bad?"

Lukas snorted a laugh. "Maybe my self-perception has."

She patted his hand in an exaggerated gesture. "The first step is admitting it."

"I did say *maybe.*"

"Hmmm . . ." was all she said in response.

At that moment, a blond bear of a man roughly their age walked up to the table. "Emmy-bo-bemmy," he boomed, and about yanked Emily's arm out of the socket pulling her to her feet to wrap her up in a hug a polar bear would be impressed by.

Lukas had to beat down his inner caveman, who'd been making way too many appearances today. Especially when Emily

227

probably wouldn't appreciate it if he punched the guy in the face just for hugging her. Lukas eyed the bear-man, who had to be at least six three and built thick, like a wrestler. Holding his own against the guy was probably unlikely. Even if it went against his manly ego to admit that to himself.

Who was this person anyway?

Emily managed to extract herself from the smothering hug, but instead of scolding the man grinned wide. "Freddy-bo-beddy," she answered the same way he'd greeted her.

Fredrik Peltz, a man she'd never been able to take seriously for obvious reasons, ducked and then glanced around. "Better not be spreading that around. I'm here with clients."

"If they've spent any time with you, they won't be surprised."

He pulled out a wounded expression. "I'll have you know people take me seriously in the realty world."

"You're a realtor?" Lukas asked.

At some point he'd stood from their table. Emily introduced the two men, who shook hands. "Yes," Fredrik said. "My father was a realtor, and, having grown up in the area, it seemed only natural to join his firm. In fact, he's just retired."

Emily brightened. "The business is all yours, I assume?"

Fredrik produced the blinding grin he'd had since grade school. "Lock, stock, and barrel."

"Do you specialize?" Lukas asked.

Emily eyed him more closely. Why was he so interested in Fredrik's business? He couldn't be thinking of settling down, could he? Buying a house here? Given how often his agent called him, he had to be chomping at the bit to get moving.

"I'm more commercial than residential, but my firm handles both extremely well." Fredrik glanced over his shoulder, then turned to her with a grimace. "Gotta go, Emmy. Clients and Christmas wait on no man."

After another quick hug, which was much like how cars in a crusher must feel, Emily waved him off and resumed her seat.

"Emmy-bo-bemmy, huh?" Lukas raised his eyebrows, though he was staring after Fredrik's broad back.

"You want to make something of it?" She softened the challenge with a wag of her eyebrows.

Lukas snapped his gaze to hers. "Nope. I think it's totes adorbs."

The sound of the teenaged words on his

lips had her snorting an inelegant laugh. "Awww . . . You want a nickname, too? I could call you Lukey-bo-bukey?"

Lukas grimaced. "Hard pass."

"Yeah. It does sound too close to pukey. What about slow-pokey-bo-bokey?" she tried. Maybe she needed more teasing in her life. Being on this side was way too fun.

"I'm not really a nickname kind of guy." He picked up his fork and continued eating.

"That's too bad."

"Is your friend a good realtor?" Lukas asked, obviously changing the subject. Back to Fredrik, though. What was going on in that head of his?

Emily followed suit and picked up her silverware to tuck back into her meal. "He is. When I was working on that previous bakery and restaurant project, he was helping me find a space." Greg ended it before they'd signed papers, thank goodness. The impact of that kind of commitment had likely scared him off, she realized in hindsight.

"Does every man in this town feel a need to lift you off your feet with hugs?"

Emily glanced over her shoulder with a fond smile. "With four older brothers, I was basically the little sister of every guy we grew up with."

She lifted her gaze from her plate to find Lukas watching her, his head canted to the side. "Why do I get the feeling that wasn't as fun as it sounds?" he asked.

Why did he seem to see her more clearly than even her family sometimes did?

She took a sip of water, then wiped her mouth with her napkin. "It didn't make it easy to find a date. Either I was little-sister material, one of the guys, or the boy trying to date me had to face down not only four brothers but all their friends. I don't know a high school boy alive with those kind of guts."

"I've met Peter. If all your brothers are like that, I'd say most full-grown men don't have those kinds of guts," Lukas muttered.

Emily giggled at his scowl. "True. You'll get a chance soon. Christmas Eve is almost here."

"All those burly brother types might be a good resource, though. Helpful around the house? After all, Weber Haus has a long fix-it list."

When she'd first met him, Emily would've immediately jumped into irritation that Lukas could think of using people that way. Except, she knew him better now, and she could tell that wasn't how he meant it. She wagged a finger in his face. "You're just try-ing to get out of your chore list, mister. Shame on you."

He snatched her finger out of midair and didn't give it back. "Even you have to admit I've been doing a decent job around the place," he wheedled.

Emily fixated. Lukas has nice hands — strong with tapered fingers, nails cut utilitar-ian short. Capable hands. She tugged.

"I guess you're okay," she admitted reluc-tantly. "Even if you are a bit sloth-like."

Needing to look anywhere else, she raised her gaze to find him watching her with a smile she could only describe as knowing. Did he realize the effect he had on her?

Another tug.

He didn't let go.

"Me? Sloth-like? Ha."

She did not remotely trust the twinkle that lit his green eyes brighter than a Christmas tree.

Lukas used the hold on her hand to pull her closer, like he was telling her a secret. "I tell you what, turtle. When we get home, I challenge you to a race. I'll bet that I can finish hanging the outside Christmas lights before you have dinner ready."

She gulped but couldn't drag her gaze away from his. "What about the cabinets?"

"I'll do those tomorrow. Is it a bet?" A cocky smile tipped her scales.

Dang. The man had found her one weakness. Saying no went against every competitive bone in her body. "What do I get if I win?"

He raised his other hand to his face, running it over his jaw, the stubble sounding softly scratchy this close. Like it had last night when he'd been kissing her.

Stop thinking about kissing Lukas, she ordered her mind. It didn't help.

"I tell you what . . . ," he said, completely oblivious to how her world had run amok thanks to teasing eyes and a bit of hand-holding. "If you get an easy breakfast ready tonight, I'll let you sleep in, and I'll get it prepped, served, and cleaned up."

Ooh . . . Now that sounded like an offer worth considering. "And if you win?"

He leaned closer. "I get a good night kiss."

Lukas's voice dropped in a way that sent shivers traipsing down her spine. He didn't look away, and the intensity in his gaze did a fair job of stealing her breath. Maybe he wasn't so oblivious after all. Maybe this was him flirting.

The thought about knocked her out of her chair. "Lukas? What are you doing?"

She wanted to look away but couldn't

233

make herself do it. Gravity had less pull than Lukas Weber.

In answer, he leaned even closer, and she knew, without doubt, that he was going to kiss her. Forget lack of oxygen, her bigger problem was the fact that she really, really wanted him to.

"What are you doing?" she whispered.

"Showing big brothers and polar-bear-size friends that this full-grown man won't be scared off so easily," he murmured.

Dredging up a stiffer backbone from somewhere inside her, Emily put a finger to his lips, stopping him. "You haven't won anything yet, buster."

He stilled but didn't back away. "Don't tell me you don't want me to kiss you, Emily. I thought we were honest with each other, if nothing else."

Emily stared into eyes gone greener, as if reflecting his entire focus on her. "There's honest, and then there's foolish. Wanting to kiss you would fall into the foolish category."

Did his eyes lose the twinkle? She couldn't have hurt him with that statement, could she?

"Why?" he asked, still not moving away.

"Because I . . . ." She wanted to say she didn't like him, but putting that to words wouldn't feel right. It would taste rather

234

bitter on her tongue and leave her with a gaping hole inside. Honesty compelled her to admit that wasn't true anymore. In fact, if she was honest with herself at least, she liked Lukas. More than a lot.

She cleared her throat. "Because you're going back out into the world after the holidays."

Beneath her touch, his mouth shifted into a smile. "There's my honest Emmy-bo-bemmy."

But beneath the charm and light humor she'd expected, she sensed that layer of hurt hadn't gone away. He let go of her finger and sat back, pulling away more than physically. Even as she dropped her hand into her lap, she wanted to close that gap and offer a kiss anyway, one to heal whatever small sting she'd delivered.

With a wave of his hand, Lukas called the waitress over to ask for the check. "We'd better get back. I need to see how Daniel is coming, and I have a bet to win."

Emily cleared her throat again. Was it dry in here? "You mean I have a bet to win."

Only, for the first time in a long while, she'd rather stay here with Lukas and talk and not go back to her To-Do lists or even her baking.

Get your feet back on solid ground, Emily

Miss Tilly's room has the best window for seeing people coming and going from the house. It also has a cushioned window seat. Other than the warm kitchen, and the inside of Emily's purse, it's my favorite spot in the house.

Right now, I'm sitting here because Lukas and Emily aren't back yet, and they've been gone a long, long time. What on earth could two humans have to do for so long away from the house? Hopefully kissing!

If they kiss enough, they're going to get married. Just like all those other couples who come through the house. Most of them are married. Miss Tilly says the newlyweds have only just been married, and those people kiss all the time. Way more than other people.

So that has to be what kissing means.

What if, when they come home, they're married? Then they could stay in that suite.

Oh . . . Except those other people are in there right now. I might need to find a way to get them out so Lukas and Emily can use it.

My ears prick as the crunch of tires on the snow sounds before I can see the car. Sure enough, it's Emily's SUV.

About time.

I jump to my feet and watch until they pull around the side, then hop down from my perch and run out the door. I can't wait to see if they're married or not.

"Snowball," Miss Tilly's voice follows me out into the hall. "Where are you going?"

I ignore her and race to the top of the stairs. I can hear Emily's and Lukas's voices, which are getting louder. They're headed my way.

Leaning between the rails, way out over the edge, I see Lukas's dark head appear beneath me first, followed by Emily.

"We each get ten minutes to prep," he was saying.

Prep? What's he talking about.

"No getting Daniel to help you," Emily said. "That's cheating."

Were they playing a game? I like games. I like knocking all the little pieces off the board and watching them fly across the table and onto the floor. It's even more fun if I can beat a human to a piece and run away with it. The best is when the piece is sparkly.

"Do I hear my name being taken in vain?" a man's voice calls out.

I scowl, a tiny growl rumbling in my throat as the Daniel guy shows up behind me and goes down the stairs. He's wiping his hands on a rag, but mostly what makes me mad is the way he's smiling at Emily. Like he has a right to.

Lukas is allowed to smile that way at her, but not this bozo.

He stops to talk to them in the foyer and is standing right under where I'm hanging over the edge, and an idea pops into my head. I gage how far below me he is, judging the distance.

I can make that.

"Did you find everything you needed?" Daniel asks Lukas.

"I did. Thanks." Lukas holds up several bags that rustle with the movement.

"I hope you took our Emily here out for a decent lunch." Daniel pulls Emily in for a side hug.

Yeah. This guy needs to stop doing that.

As soon as he lets her go, I don't think about it, I just jump. Wiggling in the air so I keep my belly to the ground and all four paws out, I give a little war cry. My accuracy is perfect, and I land right on Daniel's head.

"Gah!" he yells, and tries to swat at me.

But Lukas beats him to it, plucking me gently from Daniel's head. From the safety of Lukas's arms, I snarl and hiss at the man who should not be touching my Emily.

"Dang it. That's twice today," Daniel snaps. "That cat has it in for me."

I snuggle into Lukas's hand and give a loud purr and even lick his thumb. The human got my message. Maybe now he'll leave.

CHAPTER 13

A loud, obnoxious clanging noise roused Lukas from a dream where he won the bet and got to kiss Emily . . . and then she let him keep kissing her.

Unfortunately, that noise was the alarm on his phone, which meant it was time to get his backside out of bed and go fix breakfast while Emily slept in. She'd won fair and square after all. He should've known hanging lights on the big house would take forever. With a groan, Lukas rubbed the sleep out of his eyes. He was never going to live this down. She'd be calling him things like pokey and sloth the rest of his life.

Or, at least, the rest of his time at home.

He reached over and flipped the switch on his lamp, blinking owlishly in the soft glow. This was way too early in the morning, and not nearly as fun without her. Sure, he'd had to get up at the crack of dawn periodically to travel or to get shots in the right early-morning light. How did Emily do this every day, all by herself?

That had to be lonely.

The glitter of something shiny on his bedside table caught his eye, and he reached out to find a button encrusted in diamond-like jewels, most likely rhinestones. Nothing like this belonged on any of his clothes or in his room. He glanced at the ball of white in the bed beside him.

Had he made it on Snowball's list of people who got shiny presents? "I'm honored, fluff face."

Getting out of bed, he was careful not to jiggle Snowball, still curled up on the pillow next to his. Not an easy feat when getting out of an antique bed and the frame could use tightening, which made it extra wiggly.

Luck was with him, and her eyes remained peacefully closed. He'd brought her in the room last night when he went to bed for two reasons. First, he figured he'd get more sleep without being woken up when she managed to open the door and sneak in anyway.

Second, Snowball was his new best friend.

That attack on Daniel the day before, after the guy had side-hugged Emily, had pretty much been the funniest dang thing Lukas had ever seen. A ball of white, screaming like a little kitty banshee, dropping down on Daniel's head like an avenging angel out for blood. Doing pretty much exactly what Lukas had wanted to do, which was remove the offending arm from around Emily.

She might think the man saw her as a little sister, but Lukas was beyond positive that Daniel had outgrown that phase and saw her now as the beautiful, kind, if overly honest, woman she was.

"Let's go feed people," Lukas said to Snowball.

The kitten blinked and took her time getting up to stretch luxuriously before she finally hopped down and pranced out of the room like a duchess. Lukas smiled on the way past Emily's door. He'd managed to sneak in again yesterday while she'd been making dinner and fill a few more days in the advent calendar with things he'd picked up in town.

Filling that darn calendar was why he'd ended up losing the bet yesterday. Which was why today's advent gift would be especially interesting.

In the kitchen, he pulled the premade casseroles — something to do with French toast — out of the fridge and started the oven preheating.

While that was going, he set the dining room table and got several pitchers filled with water, milk, and juice, respectively. Then slipped the casseroles in the oven to bake for thirty minutes each. Which meant sitting and waiting.

He dropped into a chair at the small breakfast table and was not at all surprised when Snowball bounded up to sit on the table in front of him.

"What do you want to bet Emily comes down here before breakfast is over," he murmured quietly, not wanting to disturb the early-morning peace of the kitchen.

Snowball canted her head to the side.

"After she won this bet, I bet her lunch duty that she couldn't stay away from the kitchen or chores until nine," he informed the kitten. "If she loses, I get a kiss."

Snowball gave a happy meow.

"Yeah."

She meowed again, but this one sounded questioning.

"Well, I'll tell you what. I made that bet for her sake, not mine. Emily has trouble taking time for herself. You know?"

Snowball appeared to nod.

"No way could she feel right about sleeping in when work needs to be done. But to beat me in a bet, she might just do it."

243

Lukas propped his chin in one hand. "That woman is going to wear herself into a nervous breakdown if she doesn't slow down a bit. Don't you think?"

Snowball reached out and placed her paw on top of his nose, clearly commiserating.

What am I doing having a conversation with a kitten?

Lukas gave her a pat and leaned back in his chair, checking the timer for the casseroles. "Although," he said more to himself than Snowball. "At the rate I'm going, I'll be doing all the meals and getting no kisses."

Snowball settled down into a fastidious pose, all four feet tucked neatly beneath her thick fur as she lay on her belly, watching him with curious blue eyes.

Lukas sighed. "I really want to kiss her."

And, yet again, he was talking to the cat like she were human.

Lukas eyed the baked goods piled under various container lids and towels to keep them fresh. Still more were in the refrigerator. He had at least another twenty minutes to wait on the casseroles. Might as well not just sit here.

By the time he finished boxing up all of Emily's wares for her to deliver, the timer dinged, and he pulled the piping-hot dishes out of the oven, sniffing appreciatively.

Scents of cinnamon and maple syrup filled the room, and his stomach gurgled loudly in response. Whatever concoction Emily had put together smelled incredible.

Following her painstakingly simple instructions from last night, which she'd also written down in feminine, loopy handwriting, he popped the glass bakeware into antique decorative silver holders, stuck serving spoons in each, and carried them out to the table. Next he brought out plain bran muffins, butter, and a fruit salad that he'd personally seen Emily sprinkle with lemon juice and powdered sugar.

In the kitchen, the woman was nothing short of amazing.

"Something smells delicious," Bill Hoffman said as he strolled into the room.

At the sight of Lukas, he stopped. "Why Emily. What broad shoulders you've grown since last night."

Lukas chuckled. "The better to heft casserole dishes with, my dear."

Louise entered the room as Bill laughingly settled in a chair. "Where's Emily?" she asked.

"I lost a bet and am serving breakfast while she gets to sleep in," Lukas explained.

Louise brightened. "I hope you lost the bet on purpose. That girl's as worn-down as an old pair of running shoes."

Lukas silently agreed but didn't want to say so. It would feel disloyal. "I don't think it's easy to get Emily to sit still. She's one of those people who enjoys pushing herself hard, but I'm glad she gets a break today, at least."

Unfortunately, Aunt Tilly chose that moment to enter the room, catching the last bit of conversation. Her eyebrows drew together as she slowly pulled out a chair. "I've been thinking I should hire extra help for her. She does too much."

Even across the room, Lukas couldn't miss the worry in his aunt's faded blue eyes. Lukas had zero doubt what was going through her mind. She couldn't afford more help. However, she loved Emily and wouldn't want to harm her in any way, including working her too hard.

"Well, I'm here for the time being. Let's see how much I can get done before I leave," he said, aiming her a soft smile and receiving one in return.

"You always were a good helper around the house."

Lukas snorted. "Mostly because I was avoiding the guests, and chores got me out of socializing."

The words were out before he considered

who was in the room. Quickly he turned to the Hoffmans. "Not anymore, of course."

Bill tipped his head back in a big belly laugh. "Son, I don't know a boy alive who would want to hang out with old fogies like us. I don't blame you for escaping. At least you got stuff done."

At that point a small ruckus on the stairs signaled that the Andrewses were coming down. Their kids were eight and six and tended to have only one mode — running.

"Walk down those stairs. You're going to crack your heads open if you slip," Alice Andrews could be heard yelling after them.

Lukas schooled his features as they entered the room and, instead of laughing, bent an accusing stare on the two youngsters. "You know, I *was* planning to play a game with you after dinner tonight."

"Sardines?" Jakob Andrews, the older of the two, piped up hopefully, a lock of dark hair falling over one eye.

"Not if that's how you boys are going to treat this lovely old house. Wouldn't you feel horrible if you broke something and Miss Tilly had to pay to fix it or replace it?"

Two sets of wide eyes gazed back. Zac, the younger one, appeared to be on the edge of tears, wobbly chin and all. Jakob, meanwhile, eyed Lukas like he wasn't positive this wasn't another adult exaggerating to get him to behave. "I was being careful," he insisted.

"Did you go faster than a slow walk?"

"No —"

Lukas gave him a sideways look, and Jakob, face all stubbornness and defiance, looked away. "Yes."

"Then you weren't being careful." Lukas crossed his arms and waited for Jakob to lose the stubbornness.

Finally, the kid grimaced, then nodded. "I won't run, and I'll be more careful."

"Good. I'll check back with your mother tonight to see how you two do. If she gives the thumbs-up, we can play a game." He held up a hand as Jakob opened his mouth. "Not sardines. We don't have enough people. But I'll teach you a version of hide-and-seek that I learned in Russia. We'll have to play in the stables, because it involves lots of running."

"Are you sure you want to take these two heathens on?" Alice Andrews asked doubtfully.

Lukas waved her off. "It'll be fun."

As they all sat, Katie and Miles Bauer showed up, followed by Emily.

"I'm hungry," she defended herself before Lukas could even look at her funny. "And this isn't the kitchen."

Deliberately he glanced at his phone's time display. "I didn't say a word."

"I'm going back to my room after breakfast. You haven't won anything," she insisted.

Lukas glanced around the table to find every eye trained on him and Emily with variations of curiosity and humor painted across their expressions.

"Fair enough," he allowed, rather than argue with her. Then he pulled out his camera which he'd brought down last night and left here on purpose.

The ambiance in this room, with the beautiful antiques, the perfect morning light, the gorgeous spread of food, and the happy faces was too perfect not to capture on film. He'd figured since he'd be down here anyway, might as well.

As he swung around by Emily, she leaned closer. "Don't hide behind that camera the entire time," she murmured in a low voice meant just for him. "Sit down and enjoy the meal."

Busted.

If I'm not careful, I could fall for that man.

Emily watched as Lukas finished snapping a thousand pictures from every angle the room allowed, trying not to feel self-conscious any time the camera was turned in her direction. She was just part of the group in these pictures. No big deal.

Difficult not to think about kissing when, behind the camera, he'd been so . . . focused, so professional. Very much in his element.

Only that wasn't what had her worrying about her heart.

Lukas kept surprising her at every turn. This morning, she'd woken at her usual time, despite having turned off her alarm. It might've been the hallway light filtering under her bedroom door. She'd tried to sleep but couldn't, so, despite their bet, had snuck down the stairs. Just to check and make sure he was up and getting breakfast like he'd promised, then she'd go back to bed.

Only, she'd barely made it halfway down when she caught the sounds of Lukas talking . . . to Snowball she had to assume. She talked to the kitten, too. That's when she'd learned that these silly bets were his way of trying to take care of her. It should've annoyed her. She could take care of herself, after all. Instead, those words about melted her heart to a puddle at her feet.

Hearing him say he still wanted to kiss her, even while hoping he'd lose the bet, had sent a warmth bursting through her that took Emily so off guard, she'd hurried back upstairs to her room, unable to stop herself from smiling.

She'd paced around the close confines, a sort of pent up energy not letting her sit still, then stopped at the small desk that had a mirror above it and leaned over, looking at herself seriously. "Lukas Weber is trouble you can't afford. Like Greg. Only he won't just break your heart by backing out of a deal, he'll smash it when you fall in love with him."

Then her gaze had been caught by the reflection of the advent calendar on the mantel, and curiosity burned through her like wildfire. After several seconds of debate, she'd stalked over to the thing and opened the door for today to find a small note that read, "Emily owes Lukas one kiss."

Her wayward heart took off faster than Lukas would leave as soon as Christmas was over. She'd spent the next thirty minutes debating throwing the note in the trash, in his face, or taking him up on it. She still hadn't decided when she came down the stairs to discover that Lukas not only had everything well in hand as far as breakfast was concerned but was also pretty darn amazing with kids. Jakob Andrews was a handful and a half and yet had given in to Lukas with only a small amount of resistance.

Much like me, Emily thought to herself.

As soon as she'd finished a second helping — something she never took the time to treat herself to, which was better for the size of her thighs anyway — Emily caught Lukas regarding her with raised eyebrows. If she didn't know better, she'd think he was ready to pounce if she lost that bet.

She gave him a sassy little wink, then got up and cleared her place. But rather than take it to the kitchen where she wasn't allowed yet, she dropped it off where Lukas sat, then sashayed out of the room and back upstairs where she had every intention of hiding out until her 9:00 a.m. deadline.

No kissing.

Except thirty minutes later a pounding sound pulled her out of her room early. Mostly because the noise was coming from the room down the hall. The Knight Suite. She was pretty sure she hadn't listed any repairs for in there, though several needed to happen as soon as the holidays wrapped up. Still, what was going on? Daniel, maybe?

Sticking her head inside, she found Lukas standing in front of the window, tools in hand, cursing a blue streak.

"Problems?" she asked.

He jerked his head around, and she almost laughed at his disgruntled expression. So . . . Lukas Weber *did* get annoyed from time to time. Good to know.

He pointed an accusing hammer at the window. "I can't get this darn thing to open."

Emily had to clear her throat to hide a chuckle she suspected he wouldn't appreciate. "Have you asked Daniel?"

That earned her a glare. "I can do *some* things without help, you know."

"What does the internet say?"

"The internet is not being helpful in this particular instance."

"Show me anyway."

She came farther into the room and sat on the bed, which he'd covered with a cloth. After a brief hesitation, Lukas grabbed his phone and, with a grunt, dropped onto the bed beside her. The soft mattress had her rolling toward him, and Emily about strained her back trying to stay upright and at a safe distance as they watched the video together.

"Looks pretty —"

"If you say easy, I won't vouch for my reaction, but it won't be that of a gentleman."

Emily laughed. "Gentleman, huh? I forgot

what you fellas looked like."

"Isn't that line from a movie?" he asked with narrowed eyes.

That Thing You Do.

"I do a thing?"

Which made her giggle, or maybe that was the nerves. "No. The line is from the movie *That Thing You Do.*"

Given the way he was looking at her mouth, and the way she wanted to lean closer, Emily figured now was a prudent time to get up.

Hopping to her feet, she approached the window. "Why don't you show me what you've tried?"

He huffed but followed.

"See how the wood changes color here where the stain didn't reach?" He pointed. "That means it's slightly off in the frame, which I think is why it won't open. We have to force it to sit correctly. The trick is to do that without making it worse or breaking it."

"Got it," Emily said.

Together they jimmied and soaped and pushed at that darn window. Given all the grunting going on, you'd think they were going twelve rounds in a rugby match until, finally, the window popped open.

Emily peered closely at the shade of the

wood around the edges and could no longer see the delineation between the stained wood visible and the raw wood that sat inside the frame.

She shot Lukas a giant grin. "I think we got it."

"Do you, Professor Higgins?" He nudged her over. "Let me see."

After inspecting the window, making all sorts of *hmmm* noises, he then tried sliding it up and down. The thing moved without a problem. "By George, I think you're right. Brilliant."

Chuckling, and dealing with an odd combination of satisfaction at a job well done and a shared camaraderie over doing it together, Emily turned to leave, then paused at the sight that greeted her. With a growl of frustration, she tipped her head back to glare at the ceiling. "We have another problem, though."

No. No. No. She didn't just lock herself in here with the man she was avoiding kissing.

"Hmmm?" Lukas was still admiring his handiwork.

"The bedroom door closed while we were in here."

He straightened and gave her a look that most children would find insulting. "I'm pretty sure you've used a door before," he teased.

"Ha, ha, ha. This door gets stuck and can't be opened from the inside, genius." She flung a hand at the offending situation. "It's why we haven't been putting guests in here."

"Oh."

But instead of grimacing or any normal reaction, a dangerous twinkle entered his eyes. "Maybe it's a sign."

Not trusting him further than she could toss a sack of flour, Emily plunked her hands on her hips. "A sign for what?"

"I believe you owe me a kiss." He stepped closer.

Eyes going wide, Emily stepped back, but she'd already been standing by the door and didn't have anywhere else to go. "I didn't lose the bet."

He shook his head as he took another step. "I'm talking about your Advent gift."

"The calendar?" She curled her lip, doing her best to glare at him in an intimidating way that would hide how much she wanted to take him up on his teasing. His face alight with laughter even as he was trying to school it into something sexier, the combination affecting her way more than it should. "That's cheating and doesn't count."

One more step and he'd be in her personal space. He paused, tipping his head to eye her with consideration. "I thought the mistletoe would be enough of a hint, but you didn't take me up on that. A gift is a gift." He held out a hand, palm up. "Unless you want to give it back."

The small card with his distinctive scrawl suddenly scorched a hole in the back pocket of her jeans. Despite the distraction, she still wasn't fooled. "If I give it back does that mean you think you owe me a kiss?"

Lukas grinned. "Well, that's how gifts work as I understand it."

"You're going to bug me about this all day, aren't you?" Excitement bubbled up inside her, along with an unhealthy dose of anticipation, warming her from the inside out, even though, after having the window open, this room was as cold as a deep freeze.

His grin only widened. "I want to make sure you like the gift, Emily." His voice dropped to a low rumble that skated over her skin and had her lungs tightening.

Then a wicked thought occurred to her, and she had to bite back a grin of her own.

"Fine," she pretended to huff. "Stay still."

Before he could question the command, she stepped into him and placed her hands on either side of his face. Going up on tiptoes, she hovered, her lips not quite touching his. Part of her — a bigger part than she liked — wanted to close her eyes and absorb Lukas. Absorb his warmth, the spicy scent of his aftershave combined today with soap and him, the stubble prickling her palms. But this was about teaching him a lesson.

After torturing them both for a beat, she leaned in and placed a soft kiss on his cheek, just at the corner of his mouth, then stepped back and smiled at him sweetly. "There." She spun away and jiggled the handle. "Now . . . about this door."

"Hey —"

She glanced over her shoulder and couldn't contain a snigger at the consternation written across his face in frown lines.

"That is not what I had in mind," he grumbled.

"No?" she asked, all innocence. "But it's what you're going to get."

"Emily Diemer . . ." His arms flopped to his side as he grew suddenly serious in that way that made it hard to focus on anything but him. "I would like to kiss you again. A proper kiss."

Total sincerity might just be enough to make her cross her own name off Santa's nice list and pencil it on the naughty list.

She turned away and fought with the voice in her head that urged her to take him up on a need that was starting to become an obsession. "Why?"

She couldn't help glancing over her shoulder again to find him frowning.

But he took her seriously, stepping closer to turn her around and take one of her hands in his, like he needed that connection to make sure she heard him. "Because I like the way you kiss. But I also like the way you cook, and the way you take care of everyone around you, and the way you can't sit still."

Oh . . . wow.

She swallowed around a lump forming in her throat. "But you're leaving after the holidays. I help run the inn and have my bakery to open here. Why even start something?"

He ran a hand down her other arm with the softest of touches. "I've been asking myself that exact question since the day we met."

"And?"

He shrugged. "I can't seem to keep away."

At least he acted as confused about this . . . whatever it was . . . between them as she was.

"It's a bad idea," she whispered.

But she wanted it so much she ached.

"I know," he whispered back as he lowered his head.

He moved slowly, giving Emily plenty of time to stop him or step away, but all she could do was hold her breath and wait. Wait for him to close that distance. Wait for the touch of his lips, soft and sure, moving against hers in slow, sweet brushes.

"Sugar cookies," he murmured, and smiled against her lips.

"Hmmm?"

"Never mind." He kissed her again. One hand stole around her back to press her closer, surrounding her in warmth and strength.

Why did he have to be such a good kisser, anyway?

Emily wrapped her arms around his neck, going up on tiptoe to get closer, take the kiss deeper, humming against his touch. This must be what heaven was like. Floating in a haze of pure contentment. A small whimper escaped her, and Lukas paused, sucking in a breath. After a second, he pressed a swift hard kiss to her lips before he placed his hands on her hips to step away.

"Now *that's* a Christmas present." Warmth turned his eyes a glorious shade of dark green. She could get lost in those eyes.

Emily placed a hand to her lips, happy to

see she wasn't shaking. "It's still not a good idea."

He sobered at that, then ran a hand through his hair, standing it up in spiky rows she immediately itched to fix for him. "I know," he said softly.

Which only made it worse.

I listen on the other side of the door that I had managed to shut while Emily and Lukas were distracted playing with the window, for whatever reason. Humans are weird.

I knew that handle didn't work. Miss Tilly and Emily realized it the first time I got stuck in there and they couldn't find me, but they could hear me crying. I was really little when that happened. It scared me enough that I usually avoid that room now.

What's going on in there, anyway?

I could hear them playing with the stupid window, then Emily realized the door was shut. She did not sound too happy about it, either.

Then it got real, real quiet.

I about jump out of my fur as they suddenly start pounding on the door and yelling for Tilly. Well . . . rats. I guess my master plan didn't work at all.

Except . . . no one else is in the house. So

maybe this alone time will still work after they get over being mad.

"Oh, shoot!" I hear Lukas exclaim.

"What?" Emily asks.

"There's no one in the house. All the guests left, Tilly had an errand to run, and Daniel doesn't get here for . . . another hour."

"An hour," Emily's wail makes me hop back again. "I have to make my deliveries. I'm already later than usual because of your darn bet and this darn window."

"You didn't have to stop to help me," Lukas points out.

Even I wince. I might still be a kitten, but I know when a man says things to a woman that he shouldn't. That was a silly thing for him to say.

"I suppose I shouldn't have stuck around to be kissed, either," she snaps.

They kissed! I prance in an excited circle.

The door handle jiggles loudly, and I skitter away.

"Don't bother," Emily said. "Last time, Snowball got herself stuck in here alone, and I had to climb in through the —"

"Through the window?" Lukas sounds like he's laughing.

"I guess that's how it got messed up," Emily admits in a voice low enough I have to move closer to hear. "I had to crawl back out with her. After that we managed to make the knob work from the outside, at least."

Why does she sound annoyed?

"I guess that's what I'll have to do then?" Lukas says.

"What?"

"Crawl out the window and get you out."

"Oh."

"You'll be Rapunzel to my Prince Charming."

"I'm starting to rethink the charming."

The sound of wood against wood reaches me through the door. The window opening, I guess.

Emily's voice sounds next. "You'll want to climb down the trellis, only I'm not sure it'll hold you — Be careful!"

A loud shout from outside is followed by a crash that can't be good.

"Are you okay?" Emily calls.

I can't quite make out Lukas's answer, but it sounds mostly like a muffled groan. At least he's not dead. A few minutes later, the front door slams and feet stomp up the stairs and Lukas appears at the other end of the hall. His shirt is ripped, and a twig is sticking out of his hair, which is all messed up, and his face looks like the clouds right

263

before one of those thunderstorms that make me shake and hide under Miss Tilly's bed.

As he comes up to the door, he gives me a suspicious stare. "I hope you didn't have anything to do with this little fiasco," he says.

Then he opens the door and lets Emily out. She takes one look at him and bursts into laughter. Lukas does not join in, crossing his arms to glare at her.

"I'm sorry." She waves a hand. "It's not funny. You could really be hurt." Then she laughs harder.

I'm glancing between the two of them trying to figure out what the heck is so hilarious.

"I got what I deserved. Is that what you're thinking?" Lukas grumbles.

Emily sobers at that. "Of course not." She reaches up and pulls the twig out of his hair. "My knight in shining armor."

He brushes off his shirt. "Downgraded from prince. I should be offended." Suddenly, a big grin changes his face to something even I don't trust. "Maybe you should kiss me better."

Emily's eyes go wide, then narrow. "I can't." She inches past him in the hall. "All those deliveries." She's halfway down the hall when she shoots a last parting word over her shoulder. "Maybe you could fix that door handle while I'm gone."

CHAPTER 14

"I promised a game of hide-and-seek, didn't
I?" Lukas asked as he rose from the dinner
table.

The two boys erupted into cheers, and the
adults shared smiles. Emily raised her
eyebrows at him silently.

"The way they do it in Russia," Jakob
reminded him.

"Of course." Lukas held up the plates in
his hands. "Let me help Miss Emily finish
cleaning up from dinner, then we'll get
started. Maybe see if any of the other adults
would like to join?"

He held in a secret grin at the semi-
stricken expressions that greeted that suggestion. The plates suddenly disappeared
from his hands as Emily, who'd managed to
sneak closer without him seeing, took them.
"You go play with the boys. I imagine
they're near bedtime."

He caught the look of relief Alice Andrews

266

sent Emily and chuckled, but he still didn't want to leave her, thanks to an odd sensation that was growing into a protective concern. "You don't mind not having help?"

"She's got me." Daniel wrapped her up in yet another side hug that about knocked the plates from her hands.

Immediately, a tiny but unmistakable growl sounded from the hallway. Daniel's expression comically swung from smug to worried. He grabbed a few plates from the table and hightailed it into the kitchen before Snowball could attack again.

"Okay, boys," Lukas said. "Let's go."

On the way past her, he stooped and patted the kitten who was lazing on one of the stairsteps, right where she could watch the dining room closely. "Good girl," he whispered.

"I heard that," Emily called.

Lukas sent the cat a wince. "Oops."

An hour later, all played out, Lukas made his way back to the formal living room. Except the sound of Emily's voice in the sitting room caught his attention. She sounded irritated, so he scooted closer.

"I'm dealing with the loans on my own," she was saying.

Loans? Must be for the bakery. She was irritated talking about it if her tone of voice was anything to go by. He was pretty familiar with irritated Emily by now.

"I know —" Long pause.

"I *know*," she said more forcefully. Then sigh. "Mom. I'll talk to you Christmas Eve —"

Feeling bad for eavesdropping, Lukas backed away slowly and went to find the others. In the living room, he flopped down into one of the armchairs where the adults had gathered. Including Daniel. Why hadn't the guy gone home, yet?

Malcolm Andrews chuckled as his wife took the boys upstairs to bed. "I don't know where they get the energy."

"I should've picked a different game. Running when my belly is full was a bad, bad idea." Lukas rubbed at his poor stomach.

"It looked like a lot of fun from in here," Emily commented as she strode into the room, tucking her cell phone in the back pocket of her jeans. He caught the overblown innocence to her smile and was well aware she was laughing on the inside.

"Probably not a good game for a slowpoke like you," he shot back. He softened the words with a wink, then grinned when she narrowed her eyes at him in mock irritation.

Aunt Tilly gasped. "Lukas Weber. What a

thing to say."

Emily crossed her arms and stared at him, amusement dancing in dark eyes that had a hint of gold to them. *Was* there gold in her eyes, or was it a trick of the crackling fire? And why was he realizing that right now?

Lukas pointed an accusing finger. "She started it. Just ask her."

"I have no idea what he's talking about," Emily sniffed, and picked up a magazine as she sat down, hiding her face. But her shoulders shook suspiciously.

"That's how you want to play this?" Lukas challenged.

She didn't lower the magazine. "It's your word against mine," came her muffled voice from behind it. She casually flipped a page.

Lukas shook his head sadly. "Just remember that when I exact my revenge."

Emily lowered one corner of the magazine to peep at him over it. She opened her mouth to retort, but Daniel beat her to it.

"You don't want to get on the losing side of a revenge war with this one," he warned. "She fights dirty."

"What has gotten into you boys?" Tilly frowned at them. "Slowpoke. Fights dirty, indeed."

"It's true, ma'am," Daniel defended. "I once put a frog in Emily's backpack. Her

269

version of revenge was to type up an official-looking letter on paper with our school logo that she got from the school office and make it sound like I'd been skipping. My parents grounded me for weeks and made me do extra chores."

Lukas raised his eyebrows in question at Emily, who shrugged in return but didn't deny the accusation. He tipped his head in a sign of respect. A worthy opponent, then.

"Then there was the time I put salt in the sugar bowl she used for her baking," Daniel continued. "Even as a teen, she was always in the kitchen."

Lukas couldn't wait to hear what the retaliation was for that one.

Daniel leaned over and tweaked her braid. "This *angel* snuck a jar of spiders into my room and set them loose."

"Spiders." Miss Tilly clapped a hand over her mouth in horror. "How did you get a whole jar of spiders in the first place?" She lowered her hand to ask.

Emily shrugged again, though Lukas caught a peep in his direction. "I paid the neighbor boy, who was always catching them, to fill a jar for me. They weren't poisonous." She tipped her head to aim an overly sweet smile Daniel's direction. "I think the best was the blue dye in your sports drink."

Daniel laughed at that. "It turned my teeth blue for a week. Right in time for the spring formal dance. I still don't know what I did to deserve that one."

Emily sat up straighter and plunked her hands on her hips. "You asked my best friend to the spring formal instead of me."

Daniel's face would've been a comical mix of shock and interest if Lukas hadn't been stuffing his irritation down his own throat at the comment.

"*That's* why you did that? You were jealous?" Daniel asked.

Emily opted for a prim expression, lips pursed. "Well, I was a silly teenaged girl at the time. I blame the hormones."

Daniel chuckled, then poked her in the ribs. "I blame your temper."

Something about that didn't sit right with Lukas. Maybe the fact that, despite being determined not to like Lukas when he first arrived, Emily had still been kind in a gruff way. Or maybe how the humor died from her eyes at the comment. Or maybe the way Daniel touched her like he had a right to that was bothering Lukas.

Regardless, he was bothered.

"It sounds to me like you earned most of those punishments," Lukas commented in a slow drawl. "Not that I need to defend Emily. Apparently, she is a pro at defending herself."

Daniel must've noticed the way Emily had quieted as well, because he paused. "Maybe I can make it up to you, Em. Dinner?"

It took guts, asking her out in front of an entire house full of strangers. A blush stained Emily's cheeks rosy pink, and she flicked a glance in Lukas's direction. Barely a look, but he caught it, even as he willed her to say no.

He was the one who was supposed to kiss her until she smiled. He was the one trying to make her life easier. He was the one who would make her dream of a bakery come true, not that she knew that yet. She and Daniel might have a past, but Lukas wanted her . . .

What? He wanted her future?

He gave himself a mental shake, because he knew that wasn't possible. Christmas was a week away. He'd be gone not long after that, as soon as he settled the house situation.

"That sounds nice," Emily said.

A chill spread through Lukas, almost as though the icicles clinging to the porch outside had dropped into his stomach, churning over and freezing his veins. Meanwhile, saying yes earned her a huge grin from Daniel, whose expression then immediately changed to a comical silent open-mouthed yelp, his face contorting even as he started wiggling as though that jar of spiders had just been dumped down his back. He reached over one shoulder, grabbing at something, then plucked Snowball from his back, her claws taking his shirt with her. Eventually, he was able to disconnect the kitten from his clothing and gently handed her to Emily.

"I think that's my cue to leave," Daniel said through tight lips.

Emily, lips pinched suspiciously closed, rose and handed Snowball to Tilly. "I'll walk you out."

And give her kisses to the lumberjack?

It took everything in Lukas to keep from jumping up and following them. Instead, he watched them leave, those icicles in his stomach freezing him to the spot. A small movement flickered in the corner of his eye and had Lukas glancing at Tilly to find her watching him with a speculative twinkle in hers.

"Seems to me that if anyone around here is a slowpoke, it's you, Lukas Weber," she said.

Which meant he'd done a poor job hiding

his mental struggle over a certain feisty brunette.

"I think it's bedtime for us, too," Bill Hoffman said with a yawn.

In three seconds flat, or so it seemed, all the guests had cleared out, leaving Lukas alone with Tilly and Snowball, listening for the sound of the kitchen door to mark Emily's return.

After avoiding a good-night kiss from Daniel — a situation her teenage self would've been over the moon about — Emily returned to a quiet house and found only Lukas and Tilly and Snowball remaining in the living room.

"Where did everybody go?" she wondered.

"I think you put them in a food coma with that great dinner." Lukas patted his stomach but with such a look of contentment she chuckled.

"I guess I'll go to bed myself," she said. Except she was strangely unwilling to leave.

"After such a lazy morning?" Lukas teased.

"Lazy. We fixed a window." She paused, half turned away.

"Don't go," Lukas said. Half demand, half request. A light in his eyes told her he truly wanted her to stay.

It shouldn't make her heart trip all over itself, the thought that he wanted her to linger here with them. With him. But it did.

Stupid heart. Not even a blip standing outside with Daniel beside his car, even knowing they were going on a date. But here with a man who would never be able to stick around, her heart had turned into an Olympic gymnast, doing somersaults and getting her stomach in on the action.

Tilly patted the seat next to her. "Stay awhile. Maybe turn off the lights and we can enjoy the fire and the Christmas tree."

Emily flicked the switch, casting the room into darkness filled only with an orange glow from the fireplace and the white lights of the tree, then joined Tilly on the sofa. Lukas was right, this was not the most comfortable of sofas. She tucked her feet up under her and tried to settle into the silence broken only by the crackle of flame, and the warmth cast over the room.

Snowball got up from her spot on Tilly's lap and padded across to wiggle her head under Emily's hand. The kitten's signal for wanting to be petted, which Emily was happy to do, and a loud rumbling purr joined the sounds of the fire.

"This is nice," Lukas said. "I remember doing this when we would visit you at

275

Christmas, Aunt Tilly. I would fall asleep on the floor in front of the fire while the three of you talked quietly and Dad would carry me upstairs to my bed."

"I remember," Tilly murmured quietly, a fond smile in place.

"You spent every Christmas here?" Emily asked, truly curious.

Lukas nodded, his gaze trained on the fire and far away at the same time, no doubt lost in memories. "We were the only family we had."

Tilly cast a concerned glance in her nephew's direction but explained. "Lukas's mother had no family to speak of and I'm pretty much it on his father's side. And then of course there was the accident that took both Henry and Angela."

Emily couldn't imagine being so isolated by life.

Not only did she have her four brothers and both parents living, but of her four grandparents, only her paternal grand-mother had passed away, and even that had been recent. In the meantime, she had a myriad of aunts and uncles and cousins, and even a handful of extended family, get-ting into the twice-removed and second- and third-cousin monikers that no one could get straight.

"That sounds lonely," she said finally, not sure what the right words were.

Lukas dragged his gaze from the fire, and it was almost as though he had to chase the shadows from his eyes. "With Weber Haus being full up most holidays, 'lonely' is not the word I would use. I used to pretend like all the people here were family, too."

"Sounds like fun," Emily said with extra cheer in her voice. "Different 'family' every year and not having to worry about what Uncle Edward is going to do to upset things."

That earned her a smile without any shadows. "No Uncle Edwards. Though we had a few odd ducks." He turned to Tilly. "Remember the old gentleman who would bang his cane on the floor if he wanted room service?"

"Did you do room service then?" Emily asked doubtfully. They didn't now.

"No," Tilly chuckled. "But you couldn't tell him that. Although I think my favorite was the woman who crashed her car about half a mile away, abandoned it to walk the rest of the way here, unbeknownst to us. She got all settled in, then was shocked when the police showed up and took her to the station. Failure to control her vehicle and failure to remain with her vehicle, I vaguely remember."

"Shocked," Lukas hooted. "She was genuinely offended that they would think to do such a thing, and at the holidays, too." He raised his voice, clearly imitating the woman's posh accent.

"Our recent guests have been tame by comparison," Emily commented. "But it sounds like a fun pretend family for the holidays either way."

"It was when I was little," Lukas agreed, a fond smile tugging at his mouth in a way she found appealing, then proceeded to try to ignore.

"Granted," he continued. "People who visited were mostly elderly aunt and uncle types, but every so often I would get pretend cousins my age, like the Andrews boys. That was always the best."

"Oh!" Tilly clapped her hands. "And we would have a private family tree in the sitting room off my bedroom where we would open our Christmas presents."

Lukas straightened, eyes alight with humor. "Mom and Dad would pile those presents under the tree. I still don't know how he got that bike up the stairs and into your room without me seeing."

Tilly flapped a hand at him. "I still maintain that was Santa."

Lukas chuckled.

"But after they died, you didn't want to do that anymore," she said.

He gave a small shrug. "I didn't want to do anything that reminded me of them. It hurt too much."

"I know," Tilly said quietly.

The emotion that passed aunt and nephew was almost painful to witness — understanding, shared sorrow, and a sort of acceptance.

Snowball, who had been curled up enjoying Emily's soothing strokes, hopped off the sofa to jump into Lukas's lap to give his face a little lick. He patted the kitten, his big hands practically swallowing her whole. Capable hands. Emily hadn't been wrong about that.

"Maybe we should start that tradition again this year," he said. "Somehow, this Christmas, it feels . . . right."

"Do you mean that?" Tilly searched his face with a hopeful expression.

Lukas sent her a contented smile, not a shadow in sight. "I do."

Tilly got up from the sofa and crossed to the built-in bookshelf that took up the walls on either side of the fireplace. "Then maybe now is a good time to give you this."

She pulled a key from a hiding spot on

the top shelf and unlocked a tiny antique music box that Emily had always admired. Small and round, the trinket was adorned in an ornate scrolling design of gold and inlaid with a green stone, possibly jade. When Tilly opened the lid, she revealed an equally ornate design on the underside showing a swan with its wings extended out as though about to fly across the water. Rather than wind it up and play the music, though, Tilly pulled a ring out from inside.

After replacing the music box on the shelf, she moved to where Lukas still sat with Snowball in his lap and presented it to him.

Snowball swiped at it with her paw, so Lukas deposited her on the ground. "What is this?" he asked, reaching for it.

Tilly tipped her head. "You don't recognize it?"

He studied it more closely. From where she sat, Emily could see that the item was an engagement ring. One with a simple gold band and a beautiful emerald-cut ruby that reflected the light of the fire and the tree, coming to life in his hand.

Slowly Lukas lifted his gaze to Tilly. "This was my mother's?" A note of . . . not wonder, but a raw emotion Emily couldn't put her finger on, filled his voice.

Tilly smiled, almost with relief. "I've been

keeping it safe for you all these years. At first you were too young to give such a valuable treasure to and I held it in a safe-deposit box in a bank. Once you got older, I brought it to the house waiting for the right time to give it to you, but it didn't seem safe for you to travel with it, and you were hardly home anyway. But now . . ." She sort of nodded to herself slowly. "Now it's right."

Except he'd head back out on those travels in only a few days. A thought that made Emily grip the armrest more tightly.

Lukas stood and wrapped his aunt in a hug that he held. "Thank you," he whispered into Tilly's hair.

His gaze met Emily's over his aunt's shoulder, and she stilled, unable to look away, almost as though she were a part of the moment in some special way. Which of course, she wasn't, but tell that to her heart.

Lukas and Tilly pulled away and smiled at each other, years of understanding and pain and forgiveness passing between them.

Then Tilly grinned. "Don't let Snowball near it, though. That kitten likes to steal shiny things."

At Miss Tilly's words, I stretch my paws out in front of me, butt in the air. Then I stick

281

my tail straight up and walk calmly from the room. I don't have to hang around for insults.

Steal.

As if I'm a thief. I *never* steal. I merely move things around, present them as gifts to be treasured, or sometimes hide them in Emily's purse.

Besides, these humans clearly don't know what they're talking about. They need a long talking-to, if only I spoke human. Emily went outside with that Daniel man who won't leave her alone even though it's obvious that she doesn't want him around. And Lukas let her go out there when he should've stopped her.

I don't know what I'm going to do with these two. They're beyond help.

CHAPTER 15

Lukas pulled the door to the carriage house open and led Daniel inside the dimly lit space. With a flick, he turned on the lights, illuminating the dust-covered space with its built-in display counters and cash register area. The stale smell contributed to the overall musty feel, but insulated walls kept it from being too cold.

It had potential.

He waved a hand through the dust motes. "As you can see, this was once a small shop for knickknacks and whatnot, and I'm hoping you can use the bones of what's here for the renovations to convert it. Like maybe the new owners could use the display case?"

Daniel put his hands on his hips, looking around with a practiced eye, though Lukas had no idea what he was seeing.

When the other man said nothing, Lukas led the way farther inside. "I think the counter positioning is already good where it's located, though you'll have to tell me if you think you can use what's existing and renovate from there, or if you need to do a full rebuild."

Daniel walked around to get a closer look, opening cabinet doors and peering inside, chipping at a few spots that appeared to have been damaged, leaving handprints in the thick layer of dust, and disturbing a few spiders on their webs. "Okay" was all he said. "What else?"

"This way." Lukas took him into the room beyond that had been the storage room and back office for the shop. "This is where we'd fit the kitchen."

"Do you know what will be needed?"

Lukas grimaced. "I've started researching and will have a list of all the appliances that we'll order in the next week or so. What else will you need to know?"

Daniel kind of bobbed his head as he considered that question. "It depends on what you're setting the kitchen up for. If it's going to be a restaurant, what you need will depend on the seating capacity you're serving and the type. A grill might have different needs than a five-star gourmet."

Lukas nodded. "Got it. I'll include that in my research and have specifics to you with the list of appliances."

"Fine." Daniel unclipped a measuring tape from his belt and pulled out his phone but paused and sent Lukas a direct stare. "Is this going to be a bakery?" he asked slowly.

Lukas schooled his expression to hide his reluctance to tell Daniel the truth. He knew he was going to have to eventually, because Daniel would be building the thing out. Plus, before they were too far in, he'd need to involve Emily. Perhaps sooner rather than later, so that she could pick out what she wanted.

The not wanting to share was more about an odd need to keep this project under wraps. A gift for Emily. His Christmas gift to her.

In a short amount of time, she'd become . . . important to him. Not his most brilliant move, given their circumstances and their plans would likely never intersect again. Except he couldn't for the life of him make it stop. Or even wish for it to stop, if he was honest.

"Yes," he said finally. "It's going to be Emily's bakery."

Daniel nodded slowly. "Does Emily know?"

"Not yet, but I'll tell her soon."

"I see." Daniel glanced around, then

285

pinned Lukas with a hard stare. "She doesn't need distractions right now, you know."

Lukas rocked back on his heels. "Building her a bakery so she can pursue her dream is a distraction?"

"You're a distraction."

Coming from the overprotective-brother figure who had his own agenda where Emily was concerned, Lukas wasn't taking this too seriously. "How's that?"

"I've seen the way you look at her."

"Okaaaay." Lukas drew the word out. "How do I look at her?"

Daniel crossed his arms. "Like she's a Christmas present under your tree with a big red bow."

Lukas mimicked the other man's posture. "I'd say that's how *you've* been looking at her." *While I'm the one who has been kissing her.* Only Lukas kept that bit to himself.

"This isn't a contest." Daniel frowned. "I've known Emily practically her entire life. She likes you. I can tell."

That was semi news to Lukas, given how they'd started. He'd hoped she'd changed her tune of utter contempt, of course, but he was also well aware of his tendency to tone deafness. "I like her, too."

"Are you planning on sticking around?

Running this place with Miss Tilly?" Daniel waved in the direction of the main house. Dust motes scattered and flew through beams of light in his wake.

"I'm planning to leave after the new year but intend to be more involved than I have been."

At least, that had always been the plan. Except the way he felt flattened at the thought of not being here, someone might as well have dropped an anvil on his head. He'd become invested, doing these fixes and renovations, building the bakery. That had to be it. That part of him wanted to stay and see it through. Bethany would kill him if he did, though. She was already lining up jobs into the spring.

"Then what are you doing?" Daniel demanded.

"What do you mean?"

"Why are you pursuing her if all you're going to do is walk away?"

"I'm not the one with a date Saturday night. All I'm doing is helping Emily and Aunt Tilly fix up Weber Haus and helping Emily follow her dream of running a bakery because I believe in her."

He deliberately left off the bit about selling the place. He wouldn't broach that with anyone, other than Bethany until he'd talked with his aunt.

"And looking at her like she's strudel and you want a taste?" Daniel insisted.

More than a taste, if Lukas was honest. "That's no one's business but mine and Emily's. I know you see yourself as another big brother and protector, but, I promise you, that woman is fully capable of putting in me in my place. She does it frequently."

A narrowed-eyed stare greeted that statement. "Why would she need to?"

Done with this conversation that was going nowhere, Lukas glanced around. "Can you do this, or do I need to find another contractor?"

The other man continued to stare in silence before he dropped his arms to his sides. "I can do it. I'll get my crew out here to start a general cleanup and prep. Get me that list of specifics. We'll go from there."

"Great." Lukas spun on his booted heel and left Daniel to do his job as the guy pulled out a measuring tape.

After stomping the snow from his shoes at the back door that led into a glassed-in conservatory, he went inside, then took them off, leaving them at the door to dry rather than track snow and dirt across the aging hardwoods, even if having the floors refinished was on his list.

An angry sort of restlessness had him pacing through the house in his socked feet. The trouble was, as irritated as he wanted to be with Daniel for butting in — not to mention trying to horn in on Emily — he also had to admit that the guy was right.

Meow?

Lukas turned at the tiny sound of a kitten who seemed to be in distress.

Now I know the sound of Snowball's cries? He practically didn't recognize himself anymore.

A quick check showed she wasn't anywhere in his line of vision, so he paused to listen. Sure enough, another pathetic sound came a second later.

The kitchen door swung open, and Emily stuck her head out. "Did you hear that?"

"I hear her, but I can't tell what direction she's in." Lukas started moving carefully in the direction he thought.

Another squeak sounded, and he and Emily looked at each other. "I think she's in the dining room," she said.

He shook his head. "Sitting room."

Her turn to shake her head. "It didn't come from behind us."

"I think it did."

They blinked at each other wasting another second. Lukas had to suppress a smile, because Emily Diemer was darn adorable when she was on a mission. The bunched eyebrows, the intent dark gaze, the mouth a serious straight line.

"Split up?" Emily suggested.

He managed to yank his gaze away. Lukas moved to the doorway of the sitting room while Emily took up a post farther down the hall by the dining room and there, they both paused and waited.

A few seconds later the pathetic mewling sounded again.

"Not the sitting room." He said it at the same time Emily leaned out of her doorway to say, "Not the dining room."

The cocked their heads at each other. "Living room," they said in unison.

Once there, they paused and listened for the sad squawking. The second the sound hit them, they knew exactly where she was — inside the Christmas tree.

"Why am I not surprised?" Emily murmured, though her lips twitched.

Lukas wasn't quite as amused. Snowball was hard enough to detach from clothing with those needle-sharp claws. A tree would be trickier. Searching revealed the tiny kitten had climbed up the trunk and managed to wedge her body between two branches. Even worse. How on earth were they going to unwedge her without being torn to shreds like what she did to Aunt Tilly's newspaper in the mornings.

Lukas was too big to go in after her. After removing several ornaments, Emily managed to get her body in there, head buried in pine needles.

"I need your help," came her muffled voice.

"Okay. Ummm . . ."

"Stand behind me and reach your hands around."

He managed to do that only to have her grab him by the wrist and yank him to the side, his torso flush against hers as though hugging her. Sugar cookies. He'd never taste another one without thinking of Emily. He closed his eyes on a wave of longing, reminding himself this was a rescue mission, not another chance to steal a kiss.

While they were both being poked by pine needles and about to risk their skin. His timing was not exactly stellar.

"Here and here." She placed his hands on what felt like branches, and possibly soft fur brushed at his knuckles. Hard to tell since, even after opening his eyes again, he couldn't see a dang thing around Emily and pine branches.

"When I say, try to pull those apart," Emily instructed.

Then she sort of wiggled around beneath him, doing what, exactly, he had no clue, but as distractions went, her antics were cracking him up. Either that, or he'd lose his control and do something idiotic.

"Now," she said.

Right. Mission Rescue Kitty.

Lukas pulled on the branches, Snowball started howling as though the sky had just fallen on top of her, and Emily managed to mutter several pretty creative swear words. Suddenly, Emily burst from the tree, forcing Lukas to jump to the side. As soon as she cleared it, he could see she had Snowball, only the kitten was going berserk in her hands, clawing and scratching.

"Ah!" Emily, by some miracle, managed to set the cat on the floor rather than drop her, and Snowball took off up the stairs as though the abominable snowman was after her.

"I was trying to help her," Emily muttered, inspecting her hands and arms, which now sported several welts beading red with blood.

"Maybe you were too slow." Lukas couldn't help himself. Tease her or kiss her seemed to be his only two settings. Still, he managed to button his lips around a smile when she shot an unamused glare his way. "Not the best timing, Weber," she grumbled.

"Come on, pokey. Let's get you fixed up." Gently, he grabbed her by the wrist and led her into the kitchen, where he got out the first aid kit.

He took his time cleaning the small wounds — she looked as though she'd survived a brawl with a paper shredder — and putting bandages over the worst of them. "There," he said when he was finished. "All better."

Without thinking about it, because kissing her was becoming as natural to him as breathing, Lukas lifted one hand and dropped a kiss softly in the palm before closing her fingers around it.

Then he realized what he'd done and stilled. He raised his head slowly to find Emily staring at him with those dark eyes full of curiosity . . . and something more. For once, no wariness lingered in her gaze, which only sent his heart into a freefall.

"I really want to kiss you," he said softly, his voice a husky burr. "I mean, really. More than I've wanted anything in a long time."

Her lips twitched. "Then what are you waiting for?"

Except the conversation he'd just had with

Daniel had stuck in his head, despite the distraction Snowball had offered up. "I don't want to hurt you."

Emily stared at him for a silent beat, then leaned forward and placed her lips over his, soft and sweet and terrifying, her touch reaching inside him and wrapping around his heart. "Then don't hurt me," she whispered against him.

The banging of the kitchen door had them both jumping apart with a guilty start — guilty on his part at least — to find Daniel standing there glowering.

They said timing was everything. Between Daniel and Snowball today, Lukas was learning the truth of that the hard way.

For her part, Emily rose from the stool she'd been seated on, cool as an icicle. "Hi, Daniel. I didn't know you were going to be here today. What are you working on?"

Daniel shot a look at Lukas that clearly landed the answer to that question in his lap.

Yeah. Timing is everything.

This was a conversation he wanted to have in private. No chance of that now.

"He's converting the carriage house into a bakery for you," Lukas said, reluctance dragging at every syllable.

■ ■ ■

Buzzing filled Emily's head. Lukas hadn't just said what she thought he said. Had he? She held still, gazing at both men and taking in what could either be guilt or frustration pulling at Lukas's mouth and satisfaction in the small tilt to Daniel's.

"You're doing what?" she asked quietly.

The two men exchanged an inscrutable glance. Lukas shrugged. "Your dream of opening a bakery. We have space that could work. In fact . . ." He grinned, dimples jumping to the ready, his expression filled with an eager excitement that almost poked through the growing irritation in her breast. Almost.

"The carriage house was once used as a shop," he continued, oblivious to her ire. "And we could easily convert it. It's perfect. I'm shocked Aunt Tilly hasn't thought of this yet."

"She has," Emily said through clenched teeth, biting off both words.

Lukas's expression didn't dim, but he did peer at her more closely. "She has?" he asked. "I thought you were getting a loan to start a business in town."

Emily shook her head. "I'm getting a loan

295

to convert that space to a bakery."

"Oh." He seemed to grapple with that, then the grin was back, cocky and self-satisfied. "Even better. It means you've already thought about what you want in there."

"More than that." Was he not catching her beyond-irritated vibes? Or was he trying to power past them? "I have a business plan with everything laid out and an architect friend has already drawn up schematics for the renovations."

Lukas nodded along. "You needed that for the bank, I'm sure. Daniel can get started right away, then."

For once, even Daniel, who tended toward a frustrating male form of obliviousness, said nothing, merely watching the byplay with obvious interest.

"I didn't get the loan," Emily said, even more quietly.

Lukas stepped back, and all the excitement drained from him, stealing the dimples away with it. "Daniel, do you mind if Emily and I have a moment to talk privately?" he said, not looking away from her.

"Since I may, or may not, be doing the work, I think I should stay," Daniel insisted.

"It's okay, Daniel." Emily waved at him to leave. He didn't need to witness this conversation only to relay it back to her family, who, no doubt, would be ready with the *I told you so*s.

Daniel scowled but, after a more pointed glance from Emily, finally stomped back outside, grumbling along the way.

She turned to find Lukas had stepped closer.

"Tell me about the loan," he said.

Her first instinct, despite her anger with him, was to confess her burdens. Only that was a dumb reaction. He was leaving, not staying to share the load. She stoked her indignation higher. "I can't believe you started on construction without consulting me," she snapped.

"I didn't. We were only looking around today. My next step was to get you involved, since I have no idea what equipment needs you have." He reached out and squeezed her arm, and she frowned at him for the effort, which he ignored. "What about the loan?"

"That's none of your business." She jerked her arm back. Lukas may not judge her like her family tended to. Emily didn't like failure, and without the loan she could never have the bakery.

Lukas searched her face, solemn. "Let me guess, you didn't have enough collateral?"

Was she that transparent? Still, the fact that he looked at her with total open kindness despite the fact that she was still angry with him had her sharing despite herself.

Her hands flopped to her sides in defeat. "Exactly. My credit is fine. I knew enough to put everything on credit cards and pay them off every single month to build that, since I don't own a house. Because I don't have anything to put up against the loan, I need a cosigner."

Lukas nodded, green eyes seeing probably way more than she wanted. "Let me guess . . . You won't ask your parents?"

Emily shifted on her feet. How was it this man could understand her with such ease when people who had known her her whole life didn't? "A bakery is a high-risk business proposition. They said it helped that I had a location and only needed to do renovations rather than build and buy property. But I'm not dragging my parents' retirement through a possible bankruptcy situation if it goes under."

Lukas stepped back, crossing his arms, and stared at her as if trying to read her mind. "Why were you mad at me about starting construction if you were going to do this anyway as soon as you figured out the money?"

A hundred different answers popped into her head, but already Emily could tell that if she said them out loud, she'd feel either stupid or petty or both. The truth was this was *her* dream. *She* wanted to make the decisions, make it happen, and she wanted to do this on her own. Especially after Greg.

When she didn't answer, he narrowed his eyes in a look that pinned her to the spot. "Is it because it's me?"

The gruff growl in his voice surprised her, because it sounded as though his feelings would be hurt if she said yes. Just like that, her anger cooled like she'd been thrown into a drift of snow.

At some point since he'd come here, she'd started to think of Lukas as a partner in crime when it came to the inn, as a friend . . . more than a friend, even. Hurting him wasn't what she wanted.

"No . . . ," she started slowly. But wanted to be honest. "And yes a little bit."

Lukas's expression went completely neutral, not an emotion to be seen, not even the twinkle he usually couldn't suppress. She *had* hurt him.

"I don't mean it's because of you," she rushed to explain. "I mean that you have this habit of being slightly oblivious, and I find that . . . frustrating. Sometimes."

299

Emily wrinkled her nose. She was only making this worse. How the heck had he managed to flip this around on her and have her on the defensive?

"Oblivious," he repeated. His brows drew down over his eyes.

"Yes. Setting aside the fact that you weren't aware of your aunt's situation, you have a tendency of making decisions without asking the people involved first."

Lukas scratched his head. "We weren't going to do anything except start the cleanup and prep process. I was going to talk to you before any decisions were made."

"What if I had already bought a property in town and was preparing to make renovations there?"

He shrugged. "Then I would pay Daniel and his men for their work, and the carriage house would be ready for the next entrepreneurial baker or whoever happened along needing space."

Emily threw her hands up in the air. "You are so stubborn."

Lukas snorted. "Says the kettle to the pot."

"This is not about me."

Lukas stepped closer, getting in her space but not touching. "Yes. It is. Because I'm about to offer you your dream, and I bet your first instinct is to say no."

300

"What's that supposed to mean?" Emily tipped up her chin and refused to back down or step away, even as curiosity clawed at her like Snowball in the Christmas tree.

"It means I was already planning on investing in the renovations and paying for them myself," he informed her. "What you do with the bakery after its ready is up to you."

Lukas was wrong. Emily's first thought wasn't to say no. It was to wrap her arms around his neck because having her dream that close — where she could smell it, touch it, taste it — sent an electric current of excitement through her body.

Unfortunately, right on the heels of that, a few realizations made that electricity disappear with a fizzle.

First, she'd been here before. With Greg. Look where that had got her — savings wiped out and starting over from scratch. Second, it occurred to her that Lukas apparently had enough money to pay cash for expensive retrofitting and building a bakery while his aunt had struggled to make ends meet, letting Weber Haus fall into disrepair. Third, the fact that she could easily picture Lukas Weber in shining armor told her that her heart was more involved than she wanted to admit. Although the way she craved his kisses should've been a clue. And finally, if he did this, she would feel beholden to him for the rest of her life.

How was she supposed to get over the man who gave her her dream?

Lukas must've followed her train of thought as he watched emotions chase themselves across her no doubt wide open expression. Emily opened her mouth to say no, but he stopped her, putting a finger to her lips.

"See. I told you you'd try to say no." He lowered his hand, leaving her lips tingling. "Before you do, I have a solution to what I think your objection probably is. Do you want to hear it?"

Did she? Apparently, the man could sell snake oil to a rattler.

Sensing her hesitation, Lukas shot a gaze heavenward then took her by the arms and sat her down on one of the stools. "Just listen for a moment and try to have an open mind."

Emily folded her hands in her lap and raised her eyebrows. "Let's hear it."

"I'm going to renovate the carriage house either way. I feel as though more businesses could be brought here if we had not just the inn but a series of shops including a bakery or coffeehouse. I've even thought of bringing in a kind of petting zoo. Or doing sleigh rides. I haven't thought through those yet."

The picture Lukas was painting had Emily's blood pumping harder. She could visualize it. Maybe a pumpkin patch in the fall with a haunted maze. The small pond at the back of the property could make a nice fishing pond for children. They could do pony rides and —

Oh my God. "Snake-oil salesman" is too tame a term for Lukas Weber.

"You want my bakery to be a part of this?"

"Yes."

She glanced away, thinking hard and needing to avoid the distraction of looking directly at him. "Even so. If I were to include my bakery into any series of shops like that, the owners of those shops would expect me to pay for and arrange all the renovations needed. That's *my* responsibility."

Aggravation passed over his features, but Lukas held up his hands in a gesture of surrender. "I guess that's true. And while I have a decent amount of savings socked away, it would be nice not to have to use *all* of it for this project. Someday I might want to retire or maybe start a permanent studio of my own. So I propose this . . . I loan you the money. We'll draw it up in an official docu-

303

ment with the payment schedule, interest, and everything that would've gone with a standard bank loan."

Everything inside Emily stilled. Even her heart skipped a beat or two. "You would do that for me?"

She honestly had no idea how she felt about that.

Lukas grinned, dimples urging her to say yes. "Have you tasted your baking? As far as I'm concerned, you are a darn good investment."

I am so confused.

I mean, Emily looks shocked, too. Her jaw is practically off the hinges, so maybe I'm not the only one. Only, she doesn't know that Lukas intends to sell Weber Haus. I'm still little, and maybe I don't understand human money, but what he's talking about doesn't sound like selling to me.

"Can you give me time to think about it?" Emily asks Lukas.

She's looking away, so I don't think she realizes how disappointed he is with that answer. His smile disappears, and I want to rub against his leg to make him feel better. But he clears his throat and says, "Of course."

"Thanks." Then, gaze sort of far away, almost like she's not actually seeing where she's going, Emily gets up and leaves the kitchen.

Lukas watches her go with an expression that makes me think of the way I look at tuna when Emily opens a can. Except worse, like she then dumped the tuna in the trash without offering me any.

I don't think she should be alone right now, so I follow her. She heads upstairs to her bedroom, and I manage to slip inside before she closes the door. Then she sort of flops down on the bed and grabs a pillow that she hugs to her chest and turns her head to stare out the window, though I don't know at what. The day is gray and hazy, like Weber Haus isn't part of the world anymore but floating in its own secret, hushed space. Plus, it's not like there's a bird or a squirrel out there that needs to be scared away.

She still looks confused, and maybe a bit lost, so I hop up on the bed beside her and rub against her arm.

Emily sighs. "Oh, Snowball. I don't know what to think."

Me neither. I've heard Lukas on the phone with some woman named Bethany. He's definitely planning to sell Weber Haus.

I curl up on Emily's stomach and can't help but purr when she slowly strokes my fur. She knows exactly how I like it. At least she starts to relax a bit, the tension fading from her body in a way I can sense. Kitty senses are better than human senses.

But I'm still worried. Has Lukas changed his mind? What is he doing?

CHAPTER 16

Giving Emily time to think about what she wanted to do was just about killing Lukas. She'd been thinking about it for a couple of days, and Christmas was practically on top of them. They'd been dancing around each other in sort of a polite way, an unwritten agreement that he was giving her space.

Definitely no kissing. He missed that. He missed her.

How long did it take a woman as smart as Emily to realize that what he was offering was the best deal she'd ever get? He had no doubt she'd achieve her dream, but, after all, without him, getting there would only take longer. That was . . . unless she caved and asked her parents for help. In her eyes, maybe that was the lesser of two evils.

But he'd thought she'd changed her mind about him recently.

Speaking of which, since he was working to fix the chipped paint on the kitchen cabinets, she'd taken the fact that the kitchen was essentially closed and left him to it on his own to go visit her family.

For the umpteenth time, he turned back to the cabinet with one side open to find a bright pair of kitty eyes staring out at him from the dark interior.

"Shoo." He plucked Snowball out from under the sink yet again and kept going.

Over the buzz of the hand sander Daniel had loaned him — a fantastic time saver as it turned out — Lukas caught the ring of his phone. Probably Bethany, who'd called three times already today. Putting her off wasn't going to work. Lukas growled a little. At this rate, he'd never finish. Turning off the machine, he snatched the device from the countertop where he'd set it.

"Weber," he answered.

"I bring you a Christmas miracle," Bethany chirped in his ear.

He leaned against the counter. "I like miracles. What do you have for me this time? *Geographic International* wants to sign me to a twenty-year contract?"

"Better."

"Really? Better than career security in a career that's not all that secure?" he teased.

"You are ruining my moment."

He could practically see her scowl through

the phone.

Lukas chuckled, toeing a pile of dust from his sanding. "My apologies. What's the miracle?"

"I went one better than getting you a real estate agent. I found you a buyer."

Lukas's mind went utterly and completely blank.

"Hello? Did you hear me?" Bethany's voice sounded as though it were coming from the bottom of a deep chasm.

Lukas managed to shake himself out of his stupor and realized that he'd dropped his hand away from his ear. He raised the phone back up. "What do you mean you found a buyer?"

For a woman who was perpetually cynical, his agent sounded on the verge of bubbly with excitement. "Networking goes a long way. I have a friend of a friend who happens to be a major hotel owner."

Hotels? "And he — or she — has a friend who wants to start small?"

"No, silly boy. She is on the hunt for the perfect property to create a small, homey but exclusive getaway retreat."

Lukas stared out the window and over the snow-covered landscape, seeing but not actually taking it in as he considered Bethany's words. "And you think she would be interested in Weber Haus? I mean, it's special, but it has to be one of many Victorian homes converted to an inn on a decently large property that has already been somewhat renovated and could . . ."

He trailed off as what he was saying struck home. While Weber Haus was no Stanley Hotel, it had potential. He'd already seen that, with his plans to bring in other businesses. The location, in idyllic mountain foothills but with easy access to the quaint town as well as major metropolitan areas, did make it pretty near perfect. The only ding against the location was skiing, which wasn't exactly close but maybe close enough.

Part of him wanted to remain cautiously optimistic. The other part wanted to do a superhero pose, because that was what he was about to be dubbed.

They'll call me Luck Man.

"Now he gets it."

He could easily picture Bethany throwing her hands up in exasperation, something she did frequently when within hearing distance of him.

"I would need the bakery to be part of the contract," he said. This deal, depending on what Bethany's friend of a friend was willing to pay, sounded too good to be true.

310

"You'll have to ask her about that. She wants to come tour the property herself, along with two other members of her team. I've taken the liberty of booking them rooms in Weber Haus for one night. Luckily, whoever I was dealing with over your way was able to work something out."

Wait what? Neither Aunt Tilly nor Emily had mentioned more guests coming. He tipped his head back to make a face at the ceiling. Emily had to be wigging out if that one night coincided with Christmas Eve. She was already a little cuckoo when it came to getting ready for that.

Also, where would they put these folks? They had one room open — the one with the door that they still couldn't open properly. He'd have to get Daniel to fix that immediately. But they didn't have three rooms. What about the other two people?

"When will they be here?" he asked.

"Tomorrow."

Lukas choked. Tomorrow? That was fast. Especially given the holiday season. Which meant he needed to talk to Aunt Tilly now. He still hadn't discussed selling with her, even in a small way.

Now that he was faced with the immediacy of his idea — because telling Tilly would make it real — the wad of doubt he'd been fighting for days grew inside his stomach, like a snowball rolling down a hill, picking up steam and size, and maybe a few pine trees to skewer him with when it landed on his head. He was tempted to tell Bethany to forget it, except she'd gone to all that trouble.

Forget Luck Man, he was Calamity Man.

No, he told himself, forcing a calm he was far from reaching. *This is the right step. The right thing to do.* Otherwise the universe wouldn't have handed him the opportunity.

Aunt Tilly couldn't go on the way she was much longer, and they couldn't afford to hire more help with all his money going into renovations. He'd been stuck on that point since springing his plan on Emily. Meanwhile it sounded as though Bethany's friend of a friend would be able to do everything in her power to make Weber Haus magnificent again.

So why did he feel like how Snowball looked when she knew she was about to get in trouble — ears drooping, tail tucked, and hunkered over?

"I was expecting a tad more excitement," came the dry comment from his agent.

"Sorry, Bethany. I was thinking through all the logistics. I should probably still talk to a real estate agent in the area to get an idea of fair pricing. But you're right. You are a miracle worker." He tried to dredge up a decent amount of thrilledness for her.

"That's better."

"Santa better bring you what you want this year," he managed to tease. "You've earned it."

"Darling . . . I earn it every year."

He did laugh at that. Folks within the industry were known to call Bethany the Dragon Lady, though never to her face. Usually to his after she had wrangled him a fantastic deal on a contract.

"If that's everything you needed, I will talk to you again after the new year."

"Yes. Thanks, Bethany, and have a Merry Christmas."

"I will," she practically sang. Then the line went dead.

Slowly, his mind going a million different places, Lukas lowered his phone to the countertop. Then he gripped the edges and dropped his head between his outstretched arms to stare at the floor. "God, I hope this is the right thing."

No answering lightning bolt or whisper of wind helped clear things up, leaving him still wondering. First things first, though . . . Abandoning his project, he went in search of his aunt.

He found her with a watering can, moving from room to room to tend to each of the potted plants around the house, as well as the Christmas trees. In fact, his first sight of her was on her hands and knees, her head stuck under the branches of the Christmas tree in the formal living room, her bony behind, covered in a thick wool dress, waving in the air.

"Aunt Tilly?"

"Be right with you." After a second she started to back out from under there, very slowly.

Lukas reached out a hand to help her to her feet, steadying her as she rose. "Why don't I water the Christmas trees?" he suggested.

She slapped a hand at him. "Nonsense. I am perfectly able to water Christmas trees . . . and anything else I choose to do for that matter."

His aunt always had been the independent type. With an impressed grin, Lukas held up both hands in surrender. "Far be it for me to argue with a lady."

She just shook her head, then patted his cheek. "Smooth talker."

Right. He was gonna need all those skills for the conversation they needed to have. "Can we sit down a minute, Aunt Tilly? I

314

have something I need to discuss with you."

Her thin white eyebrows rose. "Sounds serious."

Other than that comment, she took a seat on the sofa without any noticeable concern and placed her watering can on the floor at her feet, then patted the seat beside her. Only, once he was seated, Lukas had no idea where to start the conversation. Did he start with the guests arriving tomorrow? Or the run-down state of the house?

"Have you thought about what retirement will look like for you?" he finally asked.

Tilly tipped her head, considering him with wise eyes that had always seen a little too much. "I wasn't planning on retiring. Weber Haus isn't a job to me, it's a home. One I open to others."

Not the best of starts.

He took her hands in his, hiding a wince at how frail she was under his touch. "You have to admit that without Emily, this would be too much for you. The house is in a bit of disrepair."

Tilly shrugged, clearly unconcerned. "We always have up seasons and down seasons. Times change, the economy swings, the weather brings fewer or more guests. I'll be fine."

"I have no doubt about that."

She would, even without his help. However, what would the cost to her be? Years off her life thanks to stress and worry? "But wouldn't you enjoy life a little more if you could relax, possibly travel and see the world?"

"The world comes to me. We have guests from every corner of the globe stay here and share their cultures with us. And I do travel, metaphorically, thanks to your photographs. I was always more of a homebody anyway." She eyed him in a stern way that reminded him of when he'd been a boy trying to get away with something. "Now what's this about?"

"This is about my coming home and finding things not as easy for you as I would like. I want to be able to trust that you are taken care of while I'm off taking pictures of all those faraway places."

She patted his hand, the rose scent of her perfume lighting up a hundred memories of his childhood. "Sweet boy. I'm fine. I would tell you if I needed any help. I promise."

Tilly moved to stand, but Lukas tightened his grip on her hands, though not too much, afraid he might snap a bone, and she settled back down.

"You're determined I should sell this place, aren't you?"

Lukas no doubt looked as gobsmacked as he felt because Tilly laughed outright.

"Kid, when you've been around as long as I have . . ." She winked.

"Who told?" he asked.

"A ton of people. When you have your agent asking around for realtors to sell a Victorian house on a large piece of property in this area, it's not too hard to put the pieces together."

"I see." He shook his head in an effort to clear it and get back to the topic. "In that case, you should know a woman who owns a successful chain of hotels is interested in purchasing Weber Haus and the surrounding property."

Tilly stilled, faded blue eyes focused on him, but no other visible reaction. "I see."

Lukas had to swallow down that ball of doubt that kept getting bigger. "She and two of her people will be here tomorrow."

"The three new guests?" she asked immediately.

"Yes. Will you at least talk to her and consider what she has to offer?"

Tilly turned her head to stare out the window, seeming to take in the snow-covered land she had grown up on, just like Lukas had earlier from the kitchen. Then she dropped her gaze to their clasped hands.

"If you think I should, then I will consider it."

Giving his hands a squeeze, she stood and picked up her watering can, as if this wasn't a huge moment. She didn't look at him as she left the room.

Emily wanted to throw up. Or throw something. She couldn't decide which was the stronger instinct.

After an hour of being talked at and talked around when it came to her bakery plans — not that she'd shared much of them with her family for just this reason — she'd come home. Right in time to overhear Lukas's conversation with Tilly.

She stayed in the shadows of the foyer as Tilly went up the stairs, then went and stood in the doorway of the living room, arms crossed, glaring at Lukas's down-turned head.

"Wow," she said.

He jerked his gaze up, then grimaced almost comically, guilt written across his features reminding her of Snowball after she snuck into her purse and was found out. If Emily wasn't so mad at him, she would've laughed. Instead, she wanted to thump him over the head with one of her frying pans. On second thought, maybe not a frying pan. Those were cast-iron and would probably kill him. She didn't need a murder charge heaped on her day.

"Of course *you* heard that," he muttered.

She narrowed her eyes at him. "If you were doing the right thing, then you wouldn't mind my overhearing that."

"Not when your first instinct is instant judgment," he shot back.

Ouch.

Lips flat, Lukas got to his feet and walked right past her and through to the kitchen. Emily followed to find him picking up the sander and getting back to work.

"Are we going to talk about this?" she demanded.

Lukas put the power tool down. "Talk about what, exactly?"

Except instead of cocky or proud, he looked . . . defeated — eyes tired, shoulders drooping, not even a hint of a twinkle.

For a heartbeat, she softened, before her anger bolstered her back up. Lukas had done this to himself. Anger bundled into a swell of disappointment threatened to roll over her like an avalanche.

"Why are you selling Weber Haus? This is Tilly's home, where she's happy. Why would you do that to her?"

"Because it's too big for her." He might

act defeated, but she could hear the note of finality in his voice. Lukas had made up his mind about this.

Another swell of anger rose inside her. That darn stubborn, oblivious, only-thinking-about-what-was-good-for-him man —

"She's getting old," he said.

Emily paused her mental diatribe.

Still not looking at her, he shook his head, like he was arguing with himself. "Even with your help, this place needs at least three more hands to run it in any way that makes a profit. And, as you so kindly pointed out when I arrived, she doesn't have the money for repairs as things stand, and she won't take mine. Tens of thousands are sitting in her bank, untouched."

What? Lukas had been sending Tilly money? Why hadn't he said so sooner?

Unaware of her silent questions, he continued. "What if she fell? What if she broke her hip? What if she —"

He broke off and glared at the power tool in his hands like this was its fault, fiddling with the switch, then took a breath. Emily stayed silent. She had never seen him like this. The Lukas she'd come to know was confident, easy, maybe a little thoughtless.

Or had she been the thoughtless one, assuming that he didn't take Tilly's situation seriously? The worry creasing his brow and setting his jaw so hard were not the hallmarks of a man who didn't take his responsibility seriously.

But selling the house? Couldn't he see that he would break his aunt's heart?

Lukas cleared his throat and raised his gaze, eyes hard, no give in him. "I will be building the bakery into the contract as a stipulation to move forward. Of course I'll be sharing all the ideas we discussed concerning other shops and activities with whoever buys it. I want you to know that."

Ooooh. The man could make her so dang angry faster than Santa could circle the globe. Irritation burned through her blood in a split second. "You think I'm worried about *me*?"

"I'd be a fool not to think that's part of why you're angry right now."

All Emily could do was stand there, slowly shaking her head and feeling like Lukas had gouged her heart out with her wooden slotted spoon. They hadn't known each other long, but she thought he knew her better than that. "You're a fool either way, Lukas Weber."

She walked out, letting the kitchen door swing back and forth behind her. But she stopped almost immediately and stood in the hallway for a minute as she strove to find calm, part of her hoping he'd follow and prove her wrong.

The sound of the sander buzzing to life was a definitive end to the discussion.

With feet weighed down by doubts and a heart that had dropped to her soles, she made her way up to her bedroom and sat on the edge of her bed, gazing outside but not really seeing the barren, snow-laden trees beyond, or the carriage house in the distance.

Lukas had made it plain that not only was he not open to changing this course of action but also he didn't want her input in the first place.

Maybe that hurt most of all.

A brush against her ankle had her glancing down to find Snowball winding around her feet. The kitten blinked up at her with the saddest eyes, obviously sharing Emily's pain.

"I thought he at least respected my opinion," she told the tiny cat.

Emily flopped back against her pillows and dragged her feet up so that she wasn't lying all wonky. The ceiling, with its original wood paneling, held no answers for her.

"Tilly is the heart of this place," she

murmured. "He can't sell it out from under her. She won't let him."

But maybe she would. Maybe Tilly was tired and ready for a break. After all, she hadn't argued with him, had even agreed to listen to the hotel person.

Meow.

Snowball's mewling came from across the room. Emily raised her head just in time to see the kitten leap up to the fireplace mantel in one bound.

"Holy smokes —" Emily jerked straight up, staring at the tiny animal. "How on earth did you jump that high?"

Meow, Snowball replied, and started walking, managing to navigate around the framed photos, not knocking a single one out of place let alone off, until she stood beside the advent calendar.

Emily scowled. "I don't want to see what he gave me today." She had no interest in thoughtful gestures from Lukas Weber right this second. "I don't like him very much right now."

Snowball made a sound that was suspiciously like a scoff. The kitten version. Though, more logically, it might have been a sneeze.

"I don't," Emily insisted anyway.

Now I'm arguing with a miniature version of a cat.

With a huff, she got off the bed and pulled Snowball off the mantel, putting her back down on the ground. Except by the time she'd resumed her place on the bed, the kitten was back up on the fireplace. One more round of that, and Emily buckled.

"Fine. I'll look."

She snatched the wooden carved Christmas tree from the mantel and plonked down on her bed, then opened the door for today. Inside she found a bag filled with several rolled sticks, light brown, and instantly recognizable. At least to her. Just in case she was wrong, she opened the bag and sniffed, then groaned.

Ceylon cinnamon from Sri Lanka. The man had bothered to track some down for her. Even if he'd only bought it off the internet and had it shipped, that didn't matter. He'd listened. Even at the beginning when all she'd done was glare at him and snap at him, he'd listened. She'd barely mentioned this. One time. With one small gesture he'd gone and smashed her heart to pieces.

"The big oaf," she muttered in a watery voice.

I'm in love with him.

Realization passed through her like the

ghost of Christmas future, stealing her breath and leaving her light-headed. Emily set the calendar on her dresser and dropped onto her bed, her head in her hands.

That was why she was so bothered by his actions now.

Why the disappointment ran so deep. Because somewhere along the lines, who Lukas was as a person had snuck under all her defenses and preconceived notions of him and taken up residence inside her heart. Those dimples and that smile, his easy laugh, and the way he captured the beauty of the world in his pictures, and the way he had such a big heart even if sometimes he was a little blind to how best to go about using that gift.

She loved all of it. All of him.

Except she knew, in her bones, that selling Weber Haus would be the worst mistake of his life, and she couldn't support him in that decision. Not with her bakery and not with her silence. She loved him enough that she couldn't simply let him do this.

But how the heck did she get through to that stubborn head of his?

A tiny lick on her elbow had her lifting her head to find Snowball sitting next to her. She pulled the kitten into her lap, absorbing comfort from the tiny, warm fluff-ball.

Emily closed her eyes. "I don't know what to do."

I know exactly what to do.

Emily and Lukas need a bigger hint than getting them to kiss. When I was brand-new and first came to live at Weber Haus, a man showed up and surprised a woman who was staying with us. He got down on one knee and said lovely things that made her cry happy tears. Then he gave her a ring.

They jumped up and down and squealed, and Miss Tilly said they were going to get married.

That's what Emily needs. A ring. And Lukas has one. It's nice and shiny and I've been thinking about taking it for a while. In fact, I'm not sure why I haven't taken it yet.

Odd.

Either way, it's sitting on top of the table beside his bed in his room.

Good thing I can get into both their rooms. I wait for Emily to go downstairs, then run to Lukas's room. He's not there, and it doesn't take me long to snatch the glittery thing from where he left it.

Now for the tricky part.

A bat of the paw to Lukas's door and it opens enough to squeeze through. Ring in

326

my teeth, I poke my head in the hall to use all my senses to see if anyone might be coming by. I take three cautious steps, like I'm stalking a mouse, but a loud shout comes from two rooms down, and I have to scurry backward to Lukas's.

Sure enough, a few seconds later, the Andrewses all emerged, bundled up like humans seem to do when they leave the house these days. I guess they're heading into town, because that's what most people say when they go out like that. Town or the sledding hill.

I wait for the quiet to follow them out the door, then try again. Luckily, Emily isn't in her room, and she's left the wooden tree calendar thing laying on its back, with the little doors sticking up.

Perfect!

I leap onto the bed, then scoot my way to the tree. I can't read, though, and I've seen Lukas do this enough that I know it's supposed to go in a certain door. So I take a guess. The ring gives a little *plink* of sound as it drops in, and I tap all the doors closed so she can't tell that one is special.

There. I nod to myself. If they don't get the hint after this, I give up.

CHAPTER 17

Lukas had never dreaded the jangling sound of that darn bell attached to the front door more than he did today. Not even when he'd moved in with his aunt, even though that cheerful ringing had meant more strangers coming to stay.

Ridiculous to feel that way today.

This solution, as long as the price was right, was best for everyone. He could continue to travel for his job, safe in the knowledge that Aunt Tilly would be well looked after. He'd already started researching various retirement communities or options in and around town that might work, determined to find the *perfect* place for her. Although, he'd make sure he didn't go nearly so long without visiting or bringing her to visit him.

He glanced over the top of his computer at his aunt, who sat on the sofa, knitting away, appearing as though she had not a worry in the world. He still wasn't entirely sure how she felt about all this.

With Christmas Eve close, the house looked its festive best. Spotless and smelling of lemon, bleach, and pine trees, every decoration out, all the lights turned on for the "tour."

Just wait until they saw it at night all lit up from the outside. They'd fall in love with it.

"You seem nervous," Tilly said without lifting her gaze or stopping the *clack-clack* of her knitting needles.

Lukas didn't want to talk about his divergent emotions. "What are you making?"

"A teapot cozy for Mrs. Gessner. Her husband died last year, poor dear, and she doesn't get out much. But she does enjoy her tea."

Lukas managed a small smile. "The way you take care of others has always been one of my favorite things about you."

Tilly dropped her knitting to her lap and finally raised her gaze to him. The one he'd thought of in his childhood as the lie detector gaze — straightforward and unflinching. "That's lovely of you to say. Now what's got you in a tizzy?"

Lukas tossed her his most charming grin. "I don't tizzy, Aunt Tilly."

"Rubbish. Everybody tizzies now and again."

His aunt clearly wasn't going to let up on this. The thing was, logic dictated that what he was doing made total sense and was the right thing to do. Why did he have this churning sense in his gut that something was off?

"I only want to take care of you the best way I can," Lukas said. Admitting his own doubts to Tilly wouldn't help any.

Tilly's expression softened. "I know that," she murmured.

Setting her knitting aside, she got up and joined him where he was seated on the matching love seat to the sofa and put a hand to his knee. "After this many years on this good earth, I have learned that things tend to work out in the end. Even when one can't quite see the way."

Was that why she appeared unaffected by this? He almost would rather she had a strong emotion one way or the other. That might tell him if he was on the right track or not.

She patted his knee and was about to get up when his computer screen caught her attention. "Oh, those are lovely."

Tilly leaned closer, examining the large thumbnail images. He'd been sending her his pictures his whole life. Aunt Tilly had always been his biggest cheerleader, but even so, Lukas found himself waiting for her to say more. Like when he was a boy.

She pointed at an image of herself with Snowball. "Can I see this larger?"

Lukas obliged, reaching out to tap the pad and bring it up. Tilly let out a delighted laugh. "Why, I look ten years younger."

He grinned. She always said that. "You should see this one."

He brought up the image of Tilly gazing out the window when she'd been watching the snow. "I know you've said you were a beauty in your day, but I definitely think you're a beauty now," he said.

"Charmer." She batted a hand at him, but she also couldn't take her eyes from the screen. Was that a blush?

Delight that she loved the image that much filled him up in a familiar way that reminded him of why he'd loved photography to begin with. Tilly's responses to his pictures. He'd frame this one. The picture book was already done, printed on a rush job, and wrapped under the tree in her room. This one would have to be for her birthday in February.

After another minute or two, Tilly sat up straighter. "I know you've been taking lots of pictures around here. What are some of your favorites?"

Lukas had already done this exercise for her gift but couldn't go straight to the folder labeled "Tilly Christmas," so he pulled the computer nearer and spent a few minutes going through the sets, pulling out about ten that he thought were the best ones, then shuffled them in order and turned the computer to face her. He let her click through them at her own pace.

After a while, Tilly raised her gaze over the computer, blue eyes sparkling. "I think these might be your best work."

Emily had said something similar. "I was just messing around. I've never done small-town stuff."

"Except when you were here," she pointed out. "And those pictures got you into the photography program in college, if I'm not mistaken."

Huh. She's not wrong.

Lukas spun the computer back around and tried to study the images with his professional eye, studying each one for style and composition, emotional impact, salability, content.

He landed on one of Emily and the emotional impact about trampled him, like Santa landed the sleigh on top of him, and left his head ringing.

She had been in the kitchen baking.

That day, she'd left her hair partially down, only the sides tied back, loose and curling over one shoulder. She'd been wearing a red sweater that had set off her dark hair and eyes. The heat from the stove, and effort she'd been putting into kneading bread, had left her with rosy cheeks. Meanwhile Snowball wouldn't leave her alone, winding around her ankles and meowing until finally Emily had picked the kitten up and snuggled her, rubbing her cheek against the soft white fur.

Lukas hadn't been able to resist. He'd had to have a picture.

As luck would have it, his camera had been right there, and he'd snapped away. The next images in the series were almost more adorable. Emily glancing up in surprise, then frowning at him in the cutest way, then setting Snowball down only to have the kitten bat at her swinging hair.

Lukas stared at the images and struggled to force oxygen back in his lungs. Emily Diemer was about the most beautiful thing he'd ever seen.

The jangle of the bell over the front door snapped him back to reality to find Tilly watching him with deceptively mild interest. No doubt she'd been well aware of how flummoxed he was right this moment.

"That must be our new guests," she said, and went to answer the door, Lukas following more slowly behind her.

Even before they opened it, a woman's voice could easily be heard. "This will be a perfect retreat. Plus, that quaint town and the sledding hill. Just close enough, and just far enough away. I can picture it exactly."

Tilly opened the door to three people standing on the porch, fashionably dressed, though not exactly suitable for the weather. Two women and a man.

The woman in front, white hair peeping out from a fur-lined red felt hat that exactly matched her red wool peacoat, held out her hand. "You must by Matilda Weber," she said. "And this is Lukas?" She shook his hand as well. "I'm Sheila Rydel. This is my assistant, George, and my numbers genius, Adeline."

"Nice to meet you." Lukas nodded at the other two, ushering them into the house.

"Please call me Miss Tilly," his aunt said with her kindly smile. "Let's get you checked in and show you your rooms so you can settle in."

"No need," Sheila waived a careless hand. "We left our luggage in the car because we can't wait to see around this beautiful property you have."

Despite the smile Tilly sent the three, Lukas had no doubt she was reserving judgment. Usually, she was much . . . warmer . . . greeting new guests. *Never met a stranger, come on in and join us* kind of thing, but Sheila had probably put her off a bit. Visiting an inn, most people were interested in sort of stepping back in time, moving a little slower and using manners that were perhaps old-fashioned. Clearly, Sheila and her team wanted to get started.

Which is fine, he reminded himself. They weren't here for a leisurely stay. This was a business trip for them.

"Of course," Lukas said, aiming a determined beam at his aunt. "If you'll follow me."

As he turned to lead them through the foyer to the formal living room, he glanced down the hallway to the back door to the kitchen to find Emily standing there, half in shadow. As soon as their gazes met, she shook her head and disappeared back into the kitchen.

But not before he'd seen the disappointment etched into every line of her face.

"This might be the best shepherd's pie I've

335

ever tasted," Sheila said across the table.

Not that Emily was surprised. This was her go-to comfort food. She made it when she needed something warm in her belly, which made her day a little bit better. Plus she loved the recipe. One her grandmother had shared.

Not that she'd eaten much today.

Lukas brightened, nodding from Emily to Sheila, as if she needed encouragement or something.

"Just wait for dessert," he said. Only he said it slowly, an odd tone to his voice. Almost as though he wanted to believe the words but couldn't quite get there.

"And her breakfast pastries," Bill Hoffman added with an expressive eye roll. At least the other guests had taken the new additions to their group in stride. Although Lukas hadn't been too happy when he'd been informed that he'd be sleeping on the couch tonight. Emily had made sure his room was cleaned and the sheets and towels changed while he'd been running the tour.

"Thanks," Emily murmured to the table in general.

She wanted to *not* like the woman. Had tried to find reasons to stay angry. While all three were very city with their clothes that were not warm enough and their way of cutting people off when talking, they were also obviously good at what they did.

Which was the problem.

Every comment they'd made about what they'd like to do with Weber Haus and the surrounding property fell right in with the picture Lukas had painted himself. One Emily had already started believing in, despite herself. Adding shops, and perhaps converting more areas to rooms so they could house more people. Adding more events and activities to do to draw bigger crowds out this way.

Sheila had tasted a selection of baking that Emily had prepared at Lukas's suggestion and had already hinted that they would definitely be including her bakery in the plans.

I should be ecstatic.

Her dream was within her grasp. One backed by a corporation set on making Weber Haus an investment, which meant she didn't have to secure a loan, or ask her parents to cosign. Every single worry she'd had — about money, about the house itself, about her business, about her future — could be about to go poof with a signature on a piece of paper.

So why wasn't she more excited? Thrilled even? Because she still couldn't get behind

Lukas forcing his aunt out of her home.

That wasn't right, no matter how wrapped up in a pretty bow it appeared to be. *Am I going to lose this shot at my bakery, too?* Or was she just being stubborn?

She glanced across the table at Miss Tilly, who appeared relaxed if not brimming with happiness, chatting away. Was she worried? Heartbroken? Excited? Interested? Somehow Emily doubted the lovely but stubborn older woman wasn't sharing her real thoughts for a reason.

Hiding a sigh, Emily happened to glance at Lukas to find his gaze on her.

Her stomach flipped like a pancake in a skillet at the intent way he was watching her, only she couldn't look away.

He raised his eyebrows, just slightly, but in obvious question.

She had no freaking clue what she was feeling about this entire thing. Certainly not enough to give him a quick thumbs-up or thumbs-down, which is what he was asking for. So she stared back at him, mouth parted, trying to find the words. Lukas's brows drew lower and he searched her face, that intensity not leaving him.

Emily cleared her throat and forced her gaze to the woman in whose hands everything rested. "So, Sheila, tell us why your company is interested in branching out in such a unique way. I understood most of your hotels to be fairly modern and in touristy city locations."

Okay, so she might have spent last night researching the heck out of their guests. She did her best to keep her voice the right level of vaguely interested but didn't dare glance back at Lukas to see if she'd succeeded.

Sheila tapped a long, manicured nail against her water glass as though thinking through her words. "You are correct. In fact, that business has done so well, we're planning to expand. Several of our bigger clients have asked about country-style retreats, which is what we're looking for now. We already have one project underway at an exclusive beach community. Another involving a ski resort. However, we're also looking for quieter escapes." She waved a hand around. "Which is where Weber Haus could conceivably come in."

Something in that statement bothered Emily. A niggling at the back of her mind saying that it felt off. Wrong. Except she couldn't put her finger on what.

Man, she was turning into a pessimist. When had that happened? Before or after Greg?

"Are you considering any other locations?" Tilly asked.

Sheila flapped her hands. "Yes, but most no longer have the large piece of property that Weber Haus does. Or, if they do, they're so far from a town, they're not as desirable. The combination of the right ambiance, the right structures, the right land, and the right location are what we're currently searching to find."

Emily pushed a pea around on her plate, still trying to pin down that off feeling. "Beyond the repairs, and converting the other buildings into shops, and possibly more rooms, would you change much about the look and feel of Weber Haus?"

"I don't think so, though my designers will be the driving force there, but we want to keep that cozy, home-away-from-home feel with the elegance of a bygone era," Sheila said.

Emily managed a smile as the knot in her stomach untied itself a bit. Maybe she was being silly, and resistant to change, and she needed to quit.

"Of course, we'll want it to match the standards we'll be setting at our beach and ski resorts," Sheila continued.

The knot drew tighter.

"Oh?" Emily asked.

Sheila nodded. "Exclusive. High-end. An

340

experience you can't get elsewhere. I'm certain we can marry both concepts brilliantly."

The knot pulled so tight, Emily doubted she'd ever get it undone.

"Those don't sound easily blended," Lukas said slowly.

She shot him a covert glance to find him studying Sheila with a blank expression that probably fooled the woman, but Emily didn't miss the way the skin tightened around his eyes, or the lack of any smile, let alone a dimple.

Sheila sent him an easy smirk, brimming with confidence. "I'm very, very good at what I do."

"I don't doubt it," Lukas said. But he didn't smile back.

Was he having the same doubts Emily was? What if they took Weber Haus and made it into a hoity-toity playground for the über rich?

It's none of your business.

A glance at Tilly, who continued to appear unaffected, and Emily tried to force her shoulders down from around her ears and, if not untie the knot of anxiety, at least ignore it.

"I'll go get dessert ready," she said, and scooted back from the table, taking up

341

plates as she went.

In the kitchen, Snowball lay on a rug near the oven, no doubt basking in the radiated heat as the apple crisp warmed. Emily shooed her away and pulled the dish out to scoop servings into bowls, her mind only half on the task.

Snowball hopped up on that counter, and, instead of immediately putting her back on the ground, Emily scooted her away from the food, but then stood there, stroking her soft fur, and staring into the dark outside the window over the sink.

So lost in her thoughts, she didn't hear anyone open the door or enter the kitchen. She also didn't jump with surprise when a warm hand took hers, sneaking into the one dangling at her side. It felt right. Like they held hands all the time.

"It's going to be fine," Lukas said in a low voice at her ear. "I'll make sure they don't change this place."

While she had to resist the urge to tip her head slightly to the side so she could lean against his chest, Emily's shoulders still dropped another fraction at his words. She hadn't been the only one who'd been concerned with Sheila's vision?

"It's a good deal, Lukas." She turned to face him.

342

Part of her acknowledged that she should let go of his hand. But she didn't.

He cocked his head, surprise lighting his green eyes. "You think so?"

Emily's mouth quirked up on one side. "From a business angle, even I can see that. The question is Tilly. As long as Tilly's happy, I . . . shouldn't stand in your way."

Why did that feel like giving up? Like she wanted to chase the words back and find another answer to the situation?

He searched her gaze. Probably for any hint that she was being sarcastic.

Emily shook off the ominous clouds hovering over her and squeezed his hand. "I mean it. But do make sure they don't steal the soul of this place. Okay?"

Lukas stared back at her, a smile slowly growing, dimple winking at her. "Emily Diemer. One of these days, I'm going to figure you out and be able to predict your reactions."

Emily chuckled. Here was the cocky guy she'd come to know and love.

The world sort of quieted and pulled in closer until all she could see were a pair of laughing moss green eyes.

Love.

There she went again. She'd sort of been hoping the other day was an aberration, but no such luck. Somewhere along the lines, she'd lost her heart to Lukas Weber. To a man who was equal parts kind and helpful and considerate, while at the same time tunnel-visioned. A fixer, like her, though he could use a few lessons in the communicating part of those fixes. He had a tendency to make decisions without consulting anyone else. He also made her laugh, and forced her to have fun, worked hard beside her, but also made her take time to enjoy life, and see the world in beautiful colors, if his photos were anything to go by.

Not perfect, just kind of perfect for her.

As soon as he left, he'd forget all about her and Weber Haus again. Maybe not Tilly this time. He hadn't actually forgotten before. She could see that now.

Still, he *was* going to leave . . . and drag her heart right along with him.

I am an idiot.

With a small gasp, Emily stepped back, releasing his hand, and the rest of the world came rushing back in. "Um . . . We'd better get this dessert out there."

His eyebrows winged up. Had she said that too fast? Trying not to let the blush attempting to warm her cheeks to get any traction, Emily turned away to finish scooping. "It'll get cold, and it's supposed to be warm and served à la mode."

"Okaaaay." He drew the word out. "I'll get the ice cream."

"Thanks," she tossed over her shoulder.

In short order, they had dessert served and sat to enjoy it with their guests. Emily looked down the table at Lukas, chatting with a laughing Tilly, easy smile in clear view.

She scooped a bite into her mouth, hardly noticing the tangy apple, buttery crisp, and velvety cold ice cream.

How was she going to get through Christmas and then watch him walk away forever?

They are going to sell the house, and Miss Tilly is going to move away. Maybe some place she can't have cats.

Emily and Lukas are blind. The way they look at each other almost hurts to watch.

Humans can be awfully dumb.

What am I going to do? These people are supposed to be my forever family, but I don't want to leave Weber Haus. This is my home.

CHAPTER 18

A crashing sound from the kitchen followed by Emily's shout of "Snowball! Gah!" couldn't be good.

The woman had been a blizzard of preparatory activity since the crack of dawn getting ready for their big Christmas Eve dinner. Santa's elves didn't work this hard.

Lukas left the garland he'd been told to wrap up the stairs to the balcony and ran to the kitchen to find Emily already sweeping up a shattered bowl and Snowball nowhere to be seen.

"You okay?" he asked slowly.

Emily snapped her head up and flung out a hand. "That kitten is going to be the death of me."

He couldn't see bleeding or anything else that constituted a worry about real death, let alone an emergency, so Lukas buttoned his lips around a grin. Given her expression and tone of voice, he'd only tick her off

346

more. "What happened?"

"She somehow got into this cupboard. When I opened it to get a mixing bowl, she jumped out like a psychotic jack-in-the-box. Scared me to death and managed to make all these glass bowls fall out."

Lukas tried to not picture that, because he'd lose it and laugh.

Apparently, he didn't hide the urge well, because Emily's brows practically formed a unibrow as they met in the middle in a fierce scowl. "It's *not* funny," she snapped. "I have so much to do." She descended into a wail.

Lukas cleared his throat and grabbed the broom from her. "I'll clean this up. You get back to work."

He started sweeping, then frowned as realization struck. A glance at the clock confirmed it. "Do you have time to finish and err . . . get yourself ready?"

Whoops. That question put him on shaky ground. Based on the narrow-eyed stare Emily directed at him, thin ice was perhaps a more apt metaphor. He could practically feel the chilly breeze against his skin. Maybe kissing her would help.

"I'll be fine," she enunciated extra clearly.

Maybe not.

Emily snatched one of the unbroken bowls

laying haphazardly on the countertop and went to where she'd already piled up ingredients for yet another dish. With her entire family joining all the guests, they'd have at least twenty-five people tonight. It helped that Sheila and her small entourage had left yesterday, but Emily seemed to be baking enough to feed the entire town for the winter.

"What are you making?" he asked in what he assumed was a mild voice.

"Lebkuchen," she muttered. "I forgot about them. They're my grandfather's favorites because they remind him of my grandmother's baking at Christmas."

She didn't turn around to address him, entirely focused on measuring and pouring into a bowl. Apparently, Emily had the recipe memorized.

Lukas leaned on the broom handle and watched for a second, fascinated. "Is this the same grandfather who likes to have stollen at Christmas because it reminds him of your grandmother?"

Emily slammed a measuring cup on the counter, flour flying in a cloud of white dust. She whipped her head around. "Do you have a point?"

Lukas grimaced and went back to sweeping the broken bits off the floor. "Nope. No point. No kissing. Don't know what I was thinking."

"No kissing? When did that come up?"

Shoot. He hadn't meant for that to slip out. "It didn't. Why are you bringing it up?"

All he got in return was a huffy-sounding grunt as she turned back to what she was doing, and Lukas proceeded to monitor her more surreptitiously. He'd never seen Emily like this. Granted he hadn't known Emily long, but something was going on here that was bigger than simply wanting to make Christmas Eve nice for a larger than normal group of people and being stressed about it.

He just wasn't sure what.

After he finished sweeping up, Lukas took a wet paper towel over the floor to pick up any tiny shards of glass.

"I shouldn't have gone out with Daniel," Emily mumbled. More to herself than him.

No surprise the words sent a satisfied buzz through him. He hadn't been able to sleep last night until he'd heard her come home. Around midnight. She hadn't said anything about the date at breakfast, flying through her chores to start getting the house and food ready for tonight, and Lukas had about chewed his tongue off to keep from asking.

Did he dare comment now?

"Didn't you have fun?" he asked before

his brain had finished deciding what to do.

Emily, back still to him, shook her head, which sent the buzz to another level.

"That was time I needed to get ready for today," she said.

Her words managed to drop the buzz back down to a low hum. Maybe, just maybe, Lukas had been secretly hoping the date would be a disaster. He should've known better, but still.

He finished cleaning up and quietly left Emily to it, going back to the decorating she'd assigned him. A small crew of cleaners had been hired to come in earlier in the week to leave Weber Haus sparkling, so at least Emily wasn't trying to do that on top of everything else, though Tilly seemed determined to go around after them, at least with the duster. Lukas was coming to the conclusion that he should've made plans to get out of the house, out from underfoot.

Back at the stairs, a pair of blue eyes peeped out at him from beneath a length of garland laying draped on the landing. Snowball was a puff of white face amid greens and red ribbon.

"Today might not be the best day to jump out at Emily," Lukas informed her.

The kitten didn't move or make a sound, which was odd. Curious, he leaned in for a better look, only to realize that the odd twitching to her fur was Snowball shivering with fear.

"Poor baby." He scooped her out of the garland and sat on a stair, cuddling her into his chest. "That must've scared you as much as it scared Emily."

Her body, so tiny in his hands, her thick fur making her appear bigger than she truly was, which was already miniscule, shook in bouts of trembling as she tried to remain excruciatingly still, flight instinct clearly very much still in play. Lukas sat there with her until the tremors eased and her muscles relaxed. Finally, a rumbly purr sounded, vibrating against his hands.

"Lukas?" Emily appeared in the foyer and paused when she found him sitting toward the top of the stairs. "What are you doing?"

"Snowball was so scared from the bowl incident, she was shaking," he explained.

"Poor baby," Emily unknowingly mimicked his own response.

She made her way up to sit beside him, her body warm against his and smelling even more of sugar cookies than usual, along with cloves and cinnamon.

"Come here." She gently took Snowball from his grasp to hold her close. "I'm sorry if my yelling scared you, fluffball, but you scared the heck out of me, too."

Snowball nosed against her chin, almost like she was forgiving Emily. For her part, Emily giggled, the sound so different from the tension in her voice earlier, not to mention the snapping and snarling, Lukas's eyebrows raised of their own accord.

She glanced over to find Lukas watching her and still staring back in a way that made him want to kiss the taste of cookies from her lips.

"I'm sorry I yelled," she whispered.

Drawn to her like Snowball was drawn to trouble, he leaned closer. Emily blinked and sat up straighter, breaking the moment, if not the connection still strung tight as a wire between them. "Can you listen for the timer on the oven?" she asked in a hurried voice. "If I don't get in my shower now, I won't be presentable when everyone arrives."

"Sure. I'll finish up the garland here and keep an ear out."

Almost awkwardly, she held Snowball out to him. "Thanks."

She was halfway down the hallway before he called her name. When she turned back, eyebrows raised in question, he smiled.

"Don't worry. Tonight is going to be wonderful."

The hall was dimly lit, but he was fairly certain her cheeks pinkened. "I hope so," was all she said, before disappearing into her room.

Lukas looked at Snowball. "Women," he said. "I don't think I'll ever figure them out."

The kitten blinked at him for a second, then almost seemed to shrug.

The bell over the door jangled, and Emily peered at her reflection in the mirror. This was her family. She should be happy, and relaxed, and looking forward to celebrating the holiday with them. Instead, her muscles were strung so tight a violinist could pluck her.

"They are early," she said to the girl in the mirror.

Her date with Daniel last night had unfortunately put her more behind in preparations than she'd thought. She'd fidgeted and checked the clock on her phone a thousand times through dinner. Emily had thought she'd hidden it well enough, until Daniel was walking her to the door at the end. When she'd turned to face him with a polite thanks on her lips, ready to get out of the cold, she'd stopped at his expression — half-amused, half-resigned.

"What?" she'd asked.

"I get the feeling that all night you would rather have been here," he said.

"No," Emily protested. "I enjoyed spending time with you."

He gave her a look she remembered from childhood, and she'd bit her lip. "I just have so much to do to get ready for Christmas Eve."

He canted his head to the side, eyeing her closely. "And you had someone else waiting here for you."

No doubt in her mind he meant Lukas. Mortification punched through her, sending heat into her face. Had she been so obvious? "Of course not —"

Daniel reached out and put a hand on her shoulder, stopping the lie from tripping off fumbling lips. "I've known you all your life, Emily Diemer. You're in love." He reached out a hand and tucked her hair under her hat. "Just don't let him break your heart."

Emily snorted. "No worries there. He leaves soon."

Daniel had nodded, gaze searching hers. "Maybe we'll try again after that."

She'd given a half-hearted smile at that, but deep down, she knew that her feelings for Daniel would always be the same as how she felt about her brothers.

"Thanks for dinner," she'd whispered,

then hustled inside, where she'd tried not to be disappointed that every light in the house was off and Lukas wasn't waiting up.

This morning, she'd woken determined to be sensible. And she would be, darn it.

Trying to catch any sounds of her family downstairs, she rushed through her preparations, applying her makeup with a practiced hand, more than usual since tonight they'd all be dressed to go to the midnight candlelight service after a late dinner. Then she ran out of her room and down the stairs. Except the place was quiet, and her family was never, ever quiet.

"Hello?" she called out, listening.

"In here," Lukas called back from the kitchen. She pushed through to find him and Tilly there, her desserts cooling on the racks she'd set out before going up to shower . . . and a woman she'd never seen before.

Beautiful. In her mid to late twenties, with white-blond hair cut to her chin and soft gray eyes, she gave off contradicting vibes of both stubborn independence and a frail sort of helplessness.

"Hi." Emily tried not to glance at Lukas. Was this his friend? Girlfriend? Whoever she was, she was standing awfully close to him, so they likely knew each other.

One more reason to get over this silly love thing as soon as possible.

Except Tilly, not Lukas, wrapped an arm around the woman's shoulders. "Emily, this is Lara, and she's going to be staying with us for a few weeks. Her family is out of the country, so she decided to take a holiday trip at the last minute."

It sounded to Emily as though there was more to the story. Certainly looking at Lara, Emily could imagine that to be the case. But the relief that she wasn't with Lukas pretty much washed away any nagging concern. She smiled, trying to make up for her initial coolness. "Welcome. You've come just in time."

"Miss Tilly and Lukas were telling me about the party tonight." Lara bit her lip, looking like a little girl lost. "I could stay in my room. I don't want to intrude."

"Don't be silly," Tilly and Lukas said at the same time. "This is the season of togetherness."

"The more the merrier," Emily added to their objections.

Lara glanced around at their faces, not even pausing when she got to Lukas, which stupidly made Emily like her more. "If you're sure . . ."

"Of course, honey. Come with me." Tilly

led Lara off. "Let's get you settled in your room. You have plenty of time to change if you want to. We're going to church after dinner, but whatever you're comfortable in is fine." Her voice faded as they left the kitchen and went upstairs.

Emily turned back to find Lukas not watching the door, but her. As soon as he had her attention he grinned. "How'd I do?"

Do? Is he seriously asking if he'd managed to not make me jealous with another woman?

At her blank look, he waved an arm at her cooling treats.

Oh. Thank goodness. "Um . . . ." To buy herself another minute to realign her brain with reality, Emily picked one up and bit into it, testing the consistency, then gave an official nod. "Perfect. Thank you."

She walked around the center counter and snagged an apron from where it hung on a hook.

"What are you doing now?" Lukas wondered.

"The icing," she said, and rolled her eyes like he should've known that but grinned over her shoulder as she pulled two bowls of already-made icing — one vanilla and one chocolate — out of the fridge.

Dimples flashed as he shook his head. "I hope you take time to relax after the holiday

357

insanity is over."

Emily shrugged. "Relaxed isn't really my thing."

He laughed at that. "Tell me something I don't know. My turn to shower." So saying, he disappeared up the steps.

Emily flew through icing the treats and left them to set while she pulled out the various dinner items and started putting them out on the sideboard in the dining room. The salads she put on the table, which was already set with lovely china and a centerpiece of Christmas chrysanthemums and greenery.

"Smells delicious."

She jumped and spun to find Lukas standing in the doorway from the kitchen.

"Does everything look okay?" She worried at her lip with her teeth as she tweaked the angle at which she'd set one of the dishes.

Then she raised her gaze to find Lukas watching her in a way that made everything inside her yearn to get closer.

Lukas couldn't have stopped himself if he wanted to. She looked so worried, no way could he leave her that way.

He stepped closer, though not quite touching, and lifted a hand to twist a loose curl around one finger. "You have nothing to worry about. It's amazing."

The way she gazed back at him, big brown eyes solemn but with a hint of trust — more than a hint, which about brought him to his knees.

"*You're* amazing," he murmured, voice gone gruff.

Lukas tugged on that curl, slowly drawing her nearer, giving her every opportunity to put a stop to something he couldn't say no to a second longer. But she didn't walk away. Just continued to watch as his head lowered before she rose on her tiptoes, meeting him halfway.

Lukas took his time kissing Emily, trying to imprint everything about the moment — her sugar-cookie scent, the soft sweetness of her lips under his, the tiny gasp after the first touch. He deepened the kiss, slipping his other hand to the small of her back and urging her closer.

I don't want this to stop. Ever.

Lukas lifted his head to gaze down at the woman in his arms with a heady rush of wonder quickly being overtaken by a pinch of panic.

Because he had a career.

A life that didn't include a romance with a woman very much entrenched in one place and in her own career. He shouldn't be picturing things like what was going through his head. Images of Christmases spent together. Working on the house. Her getting all bent out of shape when her family came, like tonight.

Laughing. Fighting. Loving.

Home.

Emily gazed back with almost a dazed look, a small smile tugging at the corners of her mouth.

He opened his mouth to say something. Anything.

But the doorbell chose that minute to ring.

Both he and Emily stepped back from each other. Lukas grumbled quietly, both due to the interruption and because of the disappointment rolling through him that they were interrupted at all.

Emily smiled, a forced one if he was any judge, and spun away to go to the door and let her family in on a wave of noise, hugs, and introductions.

"You must be Lukas. I'm Marta." A woman who looked too much like Emily not to be her mother, came toward him with her hand outstretched.

Emily had told her mother about him?

She grasped his hand. "Peter told me Tilly's nephew was staying with her."

Served his ego right for thinking Emily

360

would do anything like tell her family about the guy who'd invaded her life.

A tall man with salt-and-pepper hair and Emily's dark eyes — obviously her dad — also grasped his hand. "Adrian. Here for the holidays?"

"Yes. I'll be heading to Morocco shortly after Christmas."

Over her father's shoulder he caught Emily's blinking frown and held in a wince. He'd just heard from Bethany today.

"Morocco. What a place," Adrian Diemer boomed in a jovial voice. Already Lukas liked her dad.

Not that he had time to comment further. Hearing the voices, Tilly made her way slowly down the stairs, looking lovely but frail in a new dress made of a shiny silver material that only seemed to make her glow. The guests staying at the house also came out of the woodwork, including Lara, who immediately was the focus of attention for Emily's unattached brothers. With so many folks being strangers to each other, an endless round — at least that's how it felt to Lukas — of introductions commenced.

Thank goodness he already knew the guests, or he'd be lost, because Emily's family was big. In addition to her parents, and Peter, he met her other three brothers —

Max, Paul, and Oscar. Two of them brought dates, whose names he thought had been Mila and Clara, but he wasn't sure if he remembered correctly.

To complicate matters, Emily's three living grandparents had come, too, and she and her brothers had been named for them. Her one living grandmother was named Paula, which was easy enough. Except grandfathers Max and Oscar and brothers Max and Oscar were getting jumbled up in his head. And, even more fun, Daniel had come, too, with his parents, Gerty and Daryl, or was it Goldie and Darren?

A little kitty banshee cry sounded a second before a streak of white flew through the legs in the foyer, and Snowball went about attacking Daniel's ankles.

Good kitty, Lukas thought.

"Hey, you." For once, Daniel didn't try to swat her off or kick her away. Instead, he gently pried her from his pants and lifted her in the air to address her face-to-face. "Someday, you and I are going to be friends."

Not likely.

Emily took the kitten from Daniel and carried her away into the kitchen before returning to complete introductions. Lukas's head was swimming with names by the time Emily got everyone seated. Because of the extra mouths, she'd set up a second dining area in the sitting room and had the foresight to use place tags. He was more than happy to see that Daniel and family had ended up in the other room.

"Emily," Tilly said as soon as she took a bite. "You've outdone yourself, honey."

Curious, Lukas took a quick bite of a fancy macaroni casserole that smelled incredible and had to stifle a groan at the cheesy tastiness. "So great," he tacked on his own agreement.

But instead of thanking them, Emily gave them a tight smile, her gaze moving around her family. She couldn't be worried about impressing them. Could she?

After a second, her mother nodded. "You always were handy in the kitchen."

Handy. That was it?

Emily was amazing in the kitchen. Such a lackluster response seemed . . . not right. What was he missing here?

"Wait until she brings out dessert," he enthused.

He might as well have thrown a wet blanket over the entire room, because not one of the Diemers seated around the table commented for a long beat.

"I hope you made lebkuchen," one of her

grandfathers said hopefully. Max, maybe?

That at least got Emily to chuckle. "Of course, and stollen."

Her grandfather shot her a delighted smile, and Emily's dad reached over to pat her hand, though the gesture was subtle.

Lukas cleared his throat. "You all must be so proud of Emily."

The Diemers all exchanged glances as though silently debating who'd answer and how. Under the table, Emily kicked his foot.

What? She was more than capable of standing up for herself, but that didn't mean she would. Family could be complicated. He may not have had much, but in his travels, he'd seen many examples of dynamics that baffled the mind.

Sometimes, it took a stranger to point it out. Since he was pointing out good stuff, he had no problem speaking up.

"Of course we're proud of our Em," Adrian Diemer said.

"My wife, Emily, who she's named for, taught her everything she knows," Grandpa Max claimed, though from the tone of his voice, this was the highest compliment he could pay.

In quick order, her brothers Peter and Max spoke up as well. Only her mother remained silent. No doubt, in Lukas's mind at least, that Marta Diemer was the driving force behind whatever this was. He aimed his most charming smile her way. "I imagine you will all be frequent visitors once she opens her bakery."

Beside him, Emily gave a sigh that probably only he and her dad caught. She grabbed one of the dishes nearest and held it out. "Mashed potatoes, Peter?"

"Sure," her brother said a little too enthusiastically as he grabbed the dish from her hand.

"Me, too," her brother Max held out a hand.

But Lukas didn't look away from Marta.

The older woman didn't return his smile. "I can see that you mean well, Lukas, but Emily is well aware that, while I support her dreams and love her with all my heart, I think a bakery is the fastest way to bankruptcy at a young age. Look at what happened the first time she tried, and she came off lucky. It could have been so much worse. Now she can't even get a loan."

Emily scowled at Peter. "You told them?"

Her brother had the grace to grimace. "I thought they'd want to cosign —"

"I told you to stay out of it," she said in a polite tone with an edge to it.

This was going downhill fast. "You didn't

tell your family?" Lukas turned his head to ask her under his breath.

"Tell us what?" her mom said, gaze dancing between them.

"Nothing," Emily said with a pointed look in his direction. "It's not a done deal yet."

Lukas stared at her. Did she mean that? Didn't she have any faith in him? He wrapped a hand around her wrist, stilling her motions mid buttering of a roll. "Even if the hotel doesn't work out, I'll still make sure the bakery happens," he insisted.

"And until I have a signed piece of paper saying so that will hold up in court, I'm not counting my chickens," she insisted back. Then she tugged her wrist from his grasp and got abruptly to her feet. "I'd better check the oven."

As soon as she disappeared behind the door, Lukas turned slowly back to her family, who were all watching him with various expressions of curiosity and irritation.

"What deal?" her mother asked.

Except Emily clearly didn't want to tell them anything yet. Which put him in a tough position.

"We are looking at selling Weber Haus to a hotel corporation who wishes to make it into a resort with several shops, including a bakery."

Tilly stepped in to save him.

"They are planning on funding the basic setup. The specifics will be up to the shop owners. As soon as they sampled her baking, they offered Emily the bakery."

As the Diemers absorbed this news, the room going heavily silent, the kitchen door swung open, and Emily stepped inside. Holding Snowball — who had green and red sparkles all over her white fur — in one hand. "This cat got into my sugar-cookie decorations," she was saying.

And every eye turned to her.

CHAPTER 19

Emily didn't know if she wanted to hug Lukas or give him a swift kick. With every single family member staring at her, faces blank with shock, she was leaning toward the kick.

Except Lukas had so obviously been trying to defend her. From her family who, though perhaps a bit stubbornly blind, loved her very much. Which was about the most wonderful thing any man had ever done for her.

"Why didn't you tell us?" her mother asked, and under the shock, Emily could hear the hurt in her voice.

Kicking Lukas was starting to win out over hugging him.

Emily sat down, hardly aware that she dropped Snowball to the floor as she did. "I was waiting until the sale is finalized, in case it falls through, or my part in it doesn't work out."

She couldn't handle another round of their disappointment and pity like after the Greg situation.

Her mother's small frown was not a good sign. "But this is a big deal. Why wouldn't you share it?"

Emily refused to glance at Lukas, who she could feel trying to burn a hole in the side of her head with his stare.

"Until there's something to tell," she said. "It's not worth getting anyone's hopes up."

Her father covered her hand with his. "I think what your mother is trying to say is that we're interested in anything big like this, even if it doesn't pan out."

Starting a family discussion in the middle of Christmas Eve dinner had not been on Emily's agenda. Dang it. Why couldn't Lukas have kept his big mouth shut. Just for tonight?

"Emily?" her mother prompted.

Emily didn't even bother to disguise her sigh. "Because every time I share my progress with the bakery, all I get are dire warnings of failure and worried looks and arguments."

"Oh, honey." Her mother rose and came around the table to stand beside her dad. "We want you to be financially secure, and a bakery is —"

"A risk, Mom. Yeah. I get it."

Her mother opened her mouth to argue but paused and shook her head. "If it failed, that's a hard way to start in life, and you've already had one big setback."

Emily had had this discussion with her parents in her head so many times. Usually, yelling was involved, sometimes a presentation to help her make her points. Except she'd never anticipated her mother backing off in any way . . . and that's what had just happened.

"Mom, I know you think of me as your little girl, but you didn't raise a dummy."

That earned her mother's fierce protective mama bear glower. "Of course not. I wanted to make sure all my children would be independent, functioning adults to make it in this world."

"Exactly. I've been planning this bakery since I was twelve. Don't you think I would have spent every one of those business classes in college applying everything to that plan? If I fail, it won't be because of stupid choices."

Except trusting the wrong man, but that was behind her.

"The people from the hotel corporation were highly impressed with her business plan," Lukas put in quietly.

Though she'd been avoiding looking at him, he'd been a steady presence beside her through this. Maybe after a good kick, she'd hug him. Kissing him was out. He was leaving for Morocco right after Christmas, apparently.

"You have a business plan?" her mother asked.

"Of course. I need it for banks to loan me the investment capital to get started. I would've had to think through all of it regardless. I don't plan to fail, and I know what I'm getting myself into."

A hush fell over the room, and under the table, Lukas put a hand over hers, linking their pinkies in a show of solidarity that somehow made her relax. No matter what, she knew her family loved her. The lack of support had never been about not loving her. More, a misguided love.

Her mother turned dark eyes like Emily's to her father, who gazed back at his wife. After forty-some-odd years of marriage they didn't need words to communicate. Then her mother took a deep breath. She bent over to take Emily's face in her hands.

"We are so proud of you, no matter what, and should tell you that more often. I'm sorry if we've . . . if *I've* ever made you feel as though we didn't support your dreams."

Emily had to take several deep breaths, made more difficult around the lump of emotion clogging up her throat. "Thanks, Mom," she whispered.

She got shakily to her feet so she could wrap her arms around her mother. Her father stood and wrapped them both up, and a choked sound escaped Emily. Maybe she'd needed this — needed to hear that she wasn't on her own in this — more than she'd realized.

"So about my lebkuchen," Grandpa Max demanded.

A tension-relieving laugh punched from her, and everyone in the room chuckled. Emily wiped tears she'd hardly noticed falling from her eyes and gave him a stern look. "You have to finish what's on your plate first, Opa."

Which was exactly what her grandmother would have said, earning her a satisfied nod from her grandfather.

After that, the buzz of conversation rose in the room, and Emily was finally able to eat without the knots in her stomach making it impossible to squeeze food in there, too.

Under the cover of everyone's general chatter, Lukas leaned closer, hand on the back of her chair, to murmur in her ear.

"Am I forgiven?"

Emily suppressed a shiver at his nearness but couldn't help turning her head to gaze into his incredible green eyes. "Remind me to thank you later."

His lips tipped in a lazy smile that did nothing to help her fluttering heart. "A good thank-you, or a bad thank-you?"

She raised her eyebrows.

"I like to be prepared," he said. "I've heard horror stories about your kind of retaliation."

His dimples made an appearance as he wrapped one of her curls around his finger, like he had earlier when he'd kissed her, and there went her heart all over again.

"You'll just have to wait and find out," she teased, turning her head away and folding her hands in her lap primly. Only to find several of her family watching them with speculation in their eyes. If Daniel had been in here, too, he probably would've been shaking his head at her, given their chat last night.

"Looking forward to it," Lukas whispered. Then unwrapped his finger and went back to eating like he hadn't just flirted outrageously with her. In front of her family no less.

He glanced at her, then around the table.

Was that a hidden grin? Better not be.

Lukas cleared his throat. "After dinner, would anyone be interested in seeing the plans for the house and grounds?"

At the other end of the table, Tilly gasped. "Already?" she asked. "You didn't tell me you had them."

"I got them right before the party, Aunt Tilly," Lukas said. "I haven't had a chance to see them myself. I've been warned they are preliminary."

At least he hadn't been keeping them to himself. Which would have been a very Lukas — operating in a vacuum — thing to do. Still, plans for the hotel version of Weber Haus only served to remind her that he was leaving.

Forever.

Unaware of how that one thought had turned her stomach sour, Lukas looked to her. "Maybe between dinner and dessert? Give everyone a chance to digest."

Which meant sitting through another thirty minutes of eating, only with her stomach back in knots. Maybe not quite as bad, but this was her future. Her entire dream laid out before her. Every what-if her mind could come up with decided to plague her until they'd moved into the family room, Lukas on the sofa with his computer

374

on his lap and Tilly beside him, and everyone else gathered around.

Emily chose to stand behind him where
she could easily see. Sitting beside him
would be overload with the knots-inducing
situations.

"Okay," he said. "Let's take a look."

With a punch of buttons, he pulled up a
fancy PDF. The logo of Sheila's hotel chain
prominently on the first page. Then he
started scrolling until he came to an image
that was clearly an illustration but realistic-
looking.

And all wrong.

Though Emily couldn't put her finger on
why. The image was of the main house, and
it looked itself . . . but didn't.

I just don't like change, she reminded
herself. That much had become obvious
these last few weeks.

The next image came up.

Never mind. It's wrong.

Sheila and her team were only hanging on
to the authentic, antique feel of the house
and grounds by a thread. The interiors were
modern in an odd way — white walls, black
trim, black and gray furniture, chrome
decorations, sharp lines.

With each image, Emily took a step backward, away from the computer. She couldn't

see Lukas's expression, or Tilly's, but the older woman's lackluster murmurs and his silence said it all. He didn't see a problem with this. He'd decided this move was right, and nothing would change his mind.

The final straw for Emily was the kitchen. Forget the old-fashioned, cozy charm. They planned to gut it and go straight modern. With cement countertops even. They wanted to steal the soul of Weber Haus and replace it with a cold, inauthentic version that made the bile rise up to sting her throat, leaving a sour taste in her mouth.

Quietly, she slipped out of the room, needing a moment to get her emotions under control. This was between Tilly and Lukas ultimately, and none of her business. And he was leaving anyway. She didn't have to have her bakery here. So she'd keep her mouth shut.

But with each flip of the screen, Lukas Weber was breaking her heart.

No one else noticed when Emily slipped out of the room and went upstairs. But I did. I'm sitting on Tilly's lap and have a terrific view of those stairs. Besides, for some reason, all the other humans, including Lukas and Tilly, are staring at his computer.

Humans are weird.

376

Excitement fizzes through me, fluffing out my fur. Maybe today Emily will finally find the ring in her calendar!

I want to see when it happens, because it's going to fix everything. Focused on following her, I leap from Tilly's lap, taking the fastest route across Lukas's keyboard and down to the floor.

"Snowball!" he hollers. I ignore him and weave through the legs of all the people, then sprint up the stairs.

Emily left her bedroom door open, and I slip inside to find her standing in the middle of her room, hands on her hips, just staring at the floor.

I cock my head, studying her. What is she doing?

She's standing very, very still, except I can hear her breathing. Kind of like one of Tilly's guests used to do every morning while she stretched her body. She called it yoga. I called it a fun morning game and a chance to bat at her hair when she was bent over. That's how Emily is breathing now, though, long and slow.

Maybe she needs a hint. She hasn't bothered to put the advent calendar back on the fireplace since she got it down. Maybe she hasn't been looking?

I hop up on the far side of the bed, pad

across the quilt.

"Snowball, he's going to mess this all up."

Her voice stops me. I pause and look at Emily, ears perking.

Emily shakes her head, though not at me. "Lukas is going to sell this place, and they're going to ruin it. He'll move you and Tilly to some horrible apartment. I won't be able to stomach having my bakery here, which puts me back to square one. And . . . alone."

She takes a deep, rattling breath.

"I knew this was too good to be true," she whispers.

But I know she's wrong. As soon as she and Lukas realize they're in love with each other, they'll fix all of that. Together.

She just needs to see the ring, and then she'll know.

So I jump to the bedside table where I put a paw on the calendar, still laying on its side. Then I give a small *mrrrowww* to get her attention.

Emily glances over slowly, blinking like she's a bit dazed. Then her lips twist. "Oh, Snowball. Get down."

She picks me up under my belly and sets me on the floor.

But I'm not giving up. Before she can turn away, I hop back up there and meow louder, pawing at the door I know the ring is in.

"Bad kitty," she snaps.

And for once she's really angry. Even more angry than when I got stuck in that cupboard and sort of jumped out at her when she opened it. I was so scared no one was ever going to find me in there. I didn't mean to knock all those things down or frighten Emily, but she sure looked mad then.

This mad is worse. Quieter.

"Shoo." She waves a hand.

I hop out of the way, onto the bed, and she picks up the calendar and goes to put it back on the shelf above the fireplace.

But the ring must've moved, because we both hear a little *tink,* and Emily pauses. Then she gives the calendar a shake. Sure enough, more *tinking* sounds.

I'm so excited, I can't sit still, my butt wiggling like I'm about to pounce and my tail is out of control.

This is it! This will definitely get Emily and Lukas to figure out their feelings and stop making dumb choices.

Emily sets the calendar back on her bedside table and tries a few doors, which are mostly empty. One has candy in it.

She holds it up to show me. "This didn't make that sound," she says.

Oh my gosh. Move faster. I can't wait for her to see the ring.

Finally, she opens the right door, and Emily goes completely still as she stares inside at the wonderful gift I've brought her.

Only she doesn't move, or even take it out. I still as well, watching her closely. What's she doing?

"How could he?" she whispers, more to herself.

Then, gingerly, like she doesn't want to touch it, she fishes the ring out. Holding it ahead of her with two fingers only, she marches out of the room.

To go tell Lukas she loves him. Despite her odd reaction, I'm sure of it.

Elation bubbles through me and I run out of the room to follow. Except Emily is going the wrong way. She marches down the hall and walks right into Lukas's room. I race to catch up and smack right into her feet because she stops just inside.

She's staring at something. Looking around her, I see several suitcases standing beside the door.

He's leaving?

"Right," Emily mutters to herself. Whatever that means.

Then I have to scurry out of the way, because she spins on her heels and heads the other way down the hall. I pass Emily on the stairs and run straight to Lukas, because now it's his turn.

What on earth are Sheila and her team thinking?
Lukas stared at the images with no small amount of horror. This was so far from what they'd discussed, Lukas couldn't even find the funny in it. Black and white and chrome? Concrete countertops? Not an antique in sight? What happened to the cozy, homey feel they'd been hyping?

As a visual artist, he could appreciate the aesthetic they were trying to achieve. A consistency throughout, rather than each room having its own personality. But this was wrong. Or, maybe more important, this was not the way *he* would do it.

No way could he encourage Tilly to sign anything if this was going to be the result.

He punched at the keys to close it but must've mistyped. Whatever key combination Snowball had hit on her way by brought up a collage of images that he'd sent to Bethany on a whim. Images of Emily, and Snowball, and Tilly, and Weber Haus, and Christmas.

He stared.

Emily . . . And Snowball . . . And Tilly . . .

And Weber Haus . . .

And Lukas.

"What's that?" Marta Diemer asked from over his shoulder.

Lukas managed to drag his chaotic thoughts together enough to respond with more than an incoherent mumble. He glanced over his shoulder. "I'm a photographer. These are pictures I've taken while I've been home."

Marta didn't pull her gaze from the screen. "That's a beautiful image of my daughter."

He smiled, returning his gaze to the picture of Emily laughing at him even as she was starting to frown at the fact that he had the camera up and turned her way. "Yes, it is. It's easy to take beautiful pictures of her."

"Would it be possible to get a copy?" she asked.

"Of course." He never sold his images to individuals, only publications. Lukas hadn't even considered that the subjects, or their families, might want a copy. "What's your email?"

As he hit Send, Snowball suddenly tore across the room as though Santa's elves had tied a string to her tail and she was trying to outrun it and leaped into his lap. He barely managed to keep her from hitting the keyboard again, wrangling her under one arm. Before he could say a word, a shadow fell over the computer.

Lukas raised his head to find Emily standing there, face as tragic as a child who woke up Christmas morning to coal in her shoes. She glared at him with eyes filled with a deep sadness. She also held out his mother's ring. "I don't think this gesture — whatever it means — is appropriate."

Lukas frowned, having no clue what she was talking about. "Um, what —"

"How could you?" she demanded in a choked voice.

With a shake of his head, Lukas handed Snowball to Tilly and stood to face whatever this was.

He pointed at the computer. "If this is about the house —"

"This is about everything," she said quietly. "You come here, and help fixing things up, and make me fall for you, and kiss me until I can't think straight."

She'd fallen for him?

"You convince me and Tilly that selling is the way to go, build all these dreams. Except that" — she waved a hand at his computer — "is not what we'd ever want to see happen to Weber Haus. And then this?" She shoved the ring in his face. "I don't even know what this means."

"I don't, either."

Emily stopped whatever words she was going to hurl at him next, her mouth open, then scowled. "If that's supposed to be a joke, it's not funny."

"No, it's not." He took the ring from her unresisting fingers. "The last I saw, that ring was in my room. Where did you get it?"

Which only earned him a deeper scowl. "I am not a thief, if that's what you —"

He put a finger over her lips before she could say something she regretted. "That's not what I said."

"Why don't you two discuss this privately," Aunt Tilly suggested.

Emily's cheeks flamed bright red, and Lukas had to keep from kissing her to make her patently miserable expression go away.

Before he could usher her out, Emily shook her head, a crushing sadness radiating at him from accusing brown eyes. "There's nothing to say. Regardless of the ring, I can't be part of your plans for Weber Haus."

Shock held Lukas immobile as she turned to Tilly. "Thank you for everything you've done for me. The dessert is ready to be served when people are ready."

She barely got the last words out before she spun on her heel and left the room.

Lukas stared after her, with not a clue how to proceed. Did he go after her and make her listen, or give her time to cool off before he attempted to explain? Did he explain to Tilly or her family first, who had to be hating him by now?

He turned to his aunt. "I would never —"

"I know. I was never going to sell the house, you silly boy." She patted his chest. "You just needed to learn how special our home was for yourself."

That's why she hadn't acted all that upset or worried about the sale thing? Lukas grinned. "Very sneaky, Aunt Tilly."

"True." She winked. "Now, if I were you, I'd follow her."

Right.

Without a word, Lukas started after the love of his life, who seemed determined to push him right out of it.

He hadn't made it halfway down the hall when Emily's voice, sharp and concerned, filled the house. "Snowball! Come back here!"

He hustled into the kitchen in time to see Emily disappear into the darkness, half-in and half-out of her coat.

CHAPTER 20

It didn't work.

I've only been really scared once in my life. When I was alone and crying for my mama. Only she never came. I was so little that my eyes and ears hadn't opened yet and I was so hungry. All I knew was that she'd tucked me into something soft that helped me not be as cold, and that she didn't come back, no matter how much I cried for her.

Miss Tilly and Emily found me on a stump of a tree, and fed me, and cared for me. I thought Weber Haus was supposed to be my forever home.

I was wrong.

Now I feel like I did that night. As the snow makes the bottoms of my paws ache, I keep running. Trying to get away from the scaredness. From the feeling that everything I knew to be true was a lie . . . and forever was a lie.

"Snowball . . ." Emily's voice follows me through the darkness, and I run faster.

I'm so mad at her and Lukas, all I want to do is hide until they go away, then find new people to live with.

I can hear her footsteps behind me, crunching in the snow, getting closer. Seeing a small gap under a building, I run under there, except it doesn't go far back. The space is barely big enough to hide my entire body. I curl up and manage to turn around so that I can see out.

"Snowball." Emily is calling my name.

She sounds really, really worried, and I think about coming out to her, but I need to run away. So I stay put.

"Snowball." Lukas's voice joins hers, and some kind of light is flashing around.

The light gets brighter and closer until it flashes over my hiding spot, and I scoot back into myself, my ears laid back flat against my head.

I hear a gasp followed by footsteps, then Emily's face appears in front of my hidey-hole. "Thank God," she whispers.

Even though I try to squish out of her way, and swipe at her hand with my claws, she reaches in and gently pulls me out, then tucks me inside her jacket, crooning and petting me. At first, I want to try to get

387

away, but her strokes calm me, and I snuggle my face under her hair against her neck.

Emily bursts into tears. Not loud ones, but her body shakes against me, and wetness gets into my fur.

Before Lukas could get to her, Emily was already holding Snowball. Relief punched through him. Against the white of the snow, they never would've been able to find the tiny kitten, and nights were too cold, even for a fluffball like her.

Emily ducked her head, and he slowed his steps as something about her didn't seem right. The second her shoulders shook, Lukas picked up the pace, almost running to get to her, because Emily crying was like a wrecking ball to the gut.

She tensed when he wrapped his arms around her, pulling her against his chest, careful of how she held Snowball. He laid his chin on the top of her head.

"What's wrong?" he asked. Were the tears about the cat, the house, his being a jerk, the ring? What?

Emily shook her head, but at least she stayed where she was. Though the tears continued to fall. His girl was a quiet crier. Only the slight shake of her shoulders told him she was still going. He ran a hand over her back in soothing circles as she continued to sniffle, and it was killing him.

"Please tell me what's wrong," he begged.

"Everything," she muttered, then huffed a bitter laugh. "No. That sounds overdramatic."

Emily lifted her head, her cheeks wet to half glare at him, except the wobble to her chin sort of took away the impact of the glare. "I'm sorry I yelled at you, then ran out like that. I was planning to come back and talk with you rationally, except Snowball escaped."

"And that's why you're crying?" he asked.

She ducked her head and gave it a shake.

Right. If she wasn't going to tell him, he'd have to guess. "I'm not letting them do that to the house."

She stilled and lifted her head, the glare disappearing as she searched his gaze. "You're not?"

He chuckled. "If you'd have just stayed for a second instead of throwing my ring at me —"

"I did not throw it," she insisted. "I handed it to you quite calmly."

"Then ran out of the room." Lukas grinned and wiped the tears from her cheeks with the pad of his thumb.

The small hitch to her breath was the only

thing giving him hope. He still didn't even know if she liked him. She said she'd fallen for him and she liked his kisses. But if she liked him as a person, even a little, she would've given him more credit tonight.

"What are you going to do with the house then?" she asked.

No suspicion lingered in her voice.

"Well . . . I haven't had much time to think about it since you chucked that ring—"

Her glare stopped him mid-sentence and he coughed to cover a laugh.

"Gave my ring back. But I have a plan A and a plan B."

"What's plan A?"

"Can we go inside?" He glanced over his shoulder at the house, brightly lit and cheery. And warm. He'd forgotten his jacket.

"No. My entire family is in there." She wrinkled her nose in such an Emily way, it took everything he had not to kiss her.

Lukas tugged her closer. For body warmth. "Plan A is to offer Sheila and her company a partnership. We still own and operate. We have final say on renovations. They partner and retain a certain percentage of the profits."

He had no idea what she thought of that,

as her expression remained blank.

"And plan B?" she asked.

"I fund the changes myself. Not having a home or living expenses as I've traveled over the years means I've saved a decent amount. I may have to put the property up as collateral against a small loan as well. I'll need to look at the math, but I think it's doable."

Emily's throat worked as she visibly swallowed. "You'll have to get a property manager to see to all that, because I won't have time, between cooking for the house and opening my bakery."

"I'm not leaving." He watched her closely for any reaction. All he got was a long blink.

"Sorry?" she asked, her brows scrunching up. "You told my parents you're going to Morocco."

She tried to pull back, but he tightened his grip. "After I wrap up a few contractual obligations, I'm staying. Here at Weber Haus with Aunt Tilly. And Snowball. And our guests. And —"

"Why?" she asked.

Had she cut him off deliberately? "Selling this place was one of the dumbest ideas I've ever had."

That earned a small, crooked smile from the woman in his arms. "Actually —"

"I said one of," he cut her off quickly.

Emily chuckled. A sound he wanted to hear for the rest of his life.

"I have this idea," he said, taking courage from that sound and the way she was looking at him. "About staying. To help Aunt Tilly transform this place and run it, but also take a new direction in my career."

Emily remained quiet, listening. He'd pay more than a penny for her thoughts about now.

Lukas continued. "I think the hometown photos I've been taking are some of my best work. I sent them to my agent, Bethany, and she agrees. She's already talking a big-city exhibit. I want to settle down here, traveling every so often maybe, but limited. I'm going to make one of the shops my studio and gallery."

He fell silent and waited, bands squeezing around his chest, anxious for her thoughts.

"Wow," she said after a minute. But without inflection, so it didn't tell him much. "Are you sure you can be happy here?"

"Yes." He'd never been more sure of anything in his life.

"What's changed?"

Lukas hesitated, wanting to pull her back into his arms. Praying this wasn't about to blow up in his face. "I fell in love."

He had no idea what he expected, but a confused frown was not it.

"With the house?" she asked.

A huff of a laugh, mostly made up of tension, puffed from him. Lukas shook his head. "No. With Snowball, and Aunt Tilly, and Weber Haus all over again . . . And you, Emily. I'm in love with you."

She gazed at him steadily, those big brown eyes wide. With what? Disbelief? Disgust?

Words poured from Lukas as he tried to sway her. "I realized as soon as we walked Sheila through the house, talking about all the things we'd change, just how much I love this place. But the thought of not having you in my life, no matter where I am, was what made me feel sick inside."

Still she didn't speak.

"The memories don't hurt anymore, and that's because of you." A small white head poked out of the top of her jacket, and Lukas smiled and reached out a finger to tickle the kitten. "And Snowball. This is home to me now. . . ."

He trailed off, because he couldn't think of anything else to convince her. Lukas searched her gaze, desperate to discover her thoughts, and terrified at the same time. Had he messed this up with her before he'd ever arrived?

Emily licked her lips as though she were nervous. Then she smiled, a true, honest smile that lit her up from the inside. "You love me?"

The tension around his chest eased a fraction as he pulled her closer. "More than I thought possible."

Her smile widened a fraction. "And you're going to stay?"

"I'm staying." He grasped her by the arms, tugging her closer. "Please tell me what you're thinking. I'm dying here."

Emily sighed, but the smile remained. "You always were a slowpoke." She shook her head. "I love you, too, Lukas Weber. I was crying and upset at the world because you were leaving me —"

He jerked her against him, kissing away the words and the hurt and the worry and replacing them with love and a future . . . and a heck of a lot of relief.

She loved him back.

A tiny meow of protest sounded from between them, and they pulled apart with a shared laugh as Snowball popped her head up again.

Lukas cupped Emily's face with one hand. "I'll never leave you again."

Shock pinged through him as she barked a loud laugh.

"What about the suitcases in your room?" she asked pointedly. Except she was smiling, so not mad.

"I mean leave for longer than what a quick job will take," he said, giving her a look that promised retribution for her deliberate misunderstanding. He held up his mother's ring, which he'd put in his pocket when he'd run after her. "I'll put this away somewhere safe from kittens who steal shiny things . . . for safekeeping."

Even in the dim glow cast by the Christmas lights on the house far away he could see the color rise into her cheeks.

"Good." She grabbed him by the lapel and pulled him down for another kiss, oblivious to the kitten squashed between them. A kiss Lukas lost himself in, because every touch, every sigh, the sugar-cookie scent of her, and even the cold and snow, were perfect.

He'd finally found his forever home.

EPILOGUE

Emily sat in the formal living room at Weber Haus, the morning sun streaming in the windows, reflecting off the pristine snow-covered landscape outside. She held one present in her lap, unopened, as she gazed over the people surrounding her, all tearing into their pile of presents. Her family had all come to stay at Weber Haus for Christmas this year.

Just this once, because the holidays were usually the best time for business. Tilly had insisted that they all be together.

The past year had brought so many changes.

After Sheila and Lukas had negotiated a partnership to his liking, things had kind of taken off. All the renovations and construction had been completed by October, allowing them to reopen the inn as well as a variety of shops. They'd kicked things off with an Octoberfest celebration — a corn maze, a pumpkin patch, fishing in the pond. Exactly how Lukas and Emily had pictured it.

Around June, he'd wrapped up the last of his longer photography contracts when it came to extensive travel. That had been hard, his being gone during a lot of the construction. His being gone at all. Now he planned to be gone only once or twice a year. His studio would open the day after New Year's and was situated right beside her bakery, which was thriving.

So many changes.

But best of all was Lukas.

She wouldn't have believed it possible, but she loved that man more every day. Even when he was being blind or making decisions without discussing with her first, she loved him.

The sofa dipped as much as the stiff material allowed as her mother sat down and wrapped an arm around Emily. "I'm so proud of you, honey. Breakfast was incredible, and the bakery is so wonderful, and now with Weber Haus and Lukas's photography studio —" She broke off with a smile. Then put her hands to Emily's face. "I've never seen you so happy. Which is the best Christmas present a mother could ask for."

Tears stung the back of Emily's eyes as

she hugged her mother. She hadn't quite realized how much she needed to hear those words until they were spoken. "I love you, Mama."

"I love you too, *liebling.*"

Emily huffed a laugh at the endearment her grandmother used to call her, then looked around for Lukas. He would understand how important this moment was to her.

She frowned as, scanning the room, she realized he was nowhere in sight.

Where had he gone?

"Okay, Snowball. Are you ready?"

Lukas scoops me up and sets me on the table in the kitchen. Then he takes a big red bow with something shiny attached to it and ties it around my neck.

Wait . . . I know what that shiny thing is. I stole it so many times this year to give to Emily that he took it and hid it somewhere away from the house. I haven't seen it in months.

His mother's ring!

I wiggle with excitement. This must mean my humans are getting married. About time, the slowpokes.

"Sit still, you little stinker," he mutters, his face pinched with concentration and . . .

worry? Is Lukas worried about giving Emily the ring?

Finally, he finishes tying the bow around my neck. He lets out a loud, long breath, then grins. "It's now or never, fluffball."

He picks me up and carries me to the living room, where all the humans have gathered to make a fairyland of wrapping paper. All for me, of course.

Lukas crouches down. "You know what to do," he whispers in my ear.

I sure do!

As soon as he lets go, I run into the room and pounce on the first ball of paper I see.

"Snowball, that's not what you were supposed to do," Lukas calls.

It's not? I stop and look up, paper in my mouth.

"Go to Emily." He points.

I look around to find Emily sitting on the couch with her mother. She's smiling and glancing between me and Lukas with confused eyes.

Oh! The ring.

I spit out the paper and run over to her and jump into her lap to get a cuddle. Emily laughs. Such a happy sound. She laughs a lot lately.

"What is this?" she asks.

Then she looks at my bow and gasps as

she sees the ring. She jerks her gaze up to Lukas who followed me across the room. "Yes," she almost shouts, making me jump a bit.

Laughing, Lukas goes down on one knee. "I haven't asked yet."

"Then hurry up." With fingers that shake, she unties the bow and takes the ring off the ribbon.

Lukas takes her hand. "Emily Diemer . . ."

I don't need to hear the rest. My forever family is finally complete. With a leap off her lap, I pounce on another piece of paper.

ACKNOWLEDGMENTS

I get to do what I love surrounded by the people I love — a blessing that I thank God for every single day. Writing and publishing a book doesn't happen without the support and help from a host of incredible people.

To my fantastic romance readers: Thank you for going on these journeys with me, for your kindness, your support, and for generally being awesome. Emily and Lukas definitely needed Snowball's help getting things figured out. That kitten is a hoot and boy does she have a nose for HEAs. I hope you fell in love with these characters and their story as much as I did. If you have a free second, please think about leaving a review. Also, I love to connect with my readers, so I hope you'll drop a line and say "howdy" on any of my social media!

To my editor, John Scognamiglio: Snowball started with you and I loved the idea so much that I couldn't wait to put her on paper. Thank you for taking a chance on me!

To my agent, Evan Marshall: Thank you for your belief in me and constant, steady guidance. You are a delight.

To the team at Kensington: I know how much work goes into each and every book, a ton of which authors never see. I thank you so much for making this book the best it could be!

To Anna and Nicole: Thank you so much for helping me make sure this first foray into sweet romance was as good as I could make it by reading and giving me spot-on feedback . . . your friendship means the world.

To my support team of writing buddies, readers, reviewers, friends, and family (you know who you are): I know I say this every time, but I mean it . . . my stories wouldn't come alive the way they do if I didn't have the wonderful experiences and support that I do. And that's all because of you.

Finally, to my husband, I love you so much. You're the template for my heroes. Someone who lifts the heroine up and inspires her every day to be the best version of who she is. To our awesome kids, I don't know how it's possible, but I love you more every day. I can't wait to see the story of your own lives.

ABOUT THE AUTHOR

Kristen McKanagh attempted to find a practical career related to her favorite pastime by earning a degree in technical writing. However, she swiftly discovered that writing without imagination is not nearly as fun as writing with it. No matter the genre, she loves to write witty heroines, worthy heroes who deserve them, and a cast of lovable characters to surround them (and maybe get their own stories). Kristen currently resides in Austin, Texas, with her own personal hero and their two children, who are growing up way too fast.